THE STORY SO FAR

THE STORY SO FAR

JANE EKLUND

BAUHAN PUBLISHING
PETERBOROUGH NEW HAMPSHIRE
2020

Library of Congress Cataloging-in-Publication Data
Names: Eklund, Jane, 1959- author.
Title: The story so far / Jane Eklund.
Description: Peterborough, New Hampshire : Bauhan Publishing, 2020. |
Summary: "Set against 25 years of cultural evolution, the love between two women outlasts a 28-year age difference, romantic dalliances, illness, and the confines of the closet. Along the way, this protagonist ponders the nature of life, death, religion, and philosophy with help from the imaginary counterparts of Socrates, Hildegard of Bingen, and Suzanne Pleshette; samples casseroles with names like Vegetables Psychosis and The Tubers Karamazov; and forges a family with her best friend, Jeff, and assorted quirky characters who wander into their lives"— Provided by publisher.
Identifiers: LCCN 2020007374 (print) | LCCN 2020007375 (ebook) | ISBN 9780872333192 (trade paperback) | ISBN 9780872333208 (ebook) | ISBN 9780872333215
Classification: LCC PS3605.K59 S76 2020 (print) | LCC PS3605.K59 (ebook) | DDC 813/.6—dc23
LC record available at https://lccn.loc.gov/2020007374
LC ebook record available at https://lccn.loc.gov/2020007375

Book design by Kirsty Anderson
Typeset in Minion Pro
Cover Design by Henry James based on a design by Clare Innes
Front cover photograph by Julie Simons
Back cover photograph by Sarah Bauhan

To reach Jane, go to her website: www.janeeklund.com

PO BOX 117 PETERBOROUGH NEW HAMPSHIRE 03458
603-567-4430

WWW.BAUHANPUBLISHING.COM

MANUFACTURED IN THE UNITED STATES

To my Beezer,
who fills my life with music

PROLOGUE

"If the gardenias can't survive a little overwatering, then God surely must be dead," she says. It's the sort of thing she likes to say, a pronouncement on the natural world filtered through some metaphor of the human condition. These kinds of statements once led me to fall in love with her; later they would leave me feeling vaguely embarrassed. Still, even now, in what might politely be called her waning years, she has dominion over certain chambers of my heart. She knows I'm not walking out the door. And she appreciates the complexity of this scene—her much younger, shall we say, companion, silhouetted against the movie screen of the bay window, watering tin in hand. Even the flowers look black and white against all that racket of daylight streaming into the room like city noise.

I know she is thinking this picture into words. It's what she's good at, what brought her a lifetime of closeted drama. I'm no better. I am as caught up as she is in her books—messy, overpopulated sagas with three generations of bodices and riding boots clashing brutally against each other. No one goes out quietly, and she won't either. I play my part well, always maintaining the illusion that I am something of an enigma, an enigma who arrives promptly when beckoned, proffering a packet of plant food like alms for the unloved.

"I think it's too late," I say. "And I thought you'd already decided that God is dead."

No response. Usually, she likes this kind of banter, but lately, she has begun to tire of the effort it takes to live inside her own enormous personality.

I prod her. "You started it."

"Oh, for God's sake, just water the damn things and get out of all that bright light."

Ah, so she's going to be the rejected matriarch today. Not my favorite, but it suits me as well as anything.

"Perhaps you'd like a little strychnine in your tea," I say, crossing the room and planting a kiss on her gardenia-red lips, something I haven't done for quite some time.

She believes that details matter. The gilded crest on a man's navy blazer glinting in sunlight, the exact degree of arc of one incredulous eyebrow, the once-grand 9:27 wheezing into the station like an old asthmatic. These are the ornaments of her life and her work, the mass-market paperbacks she typed in triplicate on the Underwood she received as a high school graduation present in 1943. Although she now uses a computer, her liner notes still read, "The author lives in the city, where she pens her historical novels on the Underwood she received as a high school graduation gift."

Being the lover of detail that she is, she naturally names the city where she lives and, of course, where I have written "the author" her own name appears. I know she would not understand my desire to make her less of a person and more of an idea.

"The author," she would say with no small degree of irony, "beds down young women in her cheerful house in an unnamed city, on a divan purchased by her long dead and much maligned mother from the Sears and Roebuck catalog in 1937, a divan that is situated across the room from the Underwood typewriter she received as a graduation gift in 1943.

"But then," she would add, "you're not so young anymore, are you?"

She does not say these things, of course. She does not know I have decided to write down what happened between us. She has no sway over what I do when I walk out of the doors of her carefully staged home and into the streets of the unnamed city, in which she lives only through the graciousness of my unlined notebook and my perverse desire to render her vaguer than she really is by turning her into words on paper.

PART ONE

THE AUTHOR / 1977

CHAPTER 1

It started at a time when everyone was twenty-two. I was twenty-two; the streets were full of twenty-two-year-olds jostling toward a future they could barely conceive of; my nights were spent with other twenty-two-year-olds in basement pubs or in three-room apartments over pizzerias. This was before yuppies, before slackers. We all had jobs to go to or master's theses to write. No one was in a particular hurry to enter the world of responsibility; neither did we make a conscious effort to put it off or pretend it did not exist.

She wasn't there, and then one day suddenly she was, and right from the beginning it seemed as if she'd been there all along.

I may have given the impression that I don't care for details; in fact, I spent my days shelving books in the library of a college—not even the college from which I'd recently graduated, and it didn't escape my (I thought) highly developed sense of irony that I had spent four years studying contemporary literature so I could organize dusty volumes in the historical archives of a second-rate school. That's where she found me, in my regulation twenty-two-year-old jeans and long hair, on the third rung of a stepladder, arms full of Victorian-era etiquette pamphlets.

I don't want to say it was the way she looked at me, but really, it was. She looked at me as if my features were arranging themselves on my face in a way that described the inner workings of my character. Later, I understood that she was creating her own narrative, one based on the ordinary exoticness of a twenty-two-year-old girl—I would have said "woman" then—in the context of yellowing pages, cracked leather, and heavy oak tables. I didn't know that then. Then, under her intense scrutiny, I couldn't remember whether I was ascending or descending the ladder.

I came down; the pamphlets toppled from my arms to the tabletop. She wanted to see the collection of antebellum diaries that had recently come into the possession of the college. It was the first errand she was to send me on. I ducked into the back office and got the librarian to unlock the glass document case containing the diaries. I took out the first three of a dozen, then carried them back into the browsing room, hardly knowing why I'd left nine volumes of a southern gentlewoman's life in the case. I found her perusing the etiquette booklets.

"One should give a slight bow when acknowledging a lady," she read, though she was looking directly into my twenty-two-year-old face.

How was I supposed to respond to that? I tipped my head. "You'll have to read these here; they're not allowed out of the room."

"And are you allowed out of the room?"

"Only when properly chaperoned." I felt vaguely absurd, like I was wearing clothing from the wrong century, and when she sat down and opened the first diary I was relieved to be able to turn away from her and attend to the nuances of the Library of Congress system.

The librarian told me later who she was, holding up a paperback from the Light Reading shelf and pointing to the photograph on the back cover. The author looked younger—not close to my age, but certainly younger than my mother—and she seemed too large for the two or so square inches allotted for the picture. The book, too, seemed to be bursting out of its binding. It had been read so often, or perhaps so carelessly, that its spine was permanently bowed, and the pages fanned out like, to use a simile she would no doubt appreciate, a skirt puffed out by a plentitude of petticoats.

The librarian and I rolled our eyes conspiratorially. This was the kind of book my friends and I mocked over pitchers of beer, the kind not worthy of derision from my English professors. Here, at the library, it wasn't even worthy of a catalog number. Like the others in Light Reading—the tawdry romances and fast-paced thrillers, the well-mannered whodunits and the spine-tingling tales of the supernatural, the kinds of genres that need to be modified with adjectives—this book would rotate in and out, shelved haphazardly, until it either fell apart or was demoted to the book sale pile or just disappeared all together.

It was the sort of book sold in supermarkets, the sort passed over the fences of suburban backyards, the sort left behind on trains or buses. It reeked of melodrama, an emotion I was familiar with as a kind of interior costume party. There was nothing interior about this book, though. The front cover was a hackneyed maritime fantasy. In the background, a three-masted schooner tilts into a raging sea. In the foreground, a ship's mate, jacket torn open to reveal the nineteenth-century version of ripped abs, grips tightly onto the arm of the privileged merchant class, as personified by a young brunette in fancy dress and what can only be described as flowing tresses. She appears distraught, clearly both repelled by and drawn to him, for as we all know attraction is a complicated thing, something that can take five or six hundred pages to play out, sometimes even dribbling down to the next generations, who have to start from scratch, in a sequel, but now they have to work out all their unresolved passion in the steamship era.

I didn't recognize the author's name; hadn't read the book or any of the other two dozen listed with the front matter. These novels weren't taught in universities, and this was before the idea caught on that popular culture could be de- and re-constructed right alongside all the highfalutin art. And so, we made a few *Gone With the Wind* jokes and shared a laugh at the author's expense, the librarian and I, neither of whom had come close to writing anything approximating a novel, and when she wasn't looking I slipped the book into my bag.

This is how it went for an entire month. She came in each afternoon and sat at the oak table. I brought the diary to her, whichever volume she was reading at the time, and presented it with an elaborate Victorian flourish. She'd spend a couple of hours reading and taking extensive notes on a legal pad. I suspected she was lifting entire passages to insert directly into her next bodice-ripper. I didn't mention that I was systematically working my way through her books, in the order they were written. She didn't mention noticing them poking out of the top of the book bag that I arranged against the small circulation desk each morning. It proceeded like this, the author filling the room with scribbling while I lurked around the edges, hauling my stepladder from shelf to shelf, repositioning books to make room for an extensive atlas collection just donated by an elderly alumnus. Every now and then, she would read aloud.

"'Something so invades me, dear diary, when he enters the room; something so piercing and yet so tender, I can but describe it as an essence wholly apart from my own that has taken up residence in my breast.' That's rather delicious, don't you think?"

"If you go for that sappy stuff," I said, knowing full well that she did.

Did I understand that this was seduction, these long afternoons spent in the shadow of an earlier era? Yes, I understood.

If she were reading this, she would stop right about here to peer at me across the horizons of her half-moon glasses. What about character development? she would say. What about description? You've got two people on an empty stage, one lugging around a stepladder and the other sitting behind an oak table like characters in a bad minimalist play. Are we supposed to be waiting for Godot? Who are these people, where did they grow up, what are their mothers' maiden names, and for God's sake, why don't you put some clothes on them? You at least have a pair of jeans, which incidentally must be getting quite ripe by now, but I would appreciate having something other than a yellow legal pad to cover up my nakedness. Oh, I stand corrected. You don't even say that the legal pad is yellow. I suppose you expect me to hide behind a lime green legal pad?

Ah, quit complaining. I gave you a pair of half-moon glasses, didn't I? And did I mention that my afternoons rose around those glasses, and my evenings set on those glasses?

She was handsome, the author, in the way of older women who'd been drop-dead gorgeous in their youth. I spent considerable time trying to come up with just the right words to describe the color of her hair, which landed above her collar and was shaped to her neck. She wore it parted on the side and tucked behind one ear. Darker than blonde, lighter than auburn, just a suggestion of red. Her face, long and angular but not sharp, made me think: *geometry*. I wanted her eyes to be dark green, but was too shy to get close enough to look. She could have shared a bloodline with her characters, the ones who lolled about on southern porches all the humid summer long without perspiring or wrinkling their clothes.

I knew her writing before I knew her. I read her books every evening when I went home. I'd begun entertaining my roommates with dramatic recitations while we smoked marijuana or sipped beer from cans. I adopted a wildly exaggerated basso or falsetto, depending on the manliness or femininity of the character in question. I also proffered a husky impersonation of the author herself, one with no trace of an accent other than a sort of ease with the world, with privilege. "What did the author say today?" they would ask me. "What was she wearing?"

"Today the author was wearing silk," I would say in her throaty voice, "a silk blouse simply blossoming with red petals, tulips I believe, or perhaps bougainvillea, and tan slacks, and delicate rope sandals that showed off her perfectly pedicured toes polished in a disarmingly brilliant red."

I did not tell my roommates about my schoolgirl crush, or that my mocking performances were a way of protesting too much. For I hardly knew why her voice had taken up lodgings in my throat. I can look back and say she was a repository of intrigue, of mystery. I was learning from her novels that layers upon layers of cotton and velvet make only the flimsiest of coverings for desire. And nothing ends happily until the house or the ranch or the woolen mill lies in ruins. This was the kind of theme I could write pages on: The Collapse of Adolescence in the Face of Five Decades of Revisionist History—A Love Story.

The author's plotting was complex. Family trees were necessary to keep track of the small hordes that wandered from chapter to chapter like bands of mercenaries looking for combat. In some plotlines, it was perfectly acceptable to marry one's cousin, complicating the relationships even further. These complications, of course, were partly smokescreen: it took me three or four novels to discern that the plots were all basically the same. The settings changed from Charleston to Boston to St. Louis to Laramie. And the characters' names and situations differed. That established, it worked like this: Start with three or four young women. One is beautiful and good-hearted, but due to some flaw in her father's constitution, say a predisposition to laziness or an inability to hang on to money, she is poor as a churchmouse. Another is lively and witty and adventuresome, prone to scandalous activities like striding unaccompanied around the family's land holdings in riding britches. The third is a bit of a gossip and suffers from the sin of envy. The fourth? Well, she's a wildcard, someone who's just arrived on the scene from England, perhaps, or a mission in China. They are sisters or cousins or neighbors.

Then, throw in four or five men of varying dispositions, social positions, and indiscretions. It's good to have a spare, so that one can be killed off in the course of the action.

Shake or stir. (Which is it you do for a mint julep? Which for a gin and tonic?) Throw in a devastating fire or two, a crippling carriage accident, a fortune lost in shady speculation. Some four hundred pages later, they're all married off to each other, though not in the couplings you'd expect, and their children are beginning to dance around each other in the parlor.

These are the kinds of things she would say to me while I opened cartons of antique atlases and sorted them by region and publication date:

"How's it coming along, this project of yours to set the world in order?"

Or: "Here's what I can tell you about mapmaking: It's a reflection of the human desire to claim property. In man's case, that would be real estate; in woman's, the territories of the heart, which are much less easily charted, don't you think?"

And once, while I was carefully unwrapping a British colonial blueprint for Africa: "Darling, you're a bit of an anachronism in your T-shirt and white gloves."

She was quite interested in the atlases, which offered up a sort of family tree of nations and continents. She'd been in her usual seat when they arrived, four large boxes carted in on dollies, the librarian happily directing the delivery men through the bustle of the lobby and into our archival sanctum like a traffic cop who can't wait to see what's in the glove compartment of the Toyota he's just pulled over. The author moved her diary and legal pad to an unoccupied chair, and the three of us began unpacking five hundred years of civilization onto the oak table.

I didn't understand why she chose me, but I could feel her there, bent over the atlases, consciously choosing me. We were talking excitedly, she and I and the librarian, for somehow her presence in the room made it into a party, a jolly archaeological expedition, this initial sorting through books of maps. It seemed logical that she was there. I'd come to think of her as living in two worlds: one was the genteel plantation in which she pulled the strings that made characters sashay across a verandah or gallop angrily through cotton fields; the other was here, in the archives, where I felt her gaze like a hand upon the small of my back as I scoured the room for books that had been reshelved into the wrong century, or the wrong continent, or the wrong language.

I was wrong, too, a twenty-two-year-old in a place of history so long past it couldn't have been mine. But here, surrounded by primary sources, I managed to find whatever there was within me of elegance and eloquence.

Perhaps this is why she chose me: Because I carried with me something of the incongruous, it was easy to envision decades clashing together in my presence. Or maybe she was simply amused by me. Or maybe she realized that she had reached the upper limit, maybe even passed the upper limit, of being able to draw young women with her gaze.

Was I naïve? Yes. Was I drawn to her gaze? Yes. So drawn I wrapped it around me like a cloak through the day and into the evening. So drawn I fell into her historical melodrama every night, and fell from there into sleep.

I no longer remember what I was thinking as the author ran her finger along the spine of a parchment-bound volume, but I remember what I felt.

"The air was charged" is the way her omniscient narrator would have described it. "Something lit up in her like a string of Christmas lights."

A string of Christmas lights wrapped around my heart, no doubt. It sounds corny, but yes, I felt my breath caught there in my throat, luminescent. I felt myself spinning around the verandah, waiting for my next compass point.

It was, of course, thrilling that this undercurrent took place under the watch of the librarian, who, like all good chaperones, was a spinster and knew little, I supposed (stupid youth that I was), about attraction, inexplicable or otherwise. I wasn't about to explain it to her; I couldn't even explain it to myself. I arched my spine, I talked, I laughed with the two older women, my boss and my soon-to-be lover, as if I could be their equal.

All afternoon stacks of atlases swelled like topography on the oak table, and my heart was mapping out a future without consulting me.

She doesn't believe in the first person, says it's manipulative to reveal the thoughts of only one character. If I let her read this, she would spit it back at me like a curse: "Unreliable narrator." She would say this because she wants every story to be her story. I am writing it because I need it to be my own.

We were co-conspirators, the author and I, meeting over the brittle geography of history like two generals of the heart. Whose capture were we negotiating? I was bolder now, and sometimes when I felt her stare I'd turn from the shelves or look up from my paperwork and return her regard. She'd hold my look for a while, then the corners of her lips would turn up, not quite imperceptibly, or she'd raise one contriving eyebrow to release me. If it was a question, my answer was yes. She sensed this, for one afternoon, while I cleaned the shelves where the atlases would come to reside, she burst into laughter.

I could see she was laughing at me. I stiffened, then looked at the feather duster in my hand and began to giggle.

"Do you own any respectable clothing?" she asked when we had both regained our composure.

"I'm not totally without couth," I replied.

"Good. Then perhaps you'd like to meet me for dinner tonight." It wasn't a question; it was a statement. She named a time and a restaurant.

"Shall I bring this?" I said, tickling the air with my feathers.

"If you'd like."

She gathered up her legal pad and fountain pen, took off her reading glasses, and tucked everything into her leather shoulder bag. She handed me the final volume of the diary—the one in which the writer falls ill and lingers for a while, then fades politely into the pages—and walked out the door. It was the last time she would come to read in the archives room. From then on, I'd be coming to her.

CHAPTER 2

"What do you think of the wine?" the author wanted to know. We were seated at a table in the back, sipping a German Riesling she'd ordered for both of us. ("You are old enough, I trust?")

"I usually figure that any bottle of wine with a cork in it has to be good. No, actually, this is much nicer than anything I could ever afford. I'm usually more of a beer drinker, but this is really good." I was babbling, a bit unnerved that she had not asked me the questions I was expecting, standard ones like Where did you grow up, What was your major, What do your parents do for a living. She seemed more interested in what I thought and felt than in who I was, which, I have to admit, was a relief. I didn't want this to be like a dinner with an aunt or a friend of my mother who was in town for a few days. On the other hand, it required me to know what I thought and felt, and to express those things in a way that sounded articulate, or at least witty. I decided I was safer with witty.

"Or am I supposed to say it's fruity?"

"You could," she said, swirling her wine into an eddy, "and you'd be right. But it's more complex than that." She smiled. "Here. Hold it like this"—she took my hand and placed it on the stem—"so the heat from your fingers won't warm it up. Now, pick it up. Don't drink it yet. Just hold the glass a few inches from your nose, swish it around, and inhale. Don't smell it, just breathe it in. Makes you a little lightheaded, doesn't it? Okay, now close your eyes. Take a sip, just a small one, and let the flavor roll through your mouth. What do you taste? Sweet?"

I nodded.

"Flowery? Grapey?"

I nodded twice. My mouth was filling with her words.

"But something else. Something spicy, something a little acidic."

"Yes," I said, surprised. "Yes, I can taste it."

"What I love about Riesling is that line it walks between acid and sugar. It creates a certain tension, you see?"

I opened my eyes. She was fingering her necklace, a delicate lasso of freshwater pearls.

"Yes." I held up my glass in a toast. "I think this could make me very dizzy."

The wine, like the tablecloths, the walls, the waiters' crisp shirts, was white. The author had chosen a restaurant that was classy but not intimidating; the kind of place my parents might take me for a special occasion. She'd arrived first and was already seated, which meant I had to walk clear across the room while she watched from the security of the table—not the oak table of the library, but a delicate table for two. She looked softer here, dressed in a linen jacket and gauzy blouse, both just a few shades darker than the tablecloth. I was feeling soft, too, in my peasant blouse and wrap-around India-print skirt. Not exactly classic, but not bad for short notice.

"You look so at home in the archives room," she said, leaning back and resting her elbows on her chair's armrests while we waited for our dinners to be served.

"Do I? Do you think I blend in nicely with the obscure books and the oddball scholars?" Stupid! Stupid thing to say. "Present company excepted, of course," I added quickly.

She seemed not at all offended. "I expect you'd blend in nicely in any number of places, but the archives do seem to suit you. Do you like working there?"

"Yes, very much." I said it because I thought it would please her, but as the words came out of my mouth I realized they were true. "The librarian keeps slipping me pamphlets about library science school."

"Would you like to do that? Go back to school, I mean?"

"Maybe. If I could scrape the money together. There are worse ways to spend your life than hanging around books."

"So I've heard." She gave me the subtlest of winks; I felt my body incline, of its own accord, into her presence.

We ate pasta, long, flat strings of it covered in a creamy sauce, hers tossed with pieces of chicken and mine with artichoke hearts. I could go into the details of how she reached over and stabbed one of my artichokes with her fork—she appreciates that kind of heavy-handed symbolism—but really, I don't recall the specifics of twirling fettuccine or cutting green beans into manageable portions. I remember we finished the bottle of wine, I remember she paid with crisp twenty-dollar bills. I remember wondering what allowing her to buy me dinner would get me in return.

I'd taken the bus from the center of town, thinking she'd offer to drive me home. But she did not offer, did not ask how I traveled to the restaurant or even where I lived. We left together, me carrying the tin foil swan containing her leftover pasta, and walked without talking to the back parking lot, where her car waited just outside a dim puddle of light cast by the one street lamp. She opened the door to the back seat, took the swan I held, and put it on the floor.

"I was hoping your eyes would be green," I said.

She crinkled them a bit. "You hoped right."

Then she took a small piece of paper from her jacket pocket and folded it into my right hand. "I'm leaving tomorrow for a book tour. I'll be back in two weeks. Will you come and see me?"

I nodded, something I found myself doing a lot around her. And then the author took my chin in her right hand, tilted her head quizzically, and kissed me. Then she got in her car and drove away, leaving me standing in the shadows holding a piece of paper with an address and a date on it. I walked the thirty minutes home, my breath filled with her lipstick, the wine, and the aroma of garlic and white pepper.

Shall I say how I spent those two weeks? It wasn't floating, exactly; more of a suspension, more like one long night walking home with her breath in my lungs and a slip of her stationery in my hand.

What if she changed her mind? What if she met someone in her travels, someone more suited to drama and decorum, someone who could hold a glass of wine to her lips and whisper the word "bouquet?"

I kept her note in my pocket, fingering it often, taking it out whenever I had a moment to myself to unfold it, smooth it out, and search her address for some indication of her intentions. I'd memorized the words the first night—the street in an upscale neighborhood, the three-digit house number that rang like a doorbell in my thoughts, the date a train coming ever closer, and me with no power to stop it or speed it up.

Every evening I fought the impulse to drive past her house. What was I afraid of? That I might find a light on and the author in silhouette behind a closed blind, gesturing to someone I couldn't see? Or that I'd find a house so ordinary in its emptiness that I wouldn't be able to imagine coming back?

At the library, I mooned over the maps of the United States, picturing her in a tiny plane hovering just above the open book, whisking from San Francisco to Chicago to Seattle. Other times she was decked out in safari clothes, rope around her waist, climbing the sheer cliffs of Lewis and Clark's geography, fording rivers from one mall bookstore to the next.

I did my best to appear busy whenever the librarian walked by, but she could sense something had changed.

"I believe I miss our hack historian," she said once, while carrying an armload of obsolete—and therefore infinitely fascinating—encyclopedias into her office in the back. "Did she say where she was going? Or had she finished with our little crinoline chronicles?"

"I think she said something about a book tour," I mumbled, keeping to myself a defense of the author's historical accuracy. Problematic as it was, that whole revisionist genre of historical romance novels, she wasn't a hack when it came to details, at least. Whether her backdrop was Colonial New England, the post-Civil War South, or Gold-Rush California, the locations, the names of historical figures, the style of dress right down to hairpins and spurs were all painstakingly researched. And if her characters embodied the exaggerated expressions of stage actors, so be it. There was truth in those emotions.

These kinds of thoughts are to be forgiven. I was, after all, young, and I was feeling, for the first time, exaggerated emotions in myself. None of the fumbling I'd done with boys in high school and college had inspired anything more than a pleasant sensation; but now, words on a scrap of paper, a car parked outside a circumference of street light, these not-quite-historical particulars could send me reeling.

At night, alone on my mattress, I replayed the kiss again and again in my mind, until it became something cinematic, something that should be accompanied by overblown symphonic music. It was a preview, I knew, and the thought of what would come after the next kiss was both electric and terrifying.

I bought a bottle of Riesling from the corner grocery and sipped demurely each evening from a juice glass while my roommates downed bottles of beer. I no longer talked about her at home, except to say, when asked, that she had finished her work at the library. This was a private passion, I told myself, the kind played out in quiet restaurants and behind the curtains of gracious homes. I kept it to myself.

And spent day after day walking in a kind of sunlight and a kind of moonlight.

The date was coming nearer, even as it faded from the now-worn slip of paper I carried in my pocket. You could say I was anxious. You could, perhaps, say I was obsessed. What would I wear to her house? How would I behave? I scoured my closet for guidance, only to find my resources lacking. She'd already seen the wrap-around skirt, and the graduation outfit my mother had purchased for me, an absurd velvet cocktail dress, made me look like a kid trying to pass as sophisticated. Should I buy something new? Or would that look like I was trying too hard?

And should I bring her a gift? A bottle of wine, flowers, a small volume of the love poems of Christina Rosetti? Maybe studied casual was my best approach: my good pair of white jeans, a bouquet of dandelions plucked from her neighbor's yard moments before I rang the doorbell. Or was that too contrived?

Besides, now I had timing to worry about. She'd indicated a date, but not an hour. Had the date fallen on a weekday, I could have assumed she would be expecting me in the evening, after work. But I'd been summoned to appear on a Sunday, which could, I realized after I thought about it for most of a sleepless night, mean almost anything. Didn't people get together for lunch on Sundays? Or even earlier, for brunch? But perhaps she'd be unpacking from her trip; perhaps she'd want to linger in the tub all morning, submerged in bath salts, a glass of tea balanced on the rim?

These kinds of thoughts could send me into a panic. What did I think I was doing, flirting with images of a woman who had to be thirty years older than I was? Yes, she had kissed me in the parking lot and then left me for two weeks to lie awake at night, turning it all into a dream. Sometimes, in the foggy hours of early morning, I'd confuse her with one of her characters—the oldest son leaving the prairie town to study law in the city, say, while his beautiful and smitten second cousin, who had been taken in by the family after her parents' tragic death in a steamboat accident, can but sit by the fireside embroidering his initials on the edges of pillowcases until he returns. Other times she was the bold widow, taking off on horseback, riding like a man in jodhpurs and cropped jacket. Does she make it to her father's estate, four days' ride across tobacco fields and through woodlands, in time to reclaim the deed to her property before her dead husband's family gets their hands on it?

At four in the morning, melodrama gets its grip on you. By midday, back among the leather-bound facts and figures of the past—among them but not in them—I could sometimes feel almost normal, almost like someone who hadn't been kissed on the mouth and wakened into reverie.

The author would come back, safely, not from crop failure or death in the family or scarlet fever, but from something more prosaic: days upon days of sitting behind tables at chain bookstores, dedicating paperbacks to people with names like Helen and Joan and Linda, the kind of women who could read her hyperbole without a trace of irony, the kind who buy their reading material at the mall or in a drugstore or in the checkout line of the grocery.

She was coming back, and I would be waiting for her, to catch whatever embrace might come my way.

And so the calendar pedaled toward Saturday, that cliff at the end of the week, and yes, just over that cliff the day arrived, with me tumbling into it gracelessly. Though I would have said I was prepared for whatever chapter opened before me, I had all the brashness and all the trepidation of a skinny kid not three years out of her teens; I was, in short, feeling a bit sick to my stomach.

There were ways out but I didn't take them. I left the muslin skirt I'd purchased in the closet. It looked too new, too anxious to please. Instead, I opted for a mix of nonchalance and eagerness—a clean pair of jeans and a silky, off-white blouse, something she could take her time unbuttoning. Would she want to unbutton me? What if she did? Where would I put my hands while she was doing it? Maybe she'd expect me to make the first move—what then? I was one big walking duality, one minute amused by this sudden turn in my life, one minute ready to be coaxed over some physical and emotional edge.

I took the huge American car handed down by my grandmother and navigated toward the far reaches of the city. I'd decided to arrive around four o'clock—not too early, not too late. That way, if she appeared to have grown tired of me as a diversion, I could visit for an hour or two and then plead a dinner engagement. I parked in the street in front of her house, rather than in the driveway. Why? Did I think I might need a quick getaway?

Okay, breathe.

I suddenly realized I had nothing in hand to offer the author. A quick check of the neighborhood—brick and clapboard houses, stately but not ostentatious. No chance of a dandelion growing on these coiffured lawns. But perhaps empty hands were better than a fistful of weeds?

Did I mention that my heart was pounding like the heart of one of her ample-bosomed maidens, some poor relation tiptoeing into her first cotillion in a patched and outdated ball gown?

Keep breathing.

Fifteen paces up the brick walk, five steps up to the porch, four to the bell. I rang it. After what seemed enough time to waltz twelve eligible bachelors around the dance floor, the door opened.

"Oh, good, you're here. Come help me with the rissole." She turned and hustled toward the back of the house. What could I do but follow?

We walked through the living room, light and airy and not a trace of the eighteenth or nineteenth centuries, and the dining room, where the table was piled with stacks and stacks of paper, folders, index cards, and reference books. She pushed through a swinging door, then held it open for me.

"The thing is, you have to be careful to portion out the filling a little at a time, otherwise you'll overload the pastry, and it'll break apart while it's frying," she said, putting one teaspoon in my right hand and another in my left. "Like this, just scoop up a bit of stuffing, then fold."

She was dressed in black: black knit pants and a loose-fitting black tunic. It occurred to me that I hadn't spoken.

"Hi," I ventured.

She stopped mid rissole and looked straight into my eyes. "Hello, you," she answered, and then she kissed me again.

It was so like her to organize a seduction scene around the preparation of food. There are things you can do in the kitchen that wouldn't be seemly in the dining room, like plunging both hands into a bowl of dough, like licking batter from your fingers. There are definite hazards in the kitchen too—paring knives, gas burners, vats of boiling water.

I was in the story now, in her kitchen among the ingredients for rissole and the pot of hot oil. I didn't want to get out of the kitchen, and, indeed, she kept me in there all evening, alternately constructing appetizers and feeding them to me, sometimes from her fork directly into my mouth. Everything tasted brand new, the rissole and the rumaki and the shiitake mushrooms. In fact, these things *were* new to me, and I rolled their names around in my mouth as I watched her chopping and stirring. We both drank beer—she'd purchased a six-pack of the imported brand I had mentioned at the restaurant.

"Rissole," I said. "Rumaki, shiitake," making her laugh and kiss me more. We were seated on stools facing each other across a narrow counter. I thought of ships pulling up to a dock.

"Tell me about your trip," I said. "Did you think about me while you were gone?"

"Oh, book tours." She got up and stretched as if to indicate boredom with the whole topic, then climbed back onto her stool, popping a mushroom into her mouth and chewing deliberately. "They're a necessary evil. People see your face, maybe listen to you read a steamy passage, and they feel like they own you just a little bit—not just your writing, but you, as a person, as a character. The upside is that they then feel obligated to purchase everything you've ever written."

"I can't imagine what that would be like, to have readers think they know you, based on some idea that's been planted in their head."

"Well, we all plant our own ideas for the world to pick up on, don't we? For instance, these earrings you're wearing"—she reached across the divide and tucked my hair behind my left ear—"lead me to believe you're a smidgen sentimental."

I touched the earring, not because I'd forgotten which pair I'd put on but because I wanted to put my hand where her hand had been. "They were my grandmother's."

"Yes, I thought they seemed a little ornate for your taste, and a little old-fashioned, so I gathered they held some appeal that went deeper than style."

"That's pretty good. What else can you surmise?"

"About you? I surmise that you are a lover of words, based on your use of the word 'surmise.'"

"Not to mention 'rissole' and 'rumaki' and 'shiitake.' "

"Ah, I thought those were only a clever ploy to get me to kiss you."

I blushed, then tried to cover it up by going to the fridge for another beer. "Well, it worked, didn't it?" I pried off the cap.

She came around behind me, enclosing me in her arms and kissing me in that territory where neck meets shoulder. "Yes, it worked." Those words whispered in my ear.

That did it. I was gone, lost in my own body. I was falling, yes, and it was scary and wonderful and I wanted her to never let me go. And I wanted never to land.

She sent me home at eleven, with the promise that later she would show me the rest of the house. "I think I've gotten you into enough trouble for one night," she said.

I was half expecting her to press another folded note into my hand, with instructions for our next meeting, but this time she did not. Nor did she indicate when next time might be. I kissed her once more under the porch light, chastely, on the cheek. "Thank you for dinner and, well . . . "

"It was lovely." She winked, then stepped inside and closed the door.

The author's hands were long and slender, well manicured. I had not taken any particular note of them up to that first evening at her house, but now, waiting for the gesture that would return me to her arms, her lips, I thought of them constantly. The preparation of food allows for careful observation of the hands, the fingers, but now I was daydreaming them onto my body, the small of my back, the back of my knee, her hands, her fingers, the shocking red of her nails. And her eyes like a sea of moss. And her voice like wine aged in a cask.

Was I a foolish girl? No, but I was young, and learning, for the first time, about longing. I hadn't expected such a physical ache. I had not understood that the heart is a compass, and even now, two-and-a-half decades later, I can't shake myself from its pull.

Toward the end of the week, a couple of days after I had begun despairing that I would not hear from her again, a letter arrived for me, via messenger, in the archives room. Fortunately, the librarian was in her office, so I had no need to invent a lie to explain the small ivory envelope that was addressed to me, using the honorific "Miss," as if I were being invited to a fancy party.

Inside, on a note card embossed with her initials, was this: "Yes, I did think about you while I was away. Come tonight after work, will you?"

I would, and I did, after a quick shower and a change of clothes. This time I stopped by a florist for one long-stemmed white rose, which she took between thumb and forefinger when she opened the door.

"Thank you, darling," she said, and the word "darling" spun around in my stomach as I walked into her kiss.

Dinner was waiting in the den, a just-delivered mushroom and pepperoni pizza to which she was adding fresh basil leaves from a pot in the window.

"I hope you don't think I'm a terrible host, but I've been working all day to meet a deadline and I haven't had a chance to shop, much less cook. I don't even have a leaf of lettuce to offer, so we'll have to make do with this bit of basil for greenery."

"This is great," I said, biting into a slice. "I usually live on this stuff. What sort of deadline?"

"The final rewrite of my latest tome is due in New York tomorrow. I put it in overnight mail two hours ago. And here you are to help me celebrate."

"Hey, congratulations."

"Thank you. People always assume it's traumatic to send a book out into the world, and I guess it was for my first books, but now I'm quite pleased whenever I can unload one and move on to the next thing."

We faced each other, cross-legged, on the couch, eating off paper plates, the pizza box warm between us. She'd put the rose in a vase on the coffee table and lit a couple of votive candles, which cast orange reflections on the closed window shades. Over her shoulder I could see two looming bookcases; I could tell by the distinctive design that the paperbacks lined up on the top shelves were her own novels.

"Do you ever get tired of writing?"

"Not of writing. But of rewriting, yes, especially when I feel it's finished and my editor doesn't agree. Sometimes you're just ready for something new."

"I'm new," I said, emboldened by the candlelight.

"You're new and I'm growing awfully fond of you."

I felt my face flush, something it did a lot lately, purely of its own accord, when I was in her presence. "I'm fond of you, too."

"Good." She touched the rim of my wineglass with hers. "Then it's unanimous."

"You are very good at setting a scene," I said, gesturing with my glass before taking a large gulp. "I was a little afraid your interest in me was some sort of research for one of your plots."

"Oh, as in the gentleman farmer has taken to flirting shamelessly with his neighbor's daughter, that sort of thing?"

I nodded, my face furiously hot.

She laughed, not unkindly. "I spend my days in that world, but my evenings belong to me. I can flirt shamelessly very well of my own accord, as you perhaps have noticed. Come here, I want to show you something."

We wiped our hands on the cloth napkins, then she took my right hand in her left and led me to the dining room.

"This is where my characters meet their fate." The tabletop, which had appeared cluttered but tidy a few days earlier, now looked like the scene of a well-plotted battle. A long roll of paper ran down the center; on it was a timeline drawn in ink and colored pencil, with some notations highlighted in yellow. Near the end of the line, a huge red magic-marker arrow pointed ominously at a key event, as if suspended in air above the horizon of the story.

"The climax?" I suggested.

"Yes. And these notes"—she pointed to a series of white index cards strewn along the top of the timeline—"are the salient points of the primary storyline."

"So these must be the subplot." I indicated the pale blue index cards laid out below the timeline.

"Very good."

"And what's in these folders?"

"These are the people. Everyone has his or her own dossier."

"You develop all this while you're writing?"

"This is more like pre-writing. I put this all together before a single word goes on the page."

"This is the book you just finished?"

"No, this is the next book. This is the story I was researching in the library, though I admit I dawdled over that diary far longer than I needed to." She paused a moment. "If you look through these files, you'll see there's no character who resembles you in the least."

"That's okay. I believe you." I felt relieved and slightly disappointed. "I'd look pretty silly in petticoats, anyway."

She put her arms around me and folded me in. "Ah, but it would be fun to write you out of them."

I leaned into her, into the scent of a perfume so subtle it might have been mist, and held on. "When are you going to show me the upstairs?"

"Don't be in such a hurry." Her voice went soft. "I want to enjoy every moment of you."

History is, by nature, revisionist. By the time it hits the page as words, it's already started its descent into mythology. Every truth in every yellowing document in the archives room had long been replaced by a new truth, and then an even newer one. I asked her once, in the early days, why she wanted to play around with the truth, and she replied that she preferred to think of her novels as playing along with the truth.

"The only real thing is sentiment," she said, "and that's the same whether it's 1876 or 1976, and for me, the sentiments of 1876 are relatively lucrative."

The truth is, the author did not bring me up to her bedroom for another month of visits. At the time, I assumed it was her way of controlling the situation, of being the one who decided exactly how our story would unfold. Or she was being gallant—giving me every chance to back out, to return to my life of twenty-two-year-old concerns. I know now—as she did then—that seduction is the best part of an affair.

I was too far fallen into the plotline to turn and walk away, or even to step back long enough to jot notes on an index card. It was enough to live life without having to catalog it or deduce its Freudian or Jungian implications. What more can I say about this? I was happy, and that was enough.

The day she finally brought me up the staircase and down the wide hallway to her bedroom, the sun was beginning its descent into autumn. It was a Sunday afternoon; we'd been walking in a small park near her house, and my senses were alert to the changing of seasons. It was exquisite torture being out in the world with the author. She kept a companionable distance between us on the sidewalk and on the paths that navigated and circumnavigated the park, letting me take her hand just once to help her up a steep incline that brought us to a lovely view of the neighborhood. The air smelled slightly burnt. I thought my skin would explode if she did not touch me, but she did not, until finally, safe behind the closed door of her house, she placed her hand on the small of my back and guided me up the stairs.

The author's bedroom was large and comfortable, with light coming in from the south and west. I stood between the bed and a small sitting area that held a couple of armchairs upholstered in a muted floral pattern, pushing the sleeves of my cotton sweater up and down while she pulled gauzy peach curtains over the windows. When she turned her eyes to me I yanked my sweater off and tossed it on one of the chairs, before I lost my nerve.

"Not so fast," she said quietly. I leaned toward her voice. "Slow down. I want to savor you."

She came over and traced the edges of the undershirt I wore

instead of a bra, then ran her fingertips down my arms so lightly I shivered. She lifted the shirt slowly, slowly, over my head.

I was acutely aware of everything around me: The slight breeze lifting the curtains, the red of the author's lipstick, the scent of my own sweat. A siren, blocks away, signaling a distant emergency.

The author stepped back and took me wholly in her regard while I stood there, shirtless and trembling in the peach-colored light. Then she let out a small, involuntary "Oh!," bringing her hand up to meet her mouth, and I felt the word erupt through my body.

Her navy blue rayon blouse was complicated by a dozen or more delicate buttons, mother-of-pearl, and as I undid them I wondered if she had chosen it deliberately for this occasion, and hoped she had. She wore silk against her skin, a simple black camisole with thin straps that emphasized the hollow of her collarbone.

Time was erratic, and I thought it might stop entirely when I finally removed the camisole and lay my palm in the center of her chest; when she bent down and took my breast into her mouth the clock careened wildly forward.

We traveled this way for the length of early evening and into the other side of nightfall, and afterwards, lying naked in the queen-size bed, she dozed a little while I held her in my arms, feeling, for the first time in my life, I was truly awake.

She was not my universe, not exactly. More like my sun, the light I orbited around. Could there have been more than two people in the world? No. For me, there was the author; everyone else was distraction or worse, annoyance. It pleased us, this private conversation our bodies carried on in the midst of everything daily, for the daily does not pause, even for longing, even for love.

I held mystery in my every activity; when my roommates asked where I spent so many evenings, I smiled at them like some robed virgin of the Reformation. Let them make up their own stories. I wasn't giving them mine.

Yes, it was a kind of game. One afternoon, I stopped by her

home unannounced to pick up a jacket I'd left there the night before. I'd never done this before; she told me when to come and I came, unquestioningly. Perhaps I'd left my jacket there on purpose; perhaps I was trying to catch her, for once, off-kilter. Perhaps I was shivering just a bit. Maybe that's why I crossed my arms, as if to keep from losing heat, as I waited for her to come to the door.

She swung it open, then stopped mid-swing when she saw me. "This isn't a good time," she said in a low voice, her right hand on the door handle and her left on the jamb. "My bridge group is here."

"You have a bridge group?" This was a new side to her. "I didn't know you had a bridge group. You are such a grownup."

"I *am* a grownup, and I have a bridge group, and we're right in the middle of a game. Don't embarrass me."

I looked past her and saw two card tables of women sporting way too much hair spray. "I left my jacket in the kitchen." I pushed my way in.

She introduced me to the group. "She's an assistant at the college library," she told them. "She's been helping me with some research."

"I left my jacket here the other day," I said stupidly to no one in particular.

"What sort of research?" asked one of the hairdos, just as I was mapping a quick escape.

"Oh, mostly on the intricacies of Victorian dress and undress. You know, what's underneath the layers of crinoline and the three or four petticoats and the buttons and corsets and silk stockings and . . . "

"Your coat is in the kitchen." The author firmly took my arm and steered me through the swinging door.

Once it was safely closed, she retrieved my jacket from the back of a chair and draped it over my shoulders.

"I was just getting to the good parts."

"You are so bad," she said quietly. Then she kissed me until I thought I might collapse, and pushed me unceremoniously out the back door.

Funny, isn't it? Now that I am nearing the age she was when we first met, now that I know how the plot continues, how the characters develop, now that I am writing this from the perspective of the girl I once was, I still can't keep the author's voice from intruding on my vision with its revision.

Where are you planning to go with this? Those are her words creeping into my manuscript. *Two chapters in and they've already been intimate. You're climaxing, if you'll pardon the expression, far too early. It's all falling action from here on in.*

Aah, pipe down. Save it for your made-up heroines.

I'm going back to the story now, back to that era of endless climax when my name was always on her lips and hers was writing itself on my heart, if I can say such a thing without sounding sentimental.

What the hell, I was sentimental. I would have been a walking Hallmark card if I hadn't held such things in disdain. On my next appointed visit, a few days after retrieving the jacket that I didn't need, as it turned out, due to an unexpected return of summer, I announced that I had brought her something.

"What is it?" she said, looking me over for evidence of a package.

"Not yet. It's for later."

We went into the kitchen, where she was assembling a salad. She picked up a serrated knife and began sawing tomatoes into wedges. I came up from behind and circled her waist in my arms. She bit one tomato wedge in half, then reached over her shoulder to pop the other half into my mouth.

"We have to talk about these unannounced visits." She picked up a cucumber and a paring knife and started shaving off the peel.

"It was one visit, and I rather enjoyed it." I swallowed the tomato and started in on her earlobe.

"Yes, I noticed that you did"—she rolled her head to the side, pulling her earlobe from my mouth—"but I need you to listen to me." Little strips of dark green cucumber skin were piling up into a Mayan ruin on the cutting board. "I have a certain . . . image to maintain. The bridge group . . . "

"Oh, fuck the bridge group." I was talking, I realized, more loudly than I needed to, but the volume adjust on my voice was apparently out of order. I let go of her waist and stepped back.

She set down the cucumber and the knife and turned to face me. I could tell from her pained look that she was about to begin speaking to me gently, in the tone one would use to explain a complicated concept to a child who was not developmentally ready to understand it.

I was not interested. "Do you love me?" I asked. It was a dare, and I knew it. And I knew she would deflect it. I watched for her face to begin moving toward something lighthearted, some funny, sidestepping comment that would allow us to go back to chopping vegetables and arranging them in bowls and carrying them to the table to eat like any two people who enjoy each other's company.

And her face did just that, and I could see the words forming on her lips, and then she froze for a moment, and then something just let go in her expression.

"Yes, I do love you. Yes." She looked simultaneously surprised and resigned.

I swallowed. "I promise I'll call before I drop by from now on."

"Thank you." And then she began to cry.

"Aren't you happy?" I wiped the tears from her cheeks with my thumbs.

"No. Yes. I don't know." She said it again, "I love you," and she was crying and I was laughing and then we were both laughing and I was dancing her around the kitchen in my arms.

Later, we sat cross-legged on her bed and I produced my gift.

"It's an antidote to the bridge club," I said.

"Is this marijuana?"

"You aren't shocked, are you?" I hoped she was.

"Darling, I sampled opium in a back room in Istanbul before you were even a spark of a spark. Am I supposed to share this with the bridge girls?" She rolled the joint between her fingers.

"It would probably be good for them. But I'd rather you share it with me."

Ten minutes later, after I showed her how to hold the smoke in her lungs until it made her cough, we were giggling like schoolgirls. Or perhaps I should say like a schoolgirl and her usually elegant and mature lover.

"Does it always make you feel so . . . I don't know . . . stupid?"

"I forget," I said, laughing like an imbecile. I took off my glasses to further blur my focus, and the flames of the candles I'd lit glowed like a little solar system atop her bureau. "I think I'm lost in the time-space continuum."

"I was thinking pre–World War II Paris."

"Not post–Civil War Atlanta?"

"That would be a little too surreal, even for me."

"Oh, come on. We could be Gertrude and Scarlett."

"Frankly, my dear, a rose is a rose is a rose."

"A rose is a what?"

"I forget." We both started laughing, and then, suddenly, we stopped.

"Did you mean it, back in the kitchen, when you said you loved me?" We lay side by side on our backs, not touching, looking up at the ceiling.

"I meant it."

"And you weren't even stoned then."

"I wasn't."

"Do you know what I'd like? I'd like to wake up next to you in the morning. What do you think? I parked around the corner."

I turned my head and saw her mouth form itself into the word "no," but it was a day for miracles, and the opposite word came out.

CHAPTER 3

She liked buying me gifts—delicate necklaces that I wore against my skin, a black wool jacket that she produced from her closet one evening when I showed up at her door shivering, my hair dusted with the first snow of the season. "So I can wrap my arms around you even when you're not here," she said.

Sometimes we ventured out together, to restaurants at the edges of town, or occasionally downtown to see films with subtitles and characters who were constantly flirting with poorly translated danger. We'd arrive after the previews started, sit in the back row and duck out just before the credits began to roll.

Once in a while, on a Saturday afternoon, we'd drive a couple of hours to a nearby city, where we'd stroll arm-in-arm through classy department stores like a girl and her favorite aunt, invariably ending up in a not-so-innocent embrace in a dressing room. I let her choose clothes for me; I let her pay for them. She had a sense of style that was a kind of perception: she'd pick something off the rack—a rayon sweater in bright red, tan linen slacks, items I would never consider for myself—and when I put them on, I'd look more like myself than I did in my own clothes.

I turned down her offer to help me rent what she called a "decent" apartment, but I did make a move on my own accord, to a studio I could afford on my salary. I had enrolled in night classes and told my roommates I needed a quiet place to study, but the truth was, I'd outgrown them. I'd long since stopped providing them with creative explanations for my evening disappearances, and they'd long since stopped asking.

My new apartment had been hacked out of a once-elegant home in a once-elegant neighborhood. I shared a side wing with a guy named Jeff, who nodded pleasantly when we passed each other in the hallway and whom I often heard climbing the staircase to his second-floor studio as I drifted off to sleep.

I spent one or two nights a week at the author's house, on occasion an entire weekend. When I was not with her, or at work, I pored through books on research methodology, trying to do what the professor suggested—not memorize the techniques, but incorporate them into a way of seeing the world as a compilation of information and theories, scientific and otherwise, as if we could understand the machinations of the universe by following a footnote or finding the right obscure journal.

Sometimes I felt her doing this sort of research, the author, when she looked into my face as if there were some explanation there that would untangle the way she felt about me.

"I'm learning you by heart," she would say, and I'd take her hand and place it on my chest so she could feel my want in its indecipherable Morse code.

"Why me?" I asked her one night while we drove back to her house after a shopping excursion.

She kept her eyes on the taillights in front of us, but took her right hand off the wheel and lay it against my cheek. "Do you mean why do I love you?"

"No, I mean what made you notice me in the first place? There must have been any number of young women hanging around the college library last summer. Why me?"

She yanked gently on my ponytail, still looking at the road. "You make me sound like an old lecher."

"A loveable old lecher. But I'm sure I'm not the first young woman you've taken up with. What was it about me that made you come back to the library every day for a month?"

"You know, you're not as smart as you think." The highway unscrolled in front of us.

"No, really, I want to know."

"The truth is, I liked the way you carried the old books with reverence. I could see you appreciated them as objects, and that you seemed to understand they have things to teach us. I liked that you spoke with precision, that you didn't use the slangy style of your generation. I can't bear hearing the word 'goes' as a substitute for 'says,' or 'like' as a verbal tick. I think that's part of a general respectfulness I sensed in you. And of course, I found you very attractive, and I could see that you knew that and were flattered by it."

"I'm still flattered."

"And you're still beautiful, and now I know that you're also funny and kind and that you sleep in your socks and you need two cups of strong tea in the morning to get going."

"My feet get cold. What else?"

"What else? Well, you appreciate irony, you play with sarcasm but you're never mean, you're intelligent . . . "

"I thought I wasn't as intelligent as I think I am."

"I said 'smart.' You're not as smart as you think you are. There's a difference."

She put her hand back on the wheel, and we were quiet for a few moments, listening to the tires humming on asphalt. I wished I had something to give her, but I didn't know what.

"I felt your eyes all over me that first day in the library. I liked it, but it made me a little off-balance on the ladder. I think I started falling in love with you that day."

The car made a little jerk forward, an involuntary motion. She was gripping the steering wheel tightly, as if she might suddenly lose control of the two-thousand-pound machine that was careening down the highway at seventy miles per hour.

Here's an interesting piece of information about her: She went to church. Not exactly religiously, but most Sundays when she was in town. And not just any church—The Church, as in The Catholic Church. I learned this when she kicked me out of bed one Sunday morning so she could make it to 10:00 a.m. Mass.

"Since when?" I asked.

"Since always."

This may sound odd coming from the pen of a lapsed Protestant, an alumna of the easygoing Congregationalists who believe in ham and bean suppers and the restorative powers of poinsettias, but I was vaguely aroused by the thought of her, dressed stylishly in black, kneeling in her solitary pew, making the sign of the cross on her torso, waiting with parted lips to accept the communion wafer, body of Christ. There'd be organ music, incantations in a language so obsolete only the blessed have it at their disposal.

"Am I terribly perverse?" I asked her later, crossing her naked body with my unconfirmed hands.

"No, you're right, it is romantic, the church, all that stained glass and dusty light and Jesus dying for our sins."

"Are we sinners?" I placed small kisses all over her forehead and cheeks.

"Oh, yes," she replied, but she didn't look as if she minded much. "I may have to give you up for Lent."

Other times I wondered if she ventured to the church on Friday afternoons, as my Catholic schoolmates had done, to sit in what I pictured as a medieval phone booth, confessing a week's worth of indiscretions to a stern and slightly bored voice. I never asked her about this. I didn't want to know if I was a sin she admitted to each week so she could come back for more.

A book should be 15 percent exposition and 85 percent scenes, she once told me. All of the scenes should advance the action, or provide new insight into the characters.

I can't call myself a writer; I'm a research librarian who's been privileged and doomed to spend the greater part of my adult life inextricably linked to not just a writer but an author, someone with a shelf full of paperbacks to stare out from, on the penultimate page, in undated retouched glory.

Her stories are linear. Yes, there are flashbacks; yes, the future is foreshadowed in the action and the dialogue, but they make chronological sense. We all know how they're going to end—either in great happiness or great sorrow.

I've passed years watching her wring the old feelings out of new characters in an orderly way, the plot marching like a good soldier toward the cinema of the housewife's heart. But now I can't organize my own story into a story. Doesn't everything really happen at once? I carry these scenes around in my pockets. They're not my history. They are who I am. Things add up in ways we don't expect and can't explain. I know this because her eyes are still on me in the college archives, she's still tossing me out of bed for 10:00 a.m. Mass, that kiss in the restaurant parking lot still lingers on my lips.

This is no apology; I'm not one to confess sins, mine or anyone else's. I'm just explaining how it is. I'm just explaining why I stayed with her so long, even though I could tell you that there's a pocket in which I am always walking away, and a pocket in which I am kissing someone else, someone more appropriate, my own age, someone I am always leaving behind for her.

I was learning new things about her all the time, even though she wouldn't talk about the past. "I have diplomatic immunity," she'd say. It was a diplomatic way of changing the subject when I asked what seemed like harmless questions. I asked anyway. Where did you grow up, Did you take a new name when you started publishing your books, Why did you never marry.

"That should be obvious," she'd say, without clarifying which question she was answering.

I learned early not to confuse her with her characters, or her life with her messy but inevitable plot lines. She knew her stuff: could describe in detail the motions required for mounting a stallion side-saddle, for instance, or the difficulties of cooking on a cast-iron stove. But she wasn't a fanatic; details were the tools of her trade, not the kind of obsession that leads some people to spend weekends re-enacting the Battle of Antietam in stiflingly authentic wool uniforms.

"It's a job," she said, "and one I'm quite good at. It pays well enough, and it offers a lot of flexibility."

She knew she wasn't a writer of great literature, but it pleased me that she didn't apologize for her books.

"I'm always swept up by your drama," I told her.

"That's as it should be."

We were seated at her kitchen table, on either side of a Scrabble board. She'd just pulled a pan of buns from the oven—treats for tomorrow's bridge session—and had threatened to teach me bridge while we waited for them to cool enough to slather on icing. I declined. "It's too much concentration," I said. "This way we can carry on a conversation while we play."

Mostly the conversations involved her tongue on the palms of my hands, or my fingers circling the delicate skin just above her wrist. Everything we did or said in those days was a seduction scene.

She spelled out DEWY and I went weak in the knees.

"That's twenty-two points, double word score," she said.

"As opposed to double entendre."

"I'm never opposed to double entendre."

"Of course, sometimes the direct approach is better." I borrowed her D and laid down BEDROOM.

"And sometimes it's better to be creative." Picking up on my B, she expanded it into TABLE.

We looked at each other across the game board and grinned.

"Are you serious?" I asked, climbing out of my chair and over the maze of language to reach her.

An hour or so later, we were sitting on the floor, naked, wrapped in a cotton blanket I'd retrieved from the den. I leaned back against the cabinets and the author nestled between my legs, leaning back into me. The kitchen smelled of cinnamon and sex.

She held up her goblet of wine and examined it the way a scientist might look at a test tube. "What was it we were talking about?"

"Some guy named Dewy," I replied, tracing the question mark of her earlobe.

"Ah, Mr. Decimal. You and he are intimate acquaintances, aren't you?"

"He's a bit outdated, but I like him anyway."

"Umph." She set her glass on the linoleum floor and squirmed around, trying to get comfortable on the throw rug. "I'm getting too old for this."

"How old are you, exactly?" I was teasing more than questioning, because in the past she'd always sidestepped this particular line of inquiry. Older than the hills, she'd say, or Old enough to know better, or some other dumb cliché.

This time she was quiet for a few moments, and I was afraid I'd ruined the mood. "It's okay; you don't have to tell me," I said, rocking her in my arms. "I think you're just the right age."

"I'm forty-nine. I'm forty-nine and I'm going to be fifty in a few weeks." She said it like a challenge.

"Then we'll have to celebrate. I'll make cake, we'll wear party hats."

"Actually, my publisher's putting on a big bash in New York City. He's timing the release of '*Constant Sorrows*' to correspond to it." She always put verbal quotation marks around the title of her new book; it had been foisted on her by an editor recently imported from the romance division.

"I wish they could have come up with a cheerier name for that one," I told her. Finding my wine glass empty, I skipped the middle man, grabbing the bottle by its neck and taking a long gulp. "I guess I'm not invited."

"I'm sorry."

"You're always sorry."

"Constantly."

She kissed me and we went upstairs to sleep, leaving the icing for the morning and the floor strewn with Scrabble letters and a half-completed score sheet.

The weekend of her birthday, I tried not to feel sorry for myself. The weather wasn't helping: Spring was making its first appearance, coaxing a thousand yellow stars from the forsythia in my neighbor's yard. People came out from their houses, mostly in pairs, and squinted into the sun. Was it possible to emerge from a shared hibernation and walk calmly together through the park?

I opened the window to my apartment and looked for an album to toss on the stereo. I instinctively reached for the Edith Piaf record the author had given me, then, on second thought, passed it over in favor of a Joni Mitchell LP I'd loved in college. No use turning a little angst into a huge French tragedy. I cranked the volume just a notch too high for my one-and-a-half rooms plus bath, then sat down and studied the space. Empty walls, a few pieces of yard-sale furniture, a futon plopped on the floor. I'd been living here since before Christmas, but hadn't felt inclined to put up my old posters or to buy new ones. Most of my books were still in boxes that did double-duty as end tables; the ones I needed for my night class were piled high on the kitchen table. Why bother fix the place up? She would never visit me here. But something—maybe Joni Mitchell's cheerful birdsong or the faint smell of coming rain in the breeze that flapped the curtains—made me want to spruce things up. I saw the one sad Swedish ivy going brown in the window, and decided I needed plants. Lots of them. Trees, maybe, something to bring in the outdoors. Conveniently overlooking my sorry history with all things green, my inability to make things grow, let alone keep them alive, I hurried into the hallway and out the back door, nearly bumping into Jeff, who was vigorously making out with another guy on the top step.

"Sorry," I said, barely audibly, and looked quickly away, though neither of them took any notice of me. I made a beeline for my car and pulled out of the parking lot, aiming toward a huge greenhouse just outside the city limits.

I admit I got a little carried away, but I felt like an urban pirate, steering my green island back through the city, its trunk popped and full of ficuses, an enormous rubber plant, and a small orange tree complete with marble-sized fruit. I imagined the story I would tell the author when she returned, about walking through the damp glass rooms, caught up in the smell of earth and fertilizer, lugging tree after tree through those tropics to the parking lot, where a fine mist had begun draping the world in fog.

By the time I arced into my designated parking space behind the apartment house, the mist was full-blown rain. I grabbed one of the pots from the trunk and made a dash for it.

Jeff was still on the porch, but now he was alone, leaning against the clapboards, smoking. "I hope they were thirsty," he said. "Do you need a hand?" He put his cigarette out in the planter that came with the house and held the door for me. I made my way to my apartment door and balanced ficus number one on my hip while I fumbled with my keys and then let myself in. I plopped the pot on the floor in the kitchen end of the studio, then headed out for more. In the hallway, I passed Jeff, who had turned into a walking vine, with one tree in each arm and leaves flapping about his face.

"Thank you. You don't have to do that."

"Oh, thank *you*. I'd do just about anything for the feel of rubber against my skin."

Another five or so trips to the parking lot and back, and the two of us plus the menagerie of plants were dripping puddles onto the linoleum. He looked around. "I love what you've done with the place. The Spartan jungle thing is very big these days."

"Can I offer you a beer?"

"I'd love one. Just give me a minute to change into something more . . . dry."

Jeff, it turned out, was a few years older than me and had been in the navy, stationed stateside.

"Oh, I saw plenty of action. Eight hundred men cooped up on a ship for weeks at a time, with nothing to do but polish their missile launchers. Well, you can imagine."

Now he waited tables at a chi-chi downtown restaurant and took courses in film production. The guy I'd seen kissing him on the porch was a doctor who lived in the suburbs with his wife and two kids.

"The bastard didn't even tell me until I'd slept with him three times and had mentally selected the monogram for the his-and-his towels that were going to hang in the bathroom of our trendy but unpretentious three-story brownstone."

"You're better off without him." I took a long pull on my third beer.

"Who said anything about being without him? He's coming over Monday night. His wife thinks he's in a basketball league."

"So you're not mad at him for being married?"

"You ask a lot of questions for someone who reveals so little. Come on, give. What's your story? I know there's more to it than this spinster librarian thing you've got going."

"Well, it's complicated," I began, pushing back in my spindly kitchen chair so I was teetering on the back legs.

"Everything is complicated. Just start at the beginning."

And then, amazingly enough, I did. I don't know if it was the beer, the thought of the author whooping it up in New York City without me, or the fact that Jeff was so far removed from the life she and I had together that it couldn't possibly matter, but I told him the whole story. The archives room, the bridge club, the birthday party to which I was not invited. I even told him about the sex on the kitchen table.

He was impressed. Not by the sex on the table—I got the feeling that was pretty mild compared to some of his own escapades—but by the fact that I was involved with the author. He'd actually read her work. I think "devoured" was the word he used.

"I got through junior high by daydreaming about the huge pecs on those captains of industry. And the costume balls and the dancing and people storming in and out of rooms. I'm telling you, that girlfriend of yours understands camp."

"She's not my girlfriend."

He shrugged. "Well, lover. Paramour. Whatever you want to call her, she's hot stuff."

"Tell me about it." I flashed for a second to our parting two nights earlier, when she'd put her mouth up to my ear and listed the places on my body she planned to caress when she returned.

By the time Jeff left, one six pack, a pizza delivery, and several hours after we'd deposited the greenery on the kitchen floor, I was an open book. An open book that I'd have to close again by morning, an open book whose narrative I made Jeff swear never to reveal to anyone, but a book whose paragraphs had been perused and whose chapters had been discussed.

I felt giddy, really, from the act of telling and from Jeff's vicarious delight and from the thought of seeing her again, in a few days, when I would present myself for her hands' perusal.

"I knew I was right about you," Jeff said as he got up to leave.

"Right about what?"

"You're a lesbian. You're family."

The word hit like cold water on my face. "Oh, no, I'm not."

"You sleep with girls, honey. You're a lesbian."

We held our own birthday celebration a few nights later. I spread a blanket on the floor of her den and set up a picnic—Chinese food and rice and my first attempt at a layer cake, a huge chocolate affair with a red frosting heart on top. I lit candles on the coffee table, placed a jug of roses in the center of the blanket and a bottle of wine in an ice bucket off to the side, then led her in.

"You really know how to rough it," she said, arranging herself gracefully on the blanket.

"It's not exactly New York City, I know, but I can guarantee you won't get mugged after dessert." I plopped down, cross-legged, beside her.

"Can you?" She picked up her chopsticks and scissored a piece of orange chicken, straight from the box. "That's too bad."

"Well, perhaps something can be arranged."

"Open up." She fed the chicken into my mouth. "Now tell me what you did without me all weekend."

"I'd rather hear about your party."

"Oh, there's nothing to tell, really. It was rather tedious. Too many people drinking too much and sucking up to anyone they assumed to be important. I'd much rather have been curled up here with you."

I doubted it, but I filled her wine glass and mine. "Well, I spent Saturday turning my apartment into a jungle. I went to the greenhouse and bought a dozen enormous plants, mostly of the indestructible variety. Now they're occupying the kitchen while I figure out which ones should live near the windows and which ones want to hide in the corners." I fumbled with a piece of pork in garlic sauce, and eventually gave up, stabbing it through the middle with one chopstick. "It's like eating with stilts."

"Think of them as extensions of your fingers. Here, hold them in your palm like this." She took my hand.

I took it back. "I know how to eat with chopsticks. I just haven't had as much practice as you have."

She looked properly rebuked. "I'm sorry, sweetheart. You must get tired of spending so much time around an old know-it-all."

"No, of course not. I'm sorry too. I just wanted this to be perfect."

"It is perfect. And I really would prefer to eat Chinese with you than go to any number of fancy cocktail parties."

Just one cocktail party would have been plenty. But I didn't want to spoil her birthday dinner. And she'd come back from New York laden with gifts for me: a tan angora V-neck, soft and boyish; a silver pen and pencil set; a pair of black leather boots with just a hint of heel. It's not as though she went off for the weekend and completely forgot about me. It's not as though she could have shown up at the restaurant where she was being welcomed into her second half-century with an awkward kid on her arm. Nor would I have felt comfortable in a setting like that.

I let her off the hook, went back to my story of plants, how I'd sailed through town with trees spilling out of my trunk; how the downpour started just as I'd reached home and let up shortly after I finished unloading. So I left out a few details. She didn't tell me everything.

For her birthday, I'd brought something from the greenhouse—an Easter lily; and something from the rare-books store in town—a worn, leather-bound copy of Elizabeth Barrett Browning's *Sonnets from the Portuguese*; and something else—a silk chemise, delicate and lacy, a few shades darker than her skin. We ate the cake, which tasted rich and moist, even though the bottom layer wasn't quite flat and the top had slid a bit, so the whole thing looked like it could collapse at any moment.

"How does it feel to be fifty?"

"A little like the second intermission at the opera, when there's nothing left but bombast and aria."

"You have such a way with metaphor." I was rinsing the plates and stacking them in her dishwasher; she sat, leonine, on the counter beside me, pouring herself another glass of wine.

"I do, don't I?"

"I expect the fat lady isn't ready to sing quite yet." And, indeed, she looked almost girlish in the soft glow of the light above the sink. I piled in the last dish, poured some powdered detergent into the little trap door, closed the dishwasher and turned it on. "But I could picture you in the opera. You have a certain stage presence, you know."

"Have you ever been to the opera?"

" 'Fraid not."

"Well, sometimes it's absolutely transcendent. Sometimes you think your heart will burst just from the idea of so much beauty and loss. And sometimes it's pretty tedious. People standing around on stage, not even bothering to act, just singing in an overly dramatic way in a language you don't understand."

"But your opera would be all heart and great legs," I said, drying my hands and running them over her thighs.

"Hmm. That's nice. Does it bother you?"

"The opera or your legs?"

"You know what I mean. My being fifty."

"Actually, I kind of like it," I said, losing my way in her green green eyes.

CHAPTER 4

I could tell you that days went by like this, in the company of a grand secret, or that weeks went by while the moon sharpened into a sickle and disappeared and came back whole again, months, years of love and all the sorrows and resentments it brings. I could tell you this, and it would be true. Not the whole truth, perhaps. Who can ever know that? Not I, in my eternal, relative youth; not the author in her state of self-imposed grace.

These days, I've replaced sensation with philosophy, and I'm not sorry—most of the time. Most of the time it's enough to remember her hand on the stem of a wine glass, or that soft corner of skin on the underside of her elbow. Such things don't need to be analyzed; can't, in fact, be accounted for in terminology other than what is written on the heart. Perhaps my dalliance with the inner side of desire lasted longer than it should have. There have, of course, been others. No one of my generation need spend years apart from the world. There are plenty of other ways to thwart one's psyche. Still, I came back, continue to come back, even now that she's genuinely old, not simply much older than I am.

"Darling, I have a surprise for you."

We were sipping our morning tea at a small table in her fenced-in backyard, wrapped in terry-cloth bathrobes. I could still feel the imprint of her hands on my body from last night's extended tryst.

"You always surprise me," I said, affecting a glamorous drawl as I was feeling a bit like a movie star in my dark glasses.

"No, this is a big surprise. I made some arrangements—I hope you don't mind." She reached into the pocket of her robe and retrieved an envelope, which she placed on the table in front of me.

I must have looked quizzical. Her surprises usually involved boxes from Bonwit Teller or pieces of jewelry secreted in certain of her pockets (and once in her brassiere). Inside the envelope were airplane tickets, two, one in her name and one in mine. The destination was a small island in the Caribbean, the kind of place you visit to snorkel among coral reefs or to launder money.

"It's the week after your night classes end. I thought we could go and celebrate and spend some time together." She spoke quickly, as if she needed to talk me into it. "I probably should have checked with you first, but I was walking past the travel agency and I saw a poster of the white sand and the green water and I suddenly wanted very much to be there with you. Is it okay?"

I looked up from the tickets. Was it okay that she needed to assuage her guilt about leaving me behind for her birthday? "You don't have to do this. But yes, it's okay. It's wonderful."

Could I do this? I'd need to get the week off from work, buy a bathing suit and something suitable for wearing to dinner in the tropics, ask Jeff to stop by and water the jungle. Maybe it was a guilt-induced vacation, but I didn't care. I rarely had an entire weekend with her; an entire week would be heaven. "I think we should celebrate right now," I said, pulling her up from her chair and waltzing her through the azaleas.

She threw her head back and laughed. "I'm going to have to put shoes on if you start in on the Charleston."

"What say we tango up to the bedroom?" My body was getting the better of me. Or maybe it was her body.

"You need to tango into your clothes if you want to make it to work on time," she said, tapping the tip of my nose with her finger to emphasize each word. "And I'm halfway through the death of a favorite daughter in childbirth."

"How *do* you write such things?" We stopped dancing and faced each other, hand in hand, barefoot on the grass.

"By holding my breath."

I kissed her on the cheek and went inside. The dining room table was cluttered with the details of imaginary lives, people who stood for large ideals like valor and compassion, or for large failings, the capacity of a brother to kill a brother. My failings were small, they involved thinking too much and understanding too little; my attributes minor, barely worth notice. I spent a lot of time trying to be good. I spent a lot of time trying to grow up. But I didn't plan on growing into a story riddled with people and lacking in reflection, a life that could be summarized on index cards and wrapped up in a tragic jumping accident or on a feather deathbed. No, I was going to spend a week on an island with an elegant, complicated, inscrutable woman, a woman much my senior. We'd wear suntan lotion and sunglasses and say witty things to each other.

"Sounds like a happy little shipwreck," Jeff said when I told him about the plan, emphasizing the movie-star eyewear and repartee. He was an appreciative audience for my elaborate recountings of my episodes with the author.

"Well, we do have return tickets. She's got to keep cranking out the torrid fiction."

"Luckily for you, truth is sometimes more torrid than fiction."

We were sitting at my table, which was far too small for expanding plotlines and timelines and character studies. It was just right for a library science text, however, or a bowl of potato chips for entertaining the upstairs neighbor. Jeff had stopped by after work to see how the jungle was doing, so I showed him the bathtub, where I was soaking the ficuses, following instructions I'd found in a 1930s houseplant manual. Then I poured him a glass of pinot grigio—I was developing a taste for wine.

"I'm not exactly sure what one does for a week on an island," I said. "Read, I suppose, walk on the beach, write postcards."

"Well, if it were me, I'd probably ferment some coconut wine, put on a grass skirt, and bushwhack through the jungle in search of the Professor. In your case, let's see . . . Ginger or Mary Ann? Mary Ann's a tad wholesome for your tastes, I'd imagine. It'll have to be Ginger. She's got that seductive glam-girl thing going. Of course, Mrs. Howell is closer to the age you seem to go for."

I threw a corn chip at him. It fell short. "I throw like a girl."

"We'll have to butch you up a little." Even in his formal waiter uniform, a white button-down shirt, black tie and black trousers, Jeff looked right at home astride the gaudy ripped vinyl chair I'd dragged in from the street on trash day. He wasn't exactly good looking, but there was a sweetness in the way his hair scraggled over his collar and his eyebrows danced around his forehead. I could understand what the married doctor saw in him: he looked perpetually delighted.

"You don't really think she'll bring a suitcase full of evening gowns, do you?"

"Who, Ginger? She has to; it's in the script. And you couldn't pull off a sensible farm dress in those sling-back high heels."

"Not Ginger." The second chip sailed over his shoulder.

"Ah, the beloved. Just hope she brings a suitcase full of money. If you're going to be kept, might as well do it in style."

I bristled. "I'm not kept."

"Oh, come on, sweetie. You're living out everyone's fantasy. A vacation in an exotic locale with a fabulous and wealthy older lover? Who'd turn that down? It's not giving up any self-respect to just enjoy it for the week. You can still come back to your lousy minimum-wage job and your Salvation Army furniture."

The thought of coming back to this was both comforting and distressing. "I'm just, I don't know. Every now and then I stop and I think, What the hell am I doing? I mean, really, what the hell *am* I doing?" I picked up the salsa bottle and waved it around like some lunatic jacked up on jalapeños. "Fancy vacation, forty dollar bottles of wine, I'm crazy in love with a woman—*a woman*—who's in a completely different league, not to mention age range, and she swears she's not just toying with me, but how do I know that for sure? And sometimes I think, This is not the life I'm supposed to be having, this is not anything like the life I'm supposed to be having."

"Hey, hey, relax. It's only a vacation. What are you so afraid of?"

"Everything. I'm afraid of everything. We've never spent a week together. What if she gets bored with me? What if I get bored with her? What if I use the wrong fork at dinner?"

"Okay, look at it this way." Jeff picked up the pencil I'd been using to underline salient points in research methodology and tapped it on the table a couple of times. "There is no 'Life you're supposed to be having.' You're having this life, and don't say you wouldn't choose it again, because I know any number of people who'd give their eye teeth to have the kind of adventure you're having. Maybe you will get bored; maybe she'll get bored. So what? So you'll have a mysterious, forbidden love in your past, and a great story to tell your grand-nieces, the queer ones anyway." He pointed the pencil at me.

I eyed him skeptically.

"And maybe neither of you will get bored, and maybe she doesn't give a shit about whether you use the right fork, and maybe she'll look so hot in her bikini and you'll look so cute in your cut-off jeans that you'll spend the whole week rolling around in bed. When you're not sipping drinks from coconut shells with those little umbrellas in them."

"So you're saying maybe a vacation is just a vacation?"

"I'm saying you think too much. Just stop analyzing and enjoy yourself. Whatever's going to happen will happen."

"You think?"

"I know. And I'm jealous as hell, I might add."

"Well, don't be. Maybe you'll find the Professor among the ficus trees while I'm gone."

"Maybe." He got up and stretched. "But for now I'm off to meet Mr. Married at the bar. Want to come? Maybe Mary Ann will be there."

"Thanks, but I think I'll hold out for Ginger."

"You know, if you overlook the frumpy dresses and the bouffy hair, Mrs. Howell's a hot little number."

I sailed the last chip at him. It went foul, crash-landing in the Swedish Ivy.

"Just like a girl," Jeff said, scooting out the door.

She brought plenty of suitcases, none of them filled with evening gowns or wads of cash (a joke I didn't share with her, knowing *Gilligan's Island* post-dated her childhood by a couple of generations). But she'd clearly spent a fortune on our little rendezvous. We had a private cabana not ten steps from the beach, designed to look like the huts the islanders lived in fifty or a hundred years earlier, only quainter and with better security. The louvered windows were fortified with screens and sliding bolts, and an intercom system would bring a waiter in crisp white shorts and Hawaiian shirt hustling down the path with a tray of daiquiris or fruit salad. Everything was devised so there'd be no reason to leave the resort until the gleaming white van carried you back to the airport through rutted roads dotted with shacks and lean-to soup stands, the rolled-up windows and air-conditioning muffling the high-volume reggae and American pop spewing forth from giant boom boxes, an occasional goat or cow crossing into traffic.

A pool, its sides and floor painted green-blue to replicate the sea, sat yards from the original. There were two open-air restaurants, one coffee shop–like for breakfast and lunch, one suitable for an elegant dinner. Both served dishes native to the island, chicken and seafood in spicy sauce, fruits with names like words from another language. You could also order steak or primly broiled scallops or tuna salad and cottage cheese. The gift shop sold T-shirts and postcards and delicate necklaces made of shells and bowls fashioned from gourds. You could ask to have a local girl come in and massage your feet or twist your hair into a torrent of braids.

This was the world we flew into, giddy with adventure and desire and at the cusp of the hot season. So why couldn't I shake off my apprehension?

"I think I could just lie here for the rest of my life." I was stretched out on a large blanket, still wet from my first rollick in the warmest ocean I'd ever encountered.

"Too bad that's not an option. Here, you're going to burn to a crisp if you're not careful." She dripped a cool puddle of sunblock onto my back and began working it into my skin.

"No? Can't we just give up our regular lives for Lent? You could even keep your typewriter—or I'll make you a new one out of coconut shells and bamboo. Mmm, that feels good."

"Actually, the idea of Lent is to suffer a little so you appreciate what you have." She spread the sunblock down one arm and then the other, then dribbled more of the stuff on the backs of my thighs.

"Oh, I appreciate what I have. Plus, I think suffering is highly overrated." I breathed deeply. The air tasted of salt and seaweed and tanning lotion, with a faint hint of the perfume she'd dabbed behind her neck and on her wrists that morning before we left for the airport.

"So we'll take the week off from suffering, since you suffer so much in your life back home. Roll over."

I did, and found myself squinting up into a sky that was deeper and brighter than any I'd ever seen. "It's like we've walked into a painting," I said to the author, who was slathering the exposed part of my chest with lotion. "Not a watercolor—they're too washed out. Acrylic, maybe. Something really saturated."

"It does make one want to wear bright colors, doesn't it?" She looked rather Gauguin-like herself, decked out in a flowered one-piece in shades of red, orange, and yellow. She'd wrapped a matching sarong around her waist. As usual, she appeared perfectly at ease in her surroundings.

"You know, I can reach that part myself." Her hand was finding its way into my bikini top. "Here I am trying to have a philosophical discussion about art, and you just want to feel me up. Or down, as the case may be." I wasn't angry; I was delighted to be out in the world with her, under the blue blue sky, while she made no attempt to hide her affection for me. Granted there was no one nearby to get a good look at what she was doing . . .

She put down the bottle of lotion and looked out toward the sea. "You, my dear one, are all the truth and beauty I need, and it doesn't get much more philosophical than that."

I sat up and put my arm around her shoulder. "Sometimes I forget how sappy and sentimental you can be, underneath that author persona of yours."

"It's a side of myself I wasn't aware I had. You seem to have brought it out in me."

"It's the setting," I said. "Don't you just feel passionate in a landscape like this? Like you're really alive; like anything is possible?"

"With you, maybe it is."

Or maybe not. But I was certain I wanted to find out.

Is it possible to toss out the apple, look away from the eye of the snake, and go back to a kind of innocence? Those first few days we tried, keeping to our little thatched-roof paradise and the beach outside, ordering platters of fruit, decanters of wine. She was plowing through a stack of women's magazines; I'd picked up a copy of the latest best-selling feminism-for-the-masses novel. In it, a woman managed to break loose of a suffocating marriage and claim a life of her own after some four hundred pages of uncertainty and tedious conversations.

I don't have to do this, I thought, turning from one chapter to the next. I'm doing this instead. The "instead" was not exactly a life, of course—rather a trip on the outskirts of a life—but it felt like the beginning of something. Who could say what? I scooped sand into my palm and saw a hundred different shades of white and tan and brown. I tasted something primordial on the back of the author's neck.

We were pleased the day the rains came and fell in cascades, punctuating the ocean, the beach, the rooftops. We spent the afternoon in bed, moving back and forth between sleep and lovemaking, those neighboring countries without borders.

Could it be that we grew tired of sharing the universe with only ourselves? Not tired, perhaps, but restive, and after several days of keeping company with the yellow sun and the green-blue sea, we were ready to get a look at the inside of paradise. Or was it the inverse? The author arranged for us to take a day trip, a ninety-minute drive to one of the island's more spectacular natural attractions: a multi-level waterfall that included a sheer drop of several hundred feet. "We'll be tourists for the day," she said. "It'll be our chance to act spoiled and ignorant, like ugly Americans."

"You're too adorable to be an ugly American."

"I don't think anyone's ever called me adorable before," she said, packing a water bottle, bathing suit, and towel into her public radio tote bag.

I found her adorable because I knew certain personal things about her, like the fact that she brushed her teeth four times a day, or that, in winter, she slept in flannel pajamas with little reindeer on them. Other people would probably call her refined, or handsome, or perhaps striking.

"Hey, Adorable," I said, tossing her my wadded-up towel. "Got room for this in your bag?"

"Flattery will get you just about anywhere you want to go," she said, and I was pleased to notice that she was actually blushing a bit through her tan. She rolled up my towel and arranged it among her things. "Anything else?"

"I guess I should bring the feminists along," I said, throwing in the paperback novel I was halfway through. "You never know when you'll need some ideas for overthrowing the patriarchy."

We wandered up the path to the resort's main building, where the smiling woman behind the front desk directed us to a car parked just outside the door. A man leaned against it, smoking a cigarette.

"Have you noticed how everyone who works here smiles constantly?" I whispered to the author as we made our way across the lawn. "Can they possibly be that happy to see us?"

"It's part of their job description. Clean rooms, bring drinks, bus tables, and provide cheerful local color."

But when we reached the car, the driver smiled so disarmingly I couldn't help but return the favor.

"Hello, Miss," he said to the author. "Very good to see you again."

Again? My smile dropped. When had they met before? We'd

been together the entire trip. I shot her a look that said Wait a minute—; she shot me one back that said Not now.

"André," she said. "It's always lovely to see you." She touched my shoulder briefly and said my name, by way of introduction, then turned back to him.

Always? He held his hand out to me but I just nodded and got in the back. The author ignored me and climbed into what would have been the driver's seat in the U.S. but here was shotgun. André put the car in gear and the author launched into a lively conversation with him, asking about his sisters and his college studies.

I rolled down my window and let the hot wind blast my face. She glanced back at me for a moment but didn't say anything. André reached over to the dashboard and adjusted the air conditioning. We headed inland, through the gates of the resort and into a kind of luxurious poverty. Away from the ocean, the air smelled of cayenne and wood smoke. Everywhere there were abandoned, half-finished concrete-block houses with lush forest growing up through what was once intended to be a roof. The finished houses looked half-finished, too—two- or three-room affairs with chickens and children and sometimes small groups of grown men idling about in the dirt yards. I caught only a glimpse of these as André was careening at a speed that felt unsafe to someone used to limits. Other cars went just as fast. Instead of slowing for curves on single-lane roads, drivers simply leaned into their horns. It seemed everyone was in a big hurry.

Around one bend, a goat was taking its time crossing the road. We came to a screeching halt, and a group of children ran up to us with their hands out. André pounded on his side window to shoo them away, though the author rolled hers down and began handing out coins from her purse. I reached into my pockets and realized I'd spent all the money she'd given me, but none of the children hit me up anyway. They could tell who was running the show. They crowded around the author's window until she ran out of coins and the goat reached the other side. André took the car out of neutral and drove on, while she sat there looking pleased with herself, as if she'd just solved Third-World hunger with her change from the breakfast buffet.

I slouched down, opened my book, and pretended to read. Up front, André told the author about his oceanography class. He was studying the manatee, sea cows that move between fresh to salt water. They traveled slowly, unlike the cars on the island. In spite of myself, I was caught up in his description, in the lilt of his voice. I closed my eyes and tried to imagine them, large, awkward, but somehow graceful creatures gliding through the moss green of a river and into the clearer green of the Caribbean. Was it like moving from one season to the next, like putting on or taking off a cotton sweater, an incremental shift in perception? Or more of a sudden jolt, stepping off a plane into another hemisphere where even time follows a different schedule? I'd been swimming several times each day, and sometimes I was part of the current and sometimes the current was part of me.

"What was that all about?" she asked. We hiked up a steep trail along the embankment of the falls. André had settled under a shade tree near the concession stand with a science text and a yellow highlighter. Two busloads of tourists who'd pulled in behind us were several hundred yards back and safely out of earshot.

"What was what all about?" I kicked at a jagged stone that had fallen into the middle of the path.

"You were very rude to André."

I didn't wait around to be scolded. I scrambled over a small boulder and took off up the path. She caught up with me a few minutes later and grabbed my arm roughly. "Stop it!" She bent over for a minute, catching her breath. "If you're upset about something, you need to tell me and we'll discuss it. Stop behaving like a petulant kid."

I swung around. "I *am* a kid!" I shouted. "I'm a kid who could never afford a vacation like this, even if I would choose a vacation like this, which I wouldn't!"

She gripped my arm tightly and hissed at me. "Keep. Your. Voice. Down."

I twisted out of her grasp and kept yelling. "I will not keep my voice down! I'm a kid, remember? This is what kids do! They yell! What, didn't any of those other kids you brought here yell?"

"Oh, good lord." She must have scraped up against a rock or a tree while chasing after me—a smudge of dirt rode above one ankle and a small tear in her knit shirt threatened to unravel into a run. "Is that what you think? You think I brought other women here?"

"Well, of course that's what I think. What else would I think?"

She threw a quick glance over her shoulder—no sign of the tour groups yet—then picked up my hand. "Come here." She led me off the trail to a small overlook where a bench made of split logs faced the middle pool of a dramatic, three-level waterfall. A sign warned "No Swimming—Dangerous Eddies," though the water looked calm. It was the same green as her eyes. She sat down on the bench and I paced back and forth, not quite ready to sit down like a grownup and discuss things.

"Have I told you I love you?" She asked it like a good prosecutor who already knows the answer.

I rolled my eyes. "Yes, I know you love me," I said, crossing my arms and tapping my sneaker against the dirt.

"No," she said, taking off her sunglasses. There was a little glob of tanning lotion just below her left eye. "You don't understand. This doesn't happen to me. I don't just fall in love with people."

"Not ever?"

"Not in a very long time."

"How long?"

She looked down at her hands, which were folded in her lap, and grinned a bit ruefully. "Not since I was a kid, like you."

"What happened?" I demanded.

"We split up."

I picked up my pacing. "Yeah, well, lots of people split up."

"Lots of people don't get kicked out of school and sent away."

"Is that what happened to her?"

"That's what happened to both of us. Her roommate walked in

on us in an intimate moment and reported us to the dean, who called our parents and booted us out."

I felt vaguely dizzy and sat down. "Shit." The tourists had caught up to us; their loud shirts drifted through my peripheral vision. One man took a tentative step toward our overlook, and I glared at him until he backed off. "It was worse for her. Her parents had her institutionalized. Mine simply handed me a wad of money and told me to go to Europe."

"Did you go?"

"Yes. But I came back." She let out a little ironic laugh. "For her."

"Did she"—the words caught in my throat—"was she waiting for you?"

"No. A few shock treatments and she jumped into the arms of the first available man, who happened to be her doctor at the sanitarium. She had the nerve to tell me I needed to get help."

She was tearing up a little, so I rummaged around in my backpack and came up with a Kleenex.

"Thanks," she said, dabbing her eyes and blowing her nose. "I'm sorry. I haven't talked about this in a very long time."

I wiped the spot of suntan lotion off her face, then aimed another warning glance at a tourist who was approaching. "It's okay. I'm glad you told me." How could it ever be okay? I said, "I'm not going to go away," but maybe that wasn't what she wanted me to say.

"I've never brought anyone else here. I've been here alone a few times, when I needed a break from work. André's family owns the resort. He's been very kind to me."

We sat quietly for a while and watched the water raining spectacularly over the cliff. Bunches of enormous red, pink, and yellow flowers ringed the basin, and a faint rainbow hovered in the mist where the falling water crashed into the calm water. The flowers, the water, the sky, everything looked oversaturated, like a postcard that had been retouched a bit too zealously.

"You've had other lovers since then," I ventured, not certain I really wanted to hear about them.

She took my hand. "Lovers, yes."

"All of them young, like me?" Again, something I could have done very well without knowing, though I was sure I already knew the answer.

"I haven't been middle-aged forever," she said, allowing the corners of her mouth to turn up slightly. "But you're right. I do find younger women attractive."

"And you find them easier to dismiss when you're done with them."

"Please don't use your Psychology 101 on me." She said this carefully, looking at the hand—my hand—that she held as if it were a map.

I jumped up, taking back the palm, which held, after all, my future, not hers. "Please don't condescend to me. I may be young but I'm not an idiot. When were you planning to send me packing? At the end of this trip? At the end of the summer?"

She grinned a rueful grin. "Well, you see, that's just my problem. I said I've had other lovers, but I wasn't in love with them. You, I love, and I don't quite know what to do about that. I can't bear the thought of not having you in my life, but I can't just move you in with me, either."

"Why? Do I embarrass you?"

"You do nothing but delight me. No, I embarrass myself."

I sat down again. Another large group of tourists passed behind us, and I gave up trying to stop them from taking pictures of our little pool—which, I should say, I was feeling quite proprietary about, especially now that we were having our first (and final?) fight along its banks. From the tumble of their words, I gathered they were mostly Germans. One or two said hello to us in heavily accented English.

The place really was beautiful. What a beautiful setting for a fight, I thought. No, that can't be true; how could I register what was happening around me when I had such a huge cloud in the pit of my stomach?

After a while, the Germans exited.

"I guess your plan backfired, huh?" I said, remembering the way she spoke to me with her eyes in the library that first day.

"You could say that."

I took a deep breath. Was I supposed to feel gratified that she had, inexplicably, fallen in love with me? Or irritated that falling in love with me had not been even a remote possibility in those early days of archival longing?

"You never ask me what I want," I said, an accusation for her and a question for myself.

She seemed surprised by this. "I guess I don't. I guess I'm not sure which scares me the most—your wanting or not wanting more from me."

"I do want more from you. But I don't want to move into your house. I also don't want to learn to play bridge. People my age do not play bridge."

"Fair enough."

Who can explain the inexplicable? She loved me; she was doing the best she could. Who among us isn't at times surprised, taken aback, by the choices our hearts make for us? Who isn't, at times, reluctant to follow the current into something as buoyant and impossible as salt water?

We finished the hike to the base of the uppermost waterfall, which was, as advertised, lush and spectacular. Rock shelves bordered a large basin of black water that caught a vertical river so high it might have come straight from the God she prayed to Sunday mornings. It seemed the island was making a gesture for our sakes, one I didn't quite know how to read. How do you make the transition from argument to beauty? She looked awed and troubled, a combination that stirred me inexplicably.

Inexplicable. There's that word again. That which can't be understood. That which whispers to us in the dark, the voices of water tumbling into a measuring pot. Her words on my body. What did she read on the map of my hand? Did she seek a way in or a way out? She loved me inexplicably. Inexplicably, it was enough.

The remainder of our sojourn to the tropics was a kind of falling action, the kind that happens in real life, where nothing is actually resolved even though you have the return tickets in your pocket, or better yet in a safebox behind the check-in desk. You're either slipping down the top of the hourglass or drowning in sand on the bottom.

We went back to our usual spot on the beach, we ventured up to the resort for breakfast and dinner, we spent another pleasant afternoon in the company of André, who drove us to the far side of the island where two manatees had been seen in an estuary. They weren't interested in being seen by us.

The author vacillated between worry and solicitation. Was I thirsty, did I need more suntan lotion, would I like some change to buy trinkets from the beach vendors? If I was quiet for a long time, she asked what I was thinking. "Nothing," I always said, which was always a lie, but I hated being asked for my thoughts, as if they were just pieces of dialogue I'd forgotten to say aloud. There's a difference between privacy and secrets. I was her secret, and I won't deny how appealing that was.

It turns out you can drive for hours on an island without ever losing sight of the ocean, if only in the mind's eye. Even miles inland, even in the hilly country of coffee plantations, even among fields of sugar cane, it's on the tongue, salt, with its suggestion of sadness, of voyage, of memory not quite remembered.

Is that what I was thinking when I said to her, "Nothing?" Could it be my mind was occupied by the aroma of salt, by the sound of a word you could dissolve in liquid? What did I know of life in a river; what did I know of moving my body from fresh to sea water? Even manatees have to come up for air. They may not let you see them, but they're just below the surface, waiting to breathe.

PART TWO

SOCRATES / 1982

CHAPTER 5

You could say love is two people moving around on a stage they've built of whatever materials they've come by, honestly or otherwise. The author and I did this well, and we did it without an audience—though neither of us could deny playing to the fourth wall. The lights come up, the lights go dim. You exit and come back having aged a year or two or five, with a smarter mouth to boot, or perhaps a slight stooping of the shoulders. You carefully prepare your acceptance speech: I'd like to thank the academy for selecting me, and the speechwriters for providing such compelling banter, and the cinematographer for bringing out that bit of mauve in the pale gray sky, and of course the sky itself for making such a panorama of longing. And, naturally, the makeup artist for accentuating the emerald midnight of her eyes, so I could properly understand what it feels like to be untethered from my spaceship and floating through the nebulae.

Is this coming across? I'm trying to demonstrate time passing. I'm trying to show how time's edges are rough, raw. What I mean is: my heart, my irregular heart, kept beating in her direction.

No matter how much you love books, no matter that you take your history unrevised, in hand-set type, there are days you have to get out of the archives. Just as a reminder that there's air out there that isn't temperature- and moisture-controlled. Just as a reminder that you're young and the world is still new enough to surprise you.

"Spring fever," said the librarian, who did not object when I volunteered to shuttle a packet across campus to the administration building, a job we'd ordinarily give one of the work-study students. Early April: not quite T-shirt weather, but you wouldn't know it from the college kids sprawled coatless on lawns and dormitory roofs, smoking cigarettes and thumbing through somebody's-discourse-on-this-or-that. Others were teaching their dogs to catch Frisbees mid-air, training them to jump up to meet the disc rather than waiting for it to crash land. I was only five years out of college, but it seemed suddenly obvious that these kids were of a different generation. It had to do with style, imperceptible changes that add up to inconceivable differences. No one wore bell bottoms any more, including me, and even I considered it absurd that we'd all felt so anti-establishment-cool to be dragging all that extra cloth through the dirt. But it was more than that: these kids looked tidy, well pressed, in polo shirts and khakis, as if they'd just stepped from the pages of a casual clothing catalog. They wore no patches on their jeans, no army surplus jackets.

For a moment I felt dislocated, unzipped in time. I knew, of course, that longing exists outside time. I could tell of the five summers of my longing, the snowfalls, the ice melt, the recurring dream of lilacs buttering the air. Today, the sun shone; colors made themselves known on the palette of the landscape. I knew who I was: the archives clerk, only one night-school semester away from becoming a full-fledged librarian, carrying a manila envelope across the small canvas of her life.

Where did the author fit in all this? She was everywhere and nowhere; author of my desire, author of my estrangement from the world and my entanglement in it. She would have used a word like "glorious" to describe the way the sun burned a hole in the remnants of winter, would have stopped for a long moment to point out the cluster of starlings among the buds on the red maple, and, had no one been around, might have slung an arm over my shoulders and whispered the idea of feathers into my ear.

I shivered, then shook it off. What was I doing, looking at the scenery through her eyes? Think about walking, one foot in front of the other. Every action is introspection. Where did that come from? Something I read, most likely: everyone was talking about zen in those days; people had long conversations on breathing, as if it were something one randomly chose to do. Breathe in, action; breathe out, reaction.

Okay, so springtime was a coy mistress. So if my jet-stream of consciousness wasn't exactly Joycean, at least it got me from one place to the next. The next being the administration building—not exactly the life breath of the university, but certainly the locus of its bureaucratic heartbeat. I took the granite steps two at a time, simply because I felt like it.

Just inside the door, I saw her: the bureaucratic center of my heart. Well, not her—a photo of her. Or, to be more precise, a photocopied reproduction of her latest jacket photo, blown up a couple hundred percent so her face looked like one of those paintings made of dots that won't come into focus until you back off. From a distance, she looked lithe and airbrushed; the poster advertised a talk she'd be giving, part of a women's studies series on local writers. I knew about the talk, of course, and was secretly pleased that she was a bit nervous about the prospect of addressing a group of people who could well be carrying around a lot of academic pretensions about literature.

Seeing her face like that—in a public place, among my regular haunts—stopped me in my zen-ohm-walking-mantra tracks. And then, I laughed out loud. Not at the poster, but at its placement. Just beneath the photocopied announcement of her talk, with her name emblazoned in huge letters across the bottom, was an announcement in equally large type of a meeting of the Gay Student Union. She would have been mortified. She would have removed, and torn up, the offending flyer.

The times I'd addressed the topic of things homosexual with her, she'd bristled. The word "gay" was absurd, she said; the word "lesbian" ugly. She wasn't those things, and neither was I. We didn't need anyone telling us who we were or what we were.

So what could I do but leave the Gay Union poster right where it was? And then take out my notebook and write down the time and place of the meeting, all the while focusing on breathing in and breathing out to keep my hands from shaking.

"Have you ever wondered what would happen if you fell out of the parentheses and into the world?" I finished off my second beer and headed to the refrigerator for number three.

"Honey, I have no idea what you're talking about. Parenthetically speaking." Jeff was already one beer ahead of me, but, as we both knew, he made a better drunk than I did.

"Some people get charming," he once told me, "some get stupid, and you just get a little sideways in your thinking."

He was right, but there was nothing I could do about it now. The two beers were gone. "It's a metaphor," I said, cupping my hands in the air like two half moons. Though come to think of it, they did sort of look like breasts.

"No shit," said Jeff. "Everything's a metaphor with you. Now you want to parse your life like a verb? Or just diagram it into a sentence?"

One more beer and sentences weren't going to matter much. We were upstairs in Jeff's apartment, since mine was more suited to plant life than human visitation. Not that Jeff's was House Beautiful. You'd never know he was gay by his furnishings, unless you considered the industrial-strength tube of K-Y jelly on his bed table to be furniture. Everything was comfortable, in a kind of mismatched way. If you asked me now, I'd tell you he decorated like a lesbian, but back then I didn't know any lesbians, unless I counted myself—which I didn't, exactly.

"But couldn't it be possible to live inside a sentence? Imagine, one day you're out strolling among the direct articles and the verb clauses, pausing every now and then to admire a nicely placed modifier or the audacious insertion of an adverbial phrase, and you hop the fence of the parenthesis and follow the words like that ball that bounces across song lyrics—"

"You're losing me," Jeff shouted from the kitchen, where I could hear him rummaging around the silverware drawer for his bottle opener.

"It's out here," I yelled, reaching around my bottle for the stainless utensil. When he came back in the room, I held it in the air, like a mime faced with an enormous invisible beer bottle. "You see, you're hopping along and pop"—I pried off the huge invisible cap—"your closing parenthesis just flies off. What do you do? Hop after it? Backpedal in mid-air like a cartoon character?"

"Words aren't metaphors; words are symbols," he said logically. "Now if you want to talk semantics . . . "

"I'm talking linguistics! I'm talking Bouncing Ball Theory!" I tossed him the bottle opener with a flourish.

He caught it with a parallel flourish. "You know, if you would smoke pot instead of drinking beer, you would forget all these queer little theories of yours before they fell out of your mouth and into the general population."

"Who said anything about queer?"

"Who indeed. And speaking of such things, how's that older woman of yours?"

"She's giving a talk at the college."

"Well, jump my parentheses. Can I come? What should I wear?"

"Something blue," I said. "You can be my date."

"So you're not showing up on the arm of the adored one?"

"In public? Are you kidding? It's more likely she'll pretend she doesn't know me."

"No wonder you've gone a little wonky on punctuation. Maybe it's time we outed the old broad. I suggest you march right up to the podium after she takes her bow and plant one smack on those historically accurate lips of hers."

This got us both giggling. I think Jeff was as crazy about the author as I was, even though he'd never met her, so it didn't feel disloyal to poke a little fun in her direction when I was with him.

"That would certainly punctuate things," I replied. "And we both know she's a little too fond of exclamation points."

"Well, then, it'd serve her right. But you will introduce me? Should she deign to acknowledge your presence?"

I winced a bit. What sort of scenario would she cook up, at the post-lecture reception, should I wander over, Jeff in tow, and ask, for instance, for her autograph? Perhaps I could request in front of the History Department chair that she sign her name with her tongue along the small of my back?

I shook my head. "I think the parenthesis that holds in the left side of my brain has come undone."

"Does that mean I can meet her?" The author was great camp for Jeff—a classy woman famous in the kinds of circles people spend their whole childhoods trying to move out of. I think he saw her as pulling off some kind of extravagant parody.

"Sure, you can meet her." I looked around for my beer, which I'd set down before briefly transmogrifying into a talking mime. "I forget what we were celebrating."

"Um—the one-month anniversary of the vernal equinox?"

"Works for me. Unless you can think up some interesting saint to drink to." He was a font of knowledge on Catholic trivia. "It's enough to let the faith lapse; I insist on hanging on to the iconography," he'd say, usually in response to my complaints that I was self-conscious peeing in front of the crucifix collection in his bathroom.

"I only drink to the virgin. The virgin of Guadalupe, the virgin of Lourdes, the virgin of the cheesy historical saga." He drank.

I located my beer on the end table and reached to pick it up, but ended up knocking it over instead. Out of some drunken good fortune, I grabbed it before any spilled. "Fucking miraculous," I said.

The author, of course, was dazzling in her address to the women's studies crowd. I'd been a bit concerned, and perhaps a bit hopeful, that the rad fems would pelt her with accusations of looking at history through men's eyes, or playing up the subjugation of one sex to the other. In fact, judging by their initial demeanor, they had plans to use her as bait for a vicious consciousness-raising session. Hah! Were they ever out of their league. By the end of the Q and A session, they would have eaten peanuts from her hand. It wasn't what she said, exactly, though she did take them on an airbrushed journey through her life that made her sound like the first wave of the revolution. Dashing, she was, and adventurous. Errol Flynn in a red dress. But really, it was her delivery that sent everyone over the edge. She was flirting shamelessly with the audience, making eye contact, I swear, with the entire four dozen of us, including, briefly, with me. I think everyone fell in love with her; I fell in love with her all over again. Even Jeff swooned a bit.

"Oh, my God," he whispered as we made our way over to the cheese platter. "You'd better keep her away from all these young things."

She had finished speaking, but was still up at the podium, the nucleus of a swarming atom of female undergraduates. I couldn't see her face, but I knew she was looking rather pleased with herself.

"I'm not sure if I'm supposed to be jealous or honored." I picked up a crusty slice of Swiss and plopped it on a Saltine. "You'd think they could spend a little money on these affairs."

"Well, it is women's studies," Jeff said, fishing an orange slice out of the punchbowl and plopping it into my drink. "When she speaks to the football team, I'm sure there'll be caviar and champagne."

"Or at least those little weenies-in-a-bun with a beer chaser."

We tapped our plastic glasses together in a toast, then he nodded toward the front of the room. "You know, I'd really love to meet her, but if you'd rather just slip quietly out the back, that's fine with me."

"You're sweet. But I do want her to meet you. She ought to know the person who tries on all the clothes she buys for me."

"Very funny. And if you ever mention that little incident with the half-slip to anyone . . . "

"Oh, don't worry. Your secret's safe with me. Really, there's no shame in being a drag queen."

"I'm not a drag queen," he stage-whispered in falsetto. "I just happen to look better in a dress than you do."

I washed down the cracker with the punch, which was seriously watered down, then grabbed the sleeve of Jeff's sweater and pulled him toward the author. The beehive that swarmed around her was breaking up, and she'd been commandeered by one of the faculty members who'd organized the speaking series. As we got closer I could hear the professor gushing about the talk, babbling about all the things older women have to teach the younger generation.

"She doesn't know the half of it," I muttered to Jeff as we waltzed right into the middle of their conversation. "How are you?" I said to the author.

She was quite gracious, and actually took my hand. "It's lovely to see you," she said, as if she hadn't just that morning seen me naked in her shower.

"And you must be Jeff. Very nice to meet you." Now she had his hand in both of hers and, turning to me, asked if I'd get her a drink.

"I need one too," said the now slightly deflated professor, who apparently wasn't interested in sharing the author with anyone.

"How do you know her?" she asked as we joined the end of the line that was now snaking toward the punchbowl.

I've been sleeping with her for five years. No, I didn't say that. "We met when she came into the library to do research."

"Oh, that's where I've seen you."

"In the archives room. I spend a lot of time blowing dust off things." I glanced over my shoulder. The author and Jeff were chatting like intimate friends, he regaling her with some apparently hilarious story, probably involving a humongous bottle of invisible beer.

"And what do you find under the dust?"

"Hmm?" The professor was talking to me. Actually, judging by her age and attire—she looked only a couple years older than me and was wearing threadbare jeans and an ill-fitting T-shirt—she was probably a teaching assistant or maybe a lecturer. "Oh, more dust, usually. History disintegrates, you know. That gives us a reason to rewrite it." What could they be talking about so animatedly? I wanted Jeff and the author to like each other, but I hadn't intended for them to become great pals, especially since they both had a lot of damaging information about me.

The prof, or lecturer, or whatever she was, must have noticed my preoccupation with the two of them. "He your boyfriend?" she asked.

I laughed. "I adore him, but he prefers his dates to have hair on their chests." We'd arrived at the refreshments, which looked even less appealing than they had in my earlier visit.

She grinned. "What do you prefer?"

I cleared my throat. "Looks like we got here just in time." The punch was nearly gone, but she tipped the bowl up and I managed to scoop out two cups' worth. I gave one to the professor then nodded toward the author. "I guess I'd better bring these to her majesty."

"She is something, isn't she? Not at all what I was expecting."

"Have you read her books?"

"Oh, God, no." She swirled the punch around in her plastic glass, forming a miniature fruit-flavored whirlpool. We both stared at it for a moment, until she looked up and jerked her hand, sending a red wave over her palm.

"Oh, shit."

"It's all right," I said, handing her my napkin. "Just a little spill."

"No, I've got to go. Would you mind?" She handed me her cup, then wiped her hand with the napkin and handed me that, too. "See you in the library?"

She hurried across the room, intercepting a heavyset woman in a leather jacket who had clearly been heading straight at us, grabbing her by the arm and spinning her around and back toward the door. The larger woman did not look happy, and the professor-lecturer was doing some fast verbal tap-dancing from what I could tell. Then they were gone, and I stood there for a moment stupidly looking at the two cups in my hand—the professor's and the author's—until I remembered I'd left the author and Jeff having a good old time at the other end of the room.

By the time I made it back there with the punch, another small crowd had gathered around, and Jeff was standing at the periphery looking amused.

"I tried to fend them off, but my charms don't seem to work well in this crowd," he whispered. "What took you so long?"

"There was a line. Let's get out of here? I just need to deliver this drink."

"Don't want to stay and keep an eye on her?"

"I think I've seen enough." I pushed through the group and set the punch glass in her hand. She was in the middle of embellishing her already-embellished autobiography, and barely managed to nod at me.

"I'll see you later?" I said, but didn't wait for an answer.

"What exactly were you two talking about?" I asked Jeff as we made our way across campus. The night was cool and I wished I'd thought to bring a jacket.

"Oh, this and that."

"I said 'exactly.' "

"Exactly this and exactly that."

"Hey, I'm the one who brought you along and introduced you to her." I didn't like the idea of the two of them being friends. Jeff was my friend, and no matter how much I loved the author, I needed him to be on my side.

"Oh, don't get your nose in a snit. You're still My Favorite Lesbian." He made an L-shaped antenna on the back of my head with his hand. It was an old joke, but I wasn't laughing. "If you must know, she was pumping me for information."

This was interesting. "Information about me?"

"But what else? I think she's afraid you might be cheating on her. Or thinking about cheating on her. She's quite the manipulator, isn't she? We were just pleasantly chatting away when I realized the conversation had swung around to your night-time activities, what sorts of people visit your apartment, that type of thing."

"I hope you didn't tell her anything."

"As if there's anything to tell. Don't worry, darlin' "—he swung an arm around my shoulder—"I can spar with the best of them. I left her guessing."

"You are so devious." I wrapped my arm around his waist.

"That's why you love me."

"Yes." Then: "She really is fabulous, don't you think?"

"Absolutely. But no more fabulous than you."

"Aw, shucks. If you were a girl, I'd kiss you."

"Kiss me anyway."

I did.

CHAPTER 6

Time doesn't slow down in a library, not exactly. But could it be that antiquity clocks along in an analog circle while outside the beveled glass, events proceed in a linear fashion, as if time might actually have somewhere to go?

Antiquity chases. It laps up against our loves, more insistently the older we get. Is it ironic that the clock of my heart started ticking in that quiet room in the summer of my twenty-second year, when I was first learning to love the words of other decades, other centuries? Perhaps ironic isn't the best choice of words; perhaps curious is more apropos. Was it a curio, an artifact, a bibelot, our romance, something hawked in the front window of an antique shop? It may have been for others, had others known of our attachment. For her? It's true she was in love with youth—mine, her own that was already lapped up in time's ebb and flow. But even now, even several years after my first foray out of the archives and into her bedroom, she wasn't able to let me loose into some linear narrative of the world. Nor did I want to drift along in ordinariness. There was no life without the scent of her perfume, the slight imprint of her lipstick on my throat. She knew what she had to offer was not always enough, and so she made up for her emotional and physical absences with pure theatricality. Hence my low tides were offset by grand performances in the form of elaborate meals, fantastical presents, surprise long weekends in the country. In exchange for this, I came when she asked, I told pretty stories about my days in the stacks. I told her she was beautiful, and it never stopped being true.

Still, I was not surprised when the double doors to the archives room swung open and she walked in—not the author but the woman who'd rushed out of the author's reading, the professor.

"Oh, it's quiet in here, even for a library."

I came out from behind my small desk. "Don't want to startle the books."

"Or the keeper of the books?"

Was she flirting with me? "She doesn't startle easily."

She was not beautiful, but she was cute, with pixie red hair and a "Ladies Terrorist Society and Sewing Circle" T-shirt. Her name was Max; she was an assistant professor on a one-year appointment, which would run out at the end of the summer, by which time, she hoped, she'd have a tenure-track slot lined up, preferably in a large city. She was sorry she'd had to run out on me so abruptly; unrequited love could be so pesky, couldn't it? This information came tumbling forth like the prelude to something larger—an orchestral movement or the preface to a memoir—but then she suddenly stopped talking and looked at me expectantly.

I offered my name and left it at that. I was adept at giving myself away in small pieces, leaving out the connectors so the entire puzzle could never be worked out. I had no interest in being solved, and when I agreed to meet Max for lunch it was with the idea of taking on more mystery rather than shedding any. Really, I let things happen to me, as if there were no complicity in following the patterns set down by others.

"That was quite a performance you put on at the college."

"Just being my charming self, darling." She didn't turn from the mirror, where she was poking a dangling silver earring with an intricate web pattern into her earlobe. The back of her red dress was unzipped to her waist, and I resisted the impulse to cross the bedroom and run my fingers down the center of her spine. She was plenty skilled at zipping herself up, even in the most unaccommodating outfits, but she liked for me to do it when we went out together.

She looked into the mirror to see my reflection leaning against the door frame, wearing the pale yellow silk pantsuit she'd presented me last weekend, along with tickets to a play in a city we could drive to in ninety minutes.

"That looks lovely."

"The clothes, or me?"

"Both. Come here and zip me up."

I don't know if it was the loose-fitting silk or my secret lunch the next day with Max, but I felt as if the wind were whispering at my skin as I moved toward her and took her in my arms.

I reached around and slid her zipper past the small of her back and to her shoulder blades. "Railroad tracks. Lips. Zippers." I breathed these words into her ear.

"Things that are parallel?"

"Things that come together at the horizon."

This was a recent game for us, answers prompted by questions. It had started a few weeks earlier, on the equinox, when I balanced an egg on its wobbly bottom, a trick I learned in childhood. "But which came first, the equinox or the egg?" she'd asked.

"The answer usually comes before the question," I said. "Think scientific method. Think hypothesis."

"You are a silly chicken," she responded, not ruffling my feathers in the least.

Now, fully zipped, she was giving me the silly chicken look again. "Railroad tracks I'll buy, but lips and zippers? At which horizon do they come together?"

"The horizon of your back," I said, running my finger up the connecting seam of her dress. "The horizon of your neck." I touched my lips to the valley where her neck met her shoulder.

"Aren't you sweet tonight. Is it a full moon?"

I howled. "I'm always sweet." This was a lie, but we were both willing to believe it for a moment.

I worked my lips up the author's neck, slowly. I knew her heart by smell—the aroma of bottled tomato sauce in the kitchen meant she would probably send me home after dinner; coconut lotion at bedtime meant cuddling but no sex. Tonight she wore a new fragrance, something I didn't recognize. A reminder that I didn't know everything about her; a reminder that the moon could rise and set on my desire for her, and that it would always rise again.

"Intoxicating," I said. "Oxymoronic. An exquisite brouhaha."

She laughed. "What do you think of my perfume?"

"Exactly." I was had, and it was she who had me.

I remember little about the play, except that it was an unhappy love story, unhappily acted. I was little interested in other people's unhappiness or lack of talent in the drama of romance. Nor did I believe that love comes in three acts—the act of falling in, the act of falling out, the act of getting on with one's life. Bow, drop curtain.

But I do remember she let me hold her hand throughout the entire third act, once the house lights went down, until she took it back to applaud the stupidly grinning thespians.

Am I adequately demonstrating the tenor of my interactions with the author? Can I describe the complexity of the garden I'd wandered into—been drawn into, really—a few years earlier? It wasn't about good and evil; no one could say we weren't both good in our own way. She was color and fragrance and leafy vines, and if she was a temptress I fell over and over for her intrigue, the machinations of her charms. I must have had charms of my own, if not intrigue, that she should want to hold my attention through the weather of a half decade.

It's true the garden had walls, and true that she knew enough to keep me primarily outside of those walls, so they would remain parentheses around a grand secret instead of brackets holding in a restrictive clause. I was free to wander; it was understood I'd return. Might that have been a miscalculation on her part? She had her garden, yes, but what other weather of gardens might I find in my perambulations on the outside?

Max was early. She stood fidgeting by the window while I answered the phone and helped a student track down a 1950s-era first edition. I watched her from my desk until the librarian returned from her lunch break and I was free for a while.

When I joined her at the window, she gave me a big grin, so

artless and genuine I knew immediately I would sleep with her if she asked.

"Where to?"

"I only have an hour."

We ended up at a crowded, noisy deli, the sort of place where the tables are so close together you feel as if you are having an intimate meal with whoever happens to sit on either side of you.

Max was expansive, comparing her hummus-and-sprouts with my roast beef on rye and with the twin ham-and-Swisses of the couple sitting to my left. She went on about the relative merits of Monterey jack vs. cheddar, shouting so as to be heard over the other voices that overran the room.

What did I think I was doing? Only a few hours earlier I had left the bed of a woman who would never speak loudly about cheese, let alone allow a stray piece of onion to bob up and down at the corner of her mouth while she talked. Max looked more like a student than a professor. Her jeans and sweatshirt were out of shape, as if they'd spent the night in a pile on her bedroom floor; her hair looked as if it hadn't been combed.

"Am I boring you?"

I started. "I'm sorry. I'm a little distracted."

"And I talk too much. Really, I can go on ad nauseum about any topic, doesn't matter whether I know the first thing about it."

"Modern art," said Mr. Ham-and-Swiss.

"I don't know a lot, but I like what I know. Women with three breasts, Marilyn Monroe, the insides of Jackson Pollack's brains splattered all over a canvas—what's not to like?"

"Peanut butter," said Mrs. Ham-and-Swiss.

"Great source of protein. Originated with Native Americans, now sticking to the roofs of our mouths due to the efforts of our recently ousted gentleman farmer president."

They all looked at me expectantly, waiting for me to throw out a topic. "Excuse me," I said, getting up and squeezing my way to the bathroom. I felt slightly nauseated, examining my already-spoken-for face in the mirror.

Okay. Calm down. A discussion of peanut butter and havarti does not an affair make. It does not even an appetizing sandwich make. I splashed water on my face and let the air out of my lungs.

"Somebody done you wrong, or you done somebody wrong; I can't decide which," said the woman leaning over the sink next to mine, applying lipstick so cautiously you'd think Andy Warhol were about to paint her three or four times.

I inhaled. There were limits to how much I would share with strangers, even in the women's room of a deli that's a little heavy handed with its sprouts.

"Wouldn't you like to know," I said, not very cleverly, then pushed my way out the door.

"Let's get out of here." I grabbed my sweater from the back of the chair.

"Scuba diving," shouted Mr. and Mrs. Ham-and-Swiss as we left the table. "Piano tuning, dog training, Eleanor Roosevelt."

Max ignored them. "I thought you had an hour?"

"I do. It's just a little claustrophobic in here."

"Sorry about the neighbors. Next time I'll bring my portable hedge."

We exited the restaurant and ambled up the sidewalk, past antique shops and florists and little boutiques that specialized in items like soap or wrapping paper—things that seem ordinary in context but absurd when given the opportunity to expand into a space big enough to house three generations of boat people. I could see she was trying hard to appear quiet and thoughtful. It was just about killing her.

I took pity. "I've always had a bit of a crush on Eleanor Roosevelt," I offered.

She jumped right in. "You should have seen her in scuba gear."

"Accompanied by her well-trained dogs, no doubt?"

"Naturally. And, of course, the ever-present piano tuner. Can you believe this neighborhood? Who would shop at a store that sells only ribbons?"

"Certainly not Eleanor," I said.

"Certainly not."

We walked up one side of the street and down the other, Max keeping up a running commentary on the sorry state of consumerism and the decline of window shopping as a spectator sport. If I found this a bit odd from someone who appeared to buy all of her clothing at Goodwill, I didn't let on. Mostly I let her talk, prompting her from time to time with an idea or a phrase that set her off on another jaunt of puppy-doggish enthusiasm.

"For a women's studies professor, you seem, well, different," I said when she dropped me off at the library door.

"Not strident enough for you, huh?"

I blushed; she laughed.

"You clearly need to get out more," she said, fumbling around in her pockets. She came up with a pen, three paperclips, a ten-dollar bill that had been through the washing machine, a shiny black stone, and a clothespin, but not a scrap of paper.

"Give me your hand."

I handed it over, neglecting to mention the small notebook I always kept in my back pocket. She wrote her phone number across my palm, and then, as an afterthought, spelled her name there too, in block letters. "Just in case some other woman gives you her number before you wash your hands."

"If she does, I'll insist she use the other palm."

"Call me." She folded my fingers around her number and skipped off down the granite steps.

I unfurled my hand, examined the number, and thought of cryptology, multiplication, the combinations of locks.

"So, one is cute, one is beautiful; one is three years older, one is thirty years older."

"Twenty-eight."

"Close enough. One is Goodwill, one is Saks Fifth Avenue, one is well-off, one will be paying off student loans for the next decade."

"Enough, already. Cataloging is *my* specialty, remember?"

Jeff and I sat at the neighborhood bar, where we fancied

ourselves queers in residence, although we blended in easily with the otherwise straight happy-hour crowd. He was working as a paralegal in those days, a position that required a tie but no jacket—pretty much the same outfit he'd worn as a waiter back when I first met him. "It's really the same job but without tips," he'd say. "You grovel, you wipe up spills. Who knew feeding egos paid more than feeding appetites?"

Now, still in our work clothes, we were camped at one end of the bar, a vantage point from which we could see everyone who came in.

"So which one do you like better," he asked, gesturing with his beer bottle, "the elegant author-about-town or the haphazard lecturer?"

It was an interesting question. I was hopelessly in love with the author, of course, and I barely knew Max, but he hadn't said "love," he'd said "like."

"It's apples and oranges."

"Surely you like one fruit more than the other. Apples and oranges, I mean."

"It depends on the time of day. Oranges in the morning, apples at lunch."

Jeff raised one eyebrow. "I sense conflict."

"I don't want to hear about conflict. I brought you here to help me rationalize. Don't try to tell me you've never dated two people at once."

"I believe the record was four, but who's counting? So, you want rationalization? Let's see." He sipped his beer thoughtfully. "You know, I'm crazy about the old relic, and she is very well preserved indeed, but it's not as though she has exclusivity rights. I mean, the woman will hardly be seen with you in public. As for the absent-minded professor, well, didn't you say she'd be leaving town at the end of the summer?"

"Probably."

"Well, then. All rationalized. Cheat to your heart's content, with my blessing." He dipped his fingertips in his beer and flicked a few drops onto my forehead, then made the sign of the cross.

I wiped my brow with a cocktail napkin. "Bless me, father, for I have sinned. Well, not yet, but soon, I hope."

"Does this mean you're going to call her?"

"Max? I can't spend my entire life sitting in bars and coffee shops and talking with a not-very-eligible bachelor. Not that you aren't witty and charming."

"Yeah. You may as well spend some of your life sitting around in bars and coffee shops with a cute babe. What are you going to tell Her Highness?"

"I wasn't planning on telling her anything. It's not like our paths ever cross outside of . . . you know . . . "

"Her bed?"

I blushed. "We do other things besides having sex."

"Yes, but that's the best thing, isn't it?"

"She is quite the limber old broad."

"Oh, come on. She's gorgeous, she's sophisticated, she's talented, and you love her. She just isn't always enough. But be careful, okay?"

What would motivate someone to become a librarian? Who would want to live in stories written by other people, in books owned by other people? Where was the justice in falling in love with a plotline, only to have to empty its leaves of bookmarks and send it back into the mail slot of circulation?

I asked these questions sometimes, fancying a little Socrates perched on my right shoulder responding to my queries with more queries. What is the nature of research? What is the nature of literature, if not to serve as the research of the heart? Now that you're nearly done with library school, now that you'll soon have three letters after your name like Library of Congress hieroglyphics on the spine of a book, might your own pages start turning?

Whose book are you reading now, are you writing now, and it's the voice of Socrates whispering in my ear.

"The questions are more interesting than the answers," says the author.

"Ask me whatever you'd like," says Max, who has an answer for everything, even if it's the wrong answer.

How did I feel? Evasive, guilty, liberated. And I hadn't even called Max yet, though her name and phone number still burned on my palm, as if she'd written them there with an etching tool and not a forty-nine-cent Bic, medium point, red ink.

I show up at the author's house with flowers—hothouse calla lilies, out of season, in the wrong latitude.

"What's this?" she says.

"Can't I bring flowers to a beautiful woman?"

More questions, fewer answers.

Où est la bibliotèque? says Socrates, fresh from his high-school French class.

Voici la bibliotèque, I answer, for I am a true bibliophile and work in the bibliotèque every day.

What have you done with your plot? says the author, who is now the size of a doll and is perched on my other shoulder, whispering in my other ear.

I need a plot. I call Max. I hang up before the phone has a chance to ring. I pour myself a glass of wine, down it like a shot of Jack Daniels. I dial again. It rings. I panic. It's too late to hang up. Someone answers. It isn't her. I panic again. Then remember: she has roommates. I ask for her by name, staring at my palm even though the writing has long since faded.

"What are you doing for dinner tomorrow night?" I say when she comes on the line, hoping she'll come up with the correct answer.

The answer was: she was cooking—for her roommates and whichever of their girlfriends might show up. "Please say you'll come. I promise to make everyone behave nicely."

"I'm not really sure I'm up for a dinner party," I told her. I'd been picturing a corner booth and a couple plates of spaghetti, maybe some garlic bread, beer in a glass to fancy it up.

"Oh, don't think dinner party. Think circus. Clowns, jugglers, trapeze artists—we've pretty much got it all."

"Which are you?"

"I'd like to say I'm the ringmaster, but in reality I'm probably more like the poor schmuck who trails after the elephants with a shovel. But honestly, we could use someone who's willing to put her head inside the lion's jaws."

Who could say no to that? I went to dinner.

Max lived with three other women in an old Victorian a few blocks from my apartment. The neighborhood was slightly overgrown; ten-speeds leaned haphazardly against chain-link fences and porch railings. Max's house was the most neglected of the lot, and after I spotted her number on the gate, I stood under a tall elm on the opposite side of the street for a while, listing to the left as if I could somehow get in sync with the house before I went in. Or maybe I was just getting my sea legs.

Turns out I needed them sooner than I thought. Just as I was about to ring the bell, the front door flew open and out stormed the woman who'd stormed in to the author's reading two weeks earlier. I jumped out of the way and mumbled something apologetic, but she was already halfway down the walkway. She kicked open the gate and kicked it closed from the other side, then huffed up the street.

The door was still open, so I walked in, poking my head into a couple of front rooms decorated in early graduate student, then found myself in the kitchen doorway. Max stood behind a butcher block, chopping onions, her eyes a little teary. She didn't seem surprised to see me standing there.

"I always forget," she said. "Is it never underestimate the wrath of a woman scorned or the fury of a woman scorned?"

"In this case it appears to be both."

The kitchen was a 1950s throwback, with a huge gas oven, scratched porcelain sink, rounded Frigidaire, almost no counter space—the kind of décor that people pay a fortune these days to replicate, but just seemed funky and hip back then. "Did I come at a bad time?"

"Oh, there's never really a good time around here," she said, pulling out a stool for me. "I'm kidding. It's great to see you. And now that the drama is out of the way, we can proceed with the circus. At center stage, yours truly, ringmaster and elephant chaser." She bowed. "The charming but currently intemperate and certainly misnamed Gigi, who runs her sideshow from the second floor rear, has opted for a previous engagement, and won't be joining us. Seabird and Augustine should be here shortly and, of course, whatever dregs wander in from the street. Present company excepted."

"Does this mean the happy ham-and-cheese couple won't be joining us?"

"Not unless they're willing to settle for tempeh bacon and cheese."

Max happily chopped any Freudian symbolism out of a bunch of carrots and started in on a convoluted explanation of the origins of the dish she was making, which was called Vegetables Psychosis. I let her words wash over me without taking them in.

Who has roommates named Gigi, Seabird, and Augustine? Don't these people understand the irony inherent in such monikers? The little philosopher was back on my shoulder again, mouthing his not-exactly-universe-bending questions directly into my left ear. Leave a guy under the ground for a couple of millennia and his priorities shift. Or perhaps the meaning of life can be divined in a run-down Victorian inhabited by people wearing T-shirts proclaiming "A woman needs a man like a fish needs a bicycle."

"So then," Max was saying, "we all spent twenty minutes picking up the chopped vegetables from the floor and the countertops and the potted plants and we rinsed them all off and baked them with a little bit of olive oil and coriander and tossed in some noodles and grated cheese over the whole mess, and ta-da—one meal of reconciliation."

"Vegetables Psychosis," I said, wishing I'd paid more attention to the plotline of this casserole, just in case I'd be quizzed later on the theme or the central metaphor. "Can I help cut vegetables? I've been known to exhibit psychotic tendencies."

"Just for future reference, you may want to keep that to yourself the next time you ask someone to hand you a knife." She looked up and winked. "Listening to my stories is enough work. Plus, I'm almost finished with the hard part."

The author, I was sure, had never prepared or eaten anything called "psychosis"; nor would she allow a food fight in her kitchen. I was also certain she would not approve of the wine Max was offering me, which came in a large jug topped with a screw cap.

I faked pompous. "Hmm. Fruity and amusing, perhaps a touch woody," I said, waving the juice glass under my nose. "Vintage?" I scanned the label, which featured an Italian peasant woman lustily eyeing a clump of purple grapes. "Ah, February. A very good year."

"Well, it has the two characteristics I find most appealing in a wine—it costs under five dollars and it has a babe on the label."

We clinked glasses and swallowed.

Dumping three cutting boards' worth of carrots, broccoli, cauliflower, mushrooms, and red peppers into a large bowl, then pouring on a liberal amount of olive oil, Max plunged her hands in and mixed, turning the vegetables over and over.

"Would you mind?" She held up her oily hands and nodded toward the sink.

I got up and turned on the faucet, leaning slightly into her body to reach the bar of soap that sat in a dish on the windowsill above the sink. I could feel the hairs on her arm brushing against my own and the sun filtering in through the dirty glass, and I'm not sure which of us was more surprised when I turned my head and landed a quick kiss—more of a question than a kiss, really—on the corner of her mouth. I can't even remember which one of us was holding the soap, but I do recall that within a few seconds we were making out like teenagers while the psychotic vegetables sat uncooked in their bowl.

"Hi, honey, we're home."

The soap dropped. We turned. Two women stood in the doorway, grinning like idiots. I looked back at Max, who sported a hands-in-the-cookie-jar look.

"Seabird and Augustine, I presume?"

Max's roommates, at least the two who showed up for dinner,

turned out to be identical twins born of entirely different gene pools. Tall and angular, Seabird had tufts of brown hair that spun out in every direction like a story too complicated to repeat. Augustine was small, round, and capped off with a thick, blonde monk's fringe. Both wore loose-fitting beige pants with untucked short-sleeve pullovers—Seabird's a pale blue and Augustine's navy.

"They're like a couple that doesn't sleep together," Max told me after they went upstairs to wash up. "Not a romantic couple; they both have girlfriends. But there are a lot of kinds of relationships. Those two are too much alike to keep any mystery going, but they're great companions. You're a terrific kisser, by the way."

I flushed. I'd positioned myself on a stool on the opposite side of the butcher block from where Max was winging cherry tomatoes into a bowl of lettuce, thinking maybe my hormones would behave if I kept a little distance between us. "I'm really sorry about that." I looked down at my hands. "Sometimes my body gets ahead of my brain."

"Mine wasn't exactly running in the other direction, as you may have noticed."

"Since we're talking about running, what's the deal with Gigi? Old girlfriend?"

"It never got that far. I prefer to be in the audience for drama, not on stage."

"Looks like you get sucked into it anyway."

"Oh, she's not so bad, really. She's just a little attached to me." And I was just a little attached to the author, and she to me, but here I was attaching my lips to those of a woman who made dinners named for mental disorders. I was the one who needed to have my head examined, not the vegetables; nonetheless, I blurted this out: "I would kiss you again, but I'm afraid your roommates would walk back in."

"Oh, that's pretty much guaranteed," she said, slipping her hands into mitts and opening the oven door. "We pretty much live by Murphy's Law around here."

"I can't wait to try the Vegetables Murphy."

"Actually, it's Murphy Fried Rice." She plopped the casserole dish on a hotplate in the center of the table. “If you’re going to kiss me, you’d better do it fast. Dinner is just about served.”

And my kiss was just about served when the door swung open. I sat down fast in the nearest chair.

“As always, your timing is impeccable,” Max said to Seabird and Augustine, who fairly tumbled into the room.

“We do pride ourselves on making an entrance,” said Seabird.

“Plus we love to see women kissing,” Augustine tossed in, playing the sidekick in the comedy duo.

“Or in this case, not kissing,” Max said. “Really”—this was directed to me—“they’re usually much better behaved.” To them: “Sit down and remember your manners, would you?”

“She’s so bossy,” Augustine stage-whispered to me, making a big show of talking behind her hand. “I just love that.”

I nodded stupidly. If we’re going to talk about manners, why not a discussion of the protocol for throwing yourself at one woman when you are bound to another?

This is not about protocol. Oh, great, now Socrates was going to make an appearance. *This is about morality, ethics, right and wrong. Now eat your vegetables.*

Seabird had just handed me the Vegetables Psychosis, which sat in a cheesy lump inside a pottery bowl that looked like someone’s first assignment for Intro to Ceramics. I set the entire bowl down on my plate, pushed back my chair, and bolted for the bathroom, where I promptly threw up.

When Max came gingerly knocking on the door several minutes later, I was sitting on the edge of the bathtub, breathing hard. I invited her in.

“You’re turning out to be a cheap date,” she said, perching on the toilet lid. “Do you always run out before the meal is finished?”

“I’m sorry. I guess I had too much wine. I just need to go home, I think.”

“I’ll drive you.”

“No thanks. I could use the fresh air.”

“Well, let me walk you then.”

"Please, just go back and finish your dinner. And apologize for me?" I got up and headed straight out the front door.

Oh shit oh shit oh shit. I breathed obscenities all the way home. The little guy in the toga wasn't helping, either. *How could you leave the author*, he'd say, followed by *How could you not leave the author.* My stomach growled at the full moon. *How could you leave her, how could you not leave her.* I never said anything about leaving her. *Were you planning to spend your whole life with a woman who's twenty-eight years older and won't be seen with you in public?* I never said that, either. Why couldn't I have an advocate for free love on my shoulder? Why did I have to be the stage for some morality play? *What do you think life is?*

Ah, shut up. I spent the remainder of the walk listening to my breath, thinking if I took up meditation, breathing would be a mantra I could focus on. Left foot, breathe, right, breathe. By the time I made it back to my apartment, I'd calmed down enough to feel embarrassed rather than panicked. Probably Max would never want to see me again. Certainly she'd never again serve anything psychotic to a date.

The phone was ringing when I opened my apartment door. Max? I nearly knocked over the orange tree running to answer it, bubbling with a bumbling apology.

It was the author. She'd been trying to call me all evening. Where had I been?

Out to dinner with friends from school, I said, a lie and not-a-lie.

She'd finished a chapter and wanted me to come over and celebrate.

When is a lie not a lie?

CHAPTER 7

By the time I knocked quietly on the door, it was after 10:00.

"You must think I'm crazy," I said when she opened it and stood for a long moment looking at me.

"That's only the vegetables talking," she answered, taking my hand and leading me down the hallway and up one winding set of stairs and then another.

Max lived under the eaves, tucked into the sloping ceiling of another century's propriety. The room sprawled comfortably toward four narrow windows, one centered on each wall. What furniture there was fell randomly into place. She took my hand and led me to the bed, a double mattress that floated like a raft on the wide floorboards, surrounded by little piers of books stacked here and there.

We sat cross-legged on a faded crazy quilt. "Do you want to talk about it?" she asked.

I felt vaguely adrift. "About running out in the middle of dinner, throwing up in your bathroom, and then bolting out the front door?"

She nodded.

"Not particularly."

I looked away from her. On the wall that rose up in a slant above her bed was a reproduction of a Reformation-era painting of the Virgin Mary. Why was it that everyone I was drawn to was infatuated with Catholicism?

"I just think she's beautiful," Max said, noticing my gaze and perhaps reading my mind. "If you want to kiss me now, I promise no one will walk in."

I understand that stories are supposed to follow certain rules, both stated and unstated. I understand plot, theme, action, protagonist, antagonist. I understand setting up characters for a fall. How do these things come into play when one is telling one's own story? Isn't it true we are each protagonist and antagonist of our individual lives? Aren't we pages, chapters, crossed-out sentences, vision and revision?

Who are you writing this for? says Socrates. *Who are you writing this against?*

Max had small hands and fidgeted awkwardly when she had no pockets to bury them in. Still, we were not careful in taking off each other's clothing. I was sorry that she wore no bra; it might have slowed me down a little, the fumbling with hooks and straps, the attentiveness to the shoulders and shoulder blades. She wasn't elegant, but was sturdy in a way I found comforting, perhaps because I knew I had the capacity to hurt her. Sex can be a reckless thing, I learned that night. Strip it of its two glasses of Chardonnay, its Bach piano etudes, its silk camisoles and promises whispered in the dark, and it's nothing but two people groping against whatever demons perch on their shoulders. It does not have to be a conversation, witty banter that challenges but does not offend. Sometimes it's an argument in which both people win.

With whom was I arguing? I didn't ask myself that. I slid Max's pants over her thighs and bit her in places that deserved to be kissed. She didn't mind. She was like a wrestler who has attempted to size up an opponent and, failing to do so, lunges in with a leg hold. No one was gentle. No one was tender. But we came to an easy truce, finally, sweating and breathing hard and lying side by side on our backs on her crazy raft.

"I guess you've done this before," she said.

And then I gave her the long, soft kiss she'd been expecting earlier, pulled on my clothes, and drifted down the two staircases and out the door.

Bravado lasts only so long. The truth is, I wasn't a desperado. But I was learning about timing my entrances and exits. Get out before there's time for questions.

It was easy enough to be evasive with the author. She was caught up in a new manuscript, one in which a tomboy southern belle dresses in boys' clothing and runs off to a California gold rush town, all to escape a love affair gone sour. This was new territory for her, and it had promise—even though we both knew our heroine would end up back in Chattanooga with the spurned gentleman. The author had to get the stereotype of the frontier just right, and she was spending a lot of time reading and researching so the motherly whore and the town drunk and the earnest marshal would be dressed appropriately and would move across the proper historical backdrop. I was happy to see her energized, working toward something new, even as I was moving across the historical backdrop of the early 1980s, a time when all things homosexual were brewing like a thunderstorm in the summer air. Or maybe I was just noticing such things: girls in work boots slumped in pairs on park benches, boys giving each other the once-over. I went to a few meetings of the gay student group, put a pink triangle button on my backpack, and officially came out to Jeff.

"Why is the best friend always the last to know?" He threw his head back, drama-queen fashion, and laid the back of his hand across his forehead. "What's your girlfriend going to say? Or your other girlfriend?"

"They don't have to know everything about me."

"Yeah, I've heard that."

Max played me albums by women singers who likened orgasms to waterfalls and had crushes on their gym teachers. I cut my hair short, a style that prompted the author to say "Oh, lord," though she then proceeded to spend the rest of the evening running her fingers through it. I let Max spend an entire night at my apartment, then sent flowers to the author in the morning. I served Max an expensive Bordeaux and baked the author tofu noodle casserole.

Those were heady times, I would say, were I the sort of person who could get away with saying things like "Those were heady times." But it's true I was a jumble of excitement and unrest: Max's mysterious lover, the author's shy tomboy. Heady times, indeed.

There are days when I sit in a coffee shop or at my kitchen table, pen in hand, notebook open, and wait for my life to play out in cursive sentences. A hundred years ago, this would have been called keeping a diary; twenty years ago, it was journaling. These days, there's a whole genre, people applying the characteristics of literature to their own lives. Everyone wants to be the main character in a book; everyone wants to wax philosophical about the mistakes they've made, then feed them to readers eager to hear about other people's screw-ups.

"The unexamined life is not worth living." Guess who said that? Socrates. Yes, it was Socrates. Of course, it would do us well to remember that he left no writing behind at all, only a system for driving each other crazy with questioning.

Still, who can fault me for wanting to be the author of my own life? Isn't this what happens in middle age, we try to make orderly fiction of the random things that have happened to us?

"Writing a novel is like constructing a building," the author said when I suggested she veer from her outline and let the gold-rush protagonist live out her life in wild-west drag. "The structure is already there; I'm just putting up the walls and staircases now, and trimming the windows. If I change the support beams at this stage, the whole thing is likely to come crashing down."

"And what's wrong with a little crashing down? Maybe you should let the characters do what they want to do."

"They're my characters. I decide what they want to do."

We were out in her yard, digging weeds from the flower bed. It was a fairly slow process, as I lacked the gene for distinguishing weeds from flowers. My idea of gardening was to provide plenty of water and then get out of the way so the greenery could run amok. "Okay, what have I got here?"

She looked out from beneath her straw hat. "Weed, weed,

daffodil," she said, pointing with a claw-like tool that was the sort of accessory a pirate might have sticking out from his shirtsleeve.

"What are the ingredients of a really bad salad?"

"Daffodils are poisonous, darling. Don't put them in your salad."

"It's my salad. I get to decide what goes in it."

"Remind me to cancel my reservations at your restaurant." She hacked away unsuccessfully at a viny-looking thing that had crept over from the stockade fence at the edge of her property. "Are you upset with me? I thought we were just talking."

"We're always just talking. You say something clever, then I say something clever back, then you say something witty, then I say something witty."

"That's what people do, sweetheart. It's called conversation."

"And then you call me sweetheart or darling and I get totally distracted and forget that I'm mad at you." I pulled the daffodil out by the roots and threw it down next to where she was kneeling, in some kind of absurd challenge.

"It doesn't seem to have worked this time," she said, setting down her claw and taking off her garden gloves.

"Oh, I'm not mad at you." I sat back on the grass and leaned against the concrete Buddha I'd given her for Christmas two years earlier. "It's just that I think people should be allowed to change if they want to change, no matter what the outline says."

"Are you talking about the character, or you?"

"I'm talking about everyone. Me, the character, you. I'm talking about you."

She looked stricken. "You seem restless lately."

"I guess I am." The Buddha's robe, where it was knotted at his shoulder, dug into my back. "I guess there's something I should tell you."

"Wait, please." She came over and sat on the ground in front of me, picking the petals off a dandelion. "Does it change anything between us? Because if it doesn't, I don't have to know everything. I don't even want to know everything."

I tried to stifle an enormous, involuntary sob. It came out, instead, as a shudder, a small seismographic event that dislodged the Buddha from his pedestal and sent him crashing face-first to the garden path.

"No," I said. "No, it doesn't change anything."

The Buddha lay there with his nose chipped off and his serene face smiling into the dirt.

We spent the rest of the afternoon making minor repairs. She replanted the daffodils while I super-glued the nose back onto the Eastern mystic. I told her I loved her, and I meant it, though it sounded like a defense, words coming out of my mouth to block other words that might have come out instead. She cooked salmon steaks on the grill, side by side with little vegetable shish kebabs. We ate on the porch, not talking much, not saying anything clever, and I was happy, at the end of the night, to climb into her bed and fall into sleep in her arms.

Library science is science in its purest sense: you venture a hypothesis, follow your notions to their conclusions, however illogical, until you find the answer that's looking for you. There's nothing exact about research, once you get past the ladder of classifications spiraling like DNA toward the next question and the next. The problem was knowing where to stop. And in fact, the joy was finding something totally unexpected that led to another thought, a new idea, some piece of history that seemed impossible to have lived without knowing, some fiction or some truth that fell off the unknown with one stroke of the jigsaw. How was it I happened upon Socrates as a person who once lived, breathed, roamed the streets of Athens with no enterprise in mind but reflecting people's queries back onto themselves, charming young men and pissing off his wife? The archivist had sent me on an errand, checking the library's main card catalog against a list of books she hoped to rescue from general circulation and bring under the aegis of her climate-controlled glass cabinet. These sorts of errands generally led to arguments at staff meetings, with the less-specialized librarians promoting their egalitarian view that books should be as accessible as possible. My boss usually lost in these cases, but I knew we had, under lock and key, several volumes that she'd pilfered from the stacks, removing their cards from the huge catalog in the lobby and refiling them in our small table-top version. I rather enjoyed this bit of library espionage, and was spending a pleasant afternoon roaming about in the card catalog when I came across his name.

For some reason, I was startled.

You forgot I existed outside of your crazed imagination? You can imagine who spoke those words.

I jotted a few Library of Congress numbers down and, on my lunch hour, made a trip into the stacks. I came out with one volume, a manageable summary of the history of philosophy and philosophers.

"So he went about prying into the human soul, uncovering assumptions and questioning certainties."

That's what I opened to that evening as I sat at my kitchen table with a plate of spaghetti and a bottle of Rolling Rock. There was a small section on Socrates, who, I learned, earned his place in history through the diligence of his student, Plato, an athletic and wealthy young man who went into the business of ideas, recording his teacher's conversations for the benefit of the souls of posterity. A "homely thinker," Socrates had an ugly but kind face and spent his days with the young, who, then as now, were disposed toward speculation about the big picture. He never worked, he never planned for the future, he neglected his wife and his children. Four hundred years BC, the gods and goddesses that had presided over everyone's behavior had begun to fade into mythology. The grand questions took on new importance—What should be the basis of morality? What sort of government should best rule?

This view of Socrates didn't quite mesh with my own experience of the Socratic method, which wasn't my own at all but was gleaned from a movie about a law student and his pompous, overbearing professor. In the face of open antagonism from this so-called learned man, what could the law student do but go to bed with the learned man's daughter?

And how is that different from your experience? asked my own personal Socrates, who apparently wanted to narrate my research into his seventy-odd years in ancient Greece.

But I was sleeping with a professor, not a professor's daughter. And I was also sleeping with a woman old enough to be my mentor. Did Socrates sleep with the young men who walked about with him in the Agora, trying to best each other with deeper questions, trying to reach the questions at the very essence of their souls?

"I'm sure he did," said Jeff, who came knocking mid-reverie with a cufflink he couldn't manage to attach to his right sleeve. "Who could resist all those boys in togas? Now wipe that spaghetti sauce off of your wrist before you come near me."

I rolled up my sleeves, went to the sink and scrubbed to my elbows like a surgeon. "How's this?"

"You missed a spot."

I threw the dish towel in his direction, keeping my aim just a bit off so I didn't actually hit him with it. He did look great, and I didn't want to spoil his outfit.

"Who's the lucky guy?" I asked as I fastened the cufflink to his sleeve.

"A lawyer from my firm. His name is Colin and he's terribly ruthless and terribly good looking. Best of all, he doesn't even have a wife to sneak out on."

"Hey, someone who could spend the whole night. Bring him down for coffee in the morning."

"Believe me, if he's here in the morning, he's not going to be drinking your coffee."

"What's wrong with my coffee?"

"It comes out of a jar and dissolves in hot water. What's with the sudden interest in Socrates?"

"Oh, he just keeps popping up in conversation. I thought I should know a little about him."

"Or perhaps you need a life not so wracked with moral dilemmas. But what do I know?" He straightened his tie and ducked out the door.

I went back to my spaghetti with philosophy, making a mental note to suggest that dish to Max's household.

You know, he's got a point there, noted Socrates, who for once didn't phrase his answer in the form of a question.

I slammed the book shut.

Max did cook me Spaghetti with Philosophy a week or so later. It turned out that philosophy was spinach-like, with a pinch of tarragon for good measure.

"You see, it opens up your mind to new possibilities," she said.

We were seated alone at her kitchen table; Seabird and Augustine, whose names no longer seemed odd to me, had gone off to a movie. Gigi, as always, had stormed off the moment I arrived.

"I don't think she likes me," I'd observed.

"What makes you say that?" Max pushed me against the hallway wall and ran her hands up the insides of my T-shirt.

"Um, I forget?"

"Forget what?"

"What's holding my feet to the ground."

"It's called gravity. We tend to frown on it around here." She squeezed my nipples between her fingers.

I gulped. "So I see."

As it happened, I was the first course. Spaghetti with Philosophy came somewhere between the apéritif and the entrée.

"So tell me," she said, twirling a huge rope of spaghetti on her fork and forking it directly into my mouth, "what is it you love most about me?"

That you're leaving at the end of the summer? No, I didn't say that; my mouth was too occupied with her philosophy to say anything.

"Is it my charm?"

I nodded.

"Style? Grace?"

I nodded twice.

She grinned mischievously, revealing a little piece of spinach stuck to her upper left bicuspid. "The fact that I never make demands, never ask you where you are all those nights you don't answer your phone?"

I kept nodding like an idiot, then realized I was nodding like an idiot and shook my head no. Then I swallowed. "You're enjoying this, aren't you?"

"I rather like making you squirm."

"You're rather good at it," I said, remembering our encounter in the hallway.

"So are you going to tell me?"

"Tell you what?" I asked, stalling for time.

"Tell me who it is that's keeping you so occupied. And don't go running off to the bathroom, either." She tapped at the air with her fork, as if to make a point. "You know, when we first got together I thought you were nervous because you hadn't been with a woman before. But that obviously isn't true. You're nervous because you're cheating on somebody. I know we've made no promises to each other. I know this is a summer romance. I certainly have no right to tell you not to see other people; I don't necessarily even want to tell you that. But I do deserve the truth, don't I?"

I looked down at my plate. A few clumps of spinach and tomato sauce lay there like seaweed left behind by the tide. "You do. I wish I could tell it to you."

"I guess that's my cue to get up and storm out the door."

"No, you don't have to. This is your house. I'll go." I rinsed my plate and set it in the sink, said "I'm sorry," and headed down the hallway to the front door.

Max cut through the living room and got there first, blocking my exit. "You're not so good at this fighting business, are you? We're supposed to yell at each other for a while, then sit on the porch sobbing and looking at the moon for a while, then go upstairs and have fabulous makeup sex."

"Maybe we could go right to the sobbing part? Since I've already started?"

She unfolded her arms from her chest, and I fell into them.

"Okay, but just this once," she said, leading me out onto the porch, where we settled on the top step. "I kind of miss the yelling part, though."

"And there's not even any moon." So I drew a waning sickle with my fingertip on her palm. "I'll tell you what I can," I said, tracing and retracing the sliver of moon. And after a while, after we had talked for an hour, the moon rose over the gable of the house across the street, and Max led me back inside and up the two flights of stairs to where her bed lay floating on the incoming tide.

"You told her?"

"Not exactly. I didn't name any names; I left out identifying characteristics."

"But she saw you together at that talk at the college." Jeff took aim and putted his ball directly through the blades of the windmill and into a miniature faux sandpit, which was made of tan Astroturf rather than green and sloped impossibly away from the hole. "Shit."

"We weren't exactly together. We were pretending to be acquaintances, as I recall." I hit my ball hard and it smacked against the metal blade.

"Remember, it's only a game." Jeff wiggled his hips and sent his ball racing uphill, over the miniature green, and into the sand trap on the opposite side. "A stupid game, but a game."

"Nice work, Slice." One more carefully aimed whack of the putter and my ball was right next to his in the pseudo sand.

In an exaggerated display of surreptitiousness, Jeff leaned over and lobbed his pink and my baby blue ball onto the green.

"Hey, that's cheating!"

"I prefer to think of it as creative problem solving." He tapped his ball into the hole and gestured toward me. "I learned from the best."

"It's not cheating if they both know about it."

"So cheating is acceptable if you keep everyone informed?"

"That's not what I said."

"I'm just speaking as someone who's been the cheated-with more than once."

My ball went back in the sand. "You've become awfully self-righteous since you got yourself a steady boyfriend." He and Colin, the cut-throat defense lawyer with a taste for expensive coffee, had become an item.

"I'm just saying that knowing about it doesn't make it feel any better when they get up in the middle of the night and go back to their wife."

"Whose idea was it to play miniature golf, anyway?" I picked up my ball and pocketed it. "Buy me a hot dog."

"You are such a cheap date."

Putters in hand, we strode off across the tiny fairways, thirteen holes into an eighteen-hole course. A few minutes later, settled back into the comfortable role of observers, we sat on a bench munching away and watching a traffic jam caused by a golf-impaired family of six.

"You know, you really are impossible," I observed.

"I know. But you love me anyway."

"Yup."

CHAPTER 8

How is it that the action in our lives seems to revolve around conversation? All these years I've risen early, watered whichever of my couple dozen trees needs water, sipped coffee and made my way to a workplace punctuated by signs that read "Quiet Please," and still what comes back to me is dialogue and its attendant segues into argument, dialectic, and sometimes something approaching grace. I had to learn all this talking, this navigating the channels of discourse. It did not come naturally. In my childhood, I preferred books and stories to interaction; it wasn't until much later that I came to understand that literature, history, philosophy, all the written disciplines, demanded a response. Hell, a bottle of wine demanded a response.

So has my life been a debate that won't let go of me? I can't say that—exactly. We all carry around our particular brand of dime-store philosophy—mine just happened to have shown up in the form of a wise-ass toga-wearing kind-but-homely martyr to the cause of ideas. And ideals. Yes, Socrates died for our sins, or perhaps for our failure to question our sins. Trespasses, the author would call them. Things to forgive. Things to ask forgiveness for. But I had my absolution: permission to digress, albeit discreetly, from one lover; grudging acceptance from another. Still, even that was problematical, especially for a non-Catholic like myself. In those days I found myself drawn to Jeff's bathroom, where I'd search out the crucifixes for different traits, depending on my disposition at the time. Sometimes I'd look for the one with the most compassionate face, the one likely to tell me with certainty that I was worthy of whatever love came my way; other times I'd stare at one of the tortured ones, the Christs contorted in pain, the ones with blood visibly dripping from the scratches etched by the crown of thorns.

Socrates believed knowledge and virtue were the same thing: armed with knowledge, people act wisely. But I couldn't figure out how to apply that aphorism to my life. Whose knowledge were we talking about here? Clearly I was a font of ignorance, but hadn't I been trying to do the right thing when I tiptoed up to the subject with the author, and when I sat on Max's porch talking while the moon lifted into the dark sky?

What is the right thing?

I don't know, old philosopher.

The truth was, I barely understood myself the depth of my connection with the author. The truth was, it was primal as my very thoughts, my very breath. I carried on a constant conversation with her in my heart. She was the secret at the beginning of everything, the muse for whom I wandered through the world, artfully and artlessly. Can I say why? In the years since, various therapists, analysts, counselors, PhDs of the human condition have hazarded guesses: insufficient mothering, fear of relationships, fear of commitment, fear of aging, fear of youth, a temporary stage, a permanent stage, inertia of the personality. I stopped going to them after a bartender asked if the author made me happy, and I replied "terribly happy and terribly unhappy," and it seemed enough to just say it without tracing it back to childhood trauma or character flaws or my inability to distinguish perception from reality.

One Sunday, on a weekend when Max was away interviewing for a job and the author had gone west to visit cowboy museums so she could accurately depict the buttons on her tomboy heroine's canvas overcoat, I did a little research of my own. I wrapped myself into a faded, flowery skirt, pulled on a simple yellow top, clothing that wouldn't call attention to itself or to me, and I went to Mass. Even now, I'm not sure what I was thinking. Maybe I thought I would feel the author's presence in a Catholic church. I knew she attended whenever she could, even when she was traveling, and so perhaps I had romantic fantasies that we would both be bathed in colored sunlight streaming through stained-glass windows at identical times, in sanctuaries hundreds of miles apart. Perhaps I just wanted to feel what she felt when she wasn't with me.

Jeff declined my offer to take him along, and not particularly graciously, so I ventured up the granite steps of Sacred Heart with my ironical sidekick on his regular perch an inch or two from my ear. I sat in the back pew, adopting the posture of a casual observer, an anthropologist, say, who is interested in a respectful way in the habits of the natives, wanting neither to adopt their culture nor modernize it.

Socrates, for once, was fascinated of his own accord. *How is it that kneeling brings one closer to heaven? If this is monotheism, then what are we to make of these saints, these angels, this mother-of-god, the father, the son, the holy ghost?*

Poor guy, he died four hundred years before Christ made his miraculous entrance in a Bethlehem manger. Always a gentleman, he'd downed a chalice of hemlock on the orders of the ruling party, whom he'd angered for numerous reasons, among them that he encouraged skepticism of the religion prevalent at the time, a religion we now refer to as myth, a religion that assigned various tasks to various gods and goddesses. One drove the sun's chariot across the sky, one pierced devotion into the hearts of the unsuspecting, one turned the seasons on and off with her comings and goings. It is said that Socrates honored the idea of one god, but kept his faith in reason, something larger and equally imprecise.

How little he must have felt we'd traveled, watching the processional to tongue the wafer, drink the wine. The priest spoke words from memory; the worshippers responded as one, as if by reflex or instinct. I'd been to a couple of Catholic weddings. I'd seen how the body of Christ became a third person in the marriage. And, once, with a Catholic friend, I'd attended midnight Mass on Christmas Eve. Those times, I understood the words didn't apply to me, and even now, in the rearmost pew of a church on the opposite side of town from the author's church, the prayers, the sermon, the Bible reading, the liturgy came across as words in another language. But in some way, I knew their intent. Ritual is a comfort, faith is a practice, something to be worked on and achieved in fleeting moments of colored sunlight.

I'd been inside Catholic churches, cathedrals, *iglesias*, grottos, and missions on a number of occasions, not as anthropologist but archaeologist, art historian, erudite tourist. Those times, there were no services under way, though often two or three people sat quietly awhile in the front benches, curtseying and crossing themselves before the altar before turning to leave. In the Southwest, in Mexico, in St. Paul's Cathedral in New York City, I'd examined the statuary, the tapestries, the saints painted on canvas and stucco and weathered boards. Why did I believe I'd walked into another era?

I'd always been struck by how interactive Catholicism appears to be. Churches put out candles for you to light; priests wait in their booths to listen to your deepest regrets, and you reveal them gratefully. A Protestant cross is a symbol, sure, but a crucifix is the real McCoy, in-your-face, the tortured, suffering martyr writhing before your very eyes, and don't you forget whom he suffered for.

I let Socrates focus on the sacraments, the ornamental scepters, the white robes of the priest and the gold embroidery on his white scarf. I thought of genuflection, the making of the cross across one's own body, and I recalled an altar boy in my junior high school geometry class telling me his secret for remembering the proper route down and over the torso: spectacles, testicles, wallet, watch. When he stood by my desk before the class bell rang, chanting his mantra and crossing himself over and over, I imagined he was making a kite of his body, something that could fly down the hallway, past the columns of lockers, out the double doors to the baseball field, and directly from there ascend in a perfect arc to heaven. Behind him, on the blackboard, Mrs. Franco had chalked a triangle at the nucleus of three squares, and it suddenly occurred to me that I had no grasp at all of the concept I'd understood perfectly the day before. How could we ever describe the nature of C, even if we could sketch C squared on a slate, even if we could calibrate it into centimeters, inches, feet, miles, light years? Because here's the thing: C doesn't stop where it intersects A and B. You can stop drawing, but the line flies out, following its trajectory to infinity.

By the end of the Mass, I realized I knew less than nothing about the nature of love, brotherly or otherwise, but somehow not knowing felt okay. Socrates was quiet; he aimed no pointed questions in my direction, even when, after all of the authentic parishioners had filed out, I stopped momentarily in the aisle and nodded awkwardly toward the altar, making the sign of the kite across my chest.

The author was particularly attentive the week she was out of town, twice sending bouquets to my apartment. The first was a delicate arrangement of lilies and ferns, the second a raucous bunch of sunflowers in shades ranging from a deep orange red to a brilliant yellow. The card, which read "You are my sunshine," was so corny it made me cry.

And she telephoned every night that I was home. If she called the other nights, she did not mention it. We had lengthy conversations, often lasting longer than an hour, and I'd tuck the phone into my shoulder and drag the cord around the apartment, puttering while we talked, watering the jungle, picking up a stray sock here, a teacup there, drying dishes and putting them away.

Just as, years ago, she had learned to ride horseback "proper," donning jodhpurs and snugging a riding crop under her arm while posting atop a steed named Ponce de León or Sir Galahad, she was now wrapping up her trip with a long weekend at a dude ranch, where she strapped herself into chaps and became one with Bronco, Buck, or Pokey.

"The idea," she said, "is to think of yourself as part of the horse."

"Forget the horse," I replied. "I want to hear about how you look in all that leather. Are you wearing a suede jacket with fringe?"

"And nothing underneath."

"You are such a liar. Tell me about the food. Are they serving you beans and boiled coffee with grounds floating in it?"

"At two hundred dollars a night? They wouldn't dare. The chef is Japanese, imported from New York City. Last night he served sea scallops in a mango-ginger sauce accompanied by *haricots verts* and a watercress salad. These cattle wranglers really know how to live."

"I'm glad you're having such an authentic experience."

"Oh, absolutely. The Norwegian masseuse even calls herself 'Slim.' Though I must say, I think 'Zaftig' would be more appropriate."

"Are you trying to make me jealous?" This came out of my mouth before I realized she had every right to turn the tables, given my behavior of the previous few weeks. She was gracious enough not to call attention to that fact, however.

"Only if you're jealous of a horse named Buck. I'm spending most of my time in the saddle, and I've got the sores to prove it."

"Poor baby. Will you be walking bowlegged when you return?"

"Just like a cowpoke. I suppose I'll have to have my cocktail dresses altered."

"Lucky thing mud-caked dungarees are perfect for any occasion. And I am jealous of the stupid horse, so don't get any ideas about buying yourself a mule and forty acres on the lone prairie, okay?"

"Okay, sweetie. I'll be home soon."

I'd long before given up feeling sorry for myself when the author was away, but this time I was rather enjoying wallowing in lonesome cowboy tunes, bolstered by her nighttime phone calls and the fact that Max was spending most of her energy on finding a job that would take her away within weeks. It was a dumb fantasy: me as the restless rustler, galloping out of town and into the sunset, one woman behind me and one in the next town. It wasn't even a good analogy: I was the one who seemed to be always stuck in town, minding my books like a good librarian, while the author went off to some adventure or other. And Max, well, Max wasn't sticking around long enough to leave a toothbrush in the bathroom. The truth was, I made a lousy desperado, with no sunset to ride into but the one in my own head. That was probably a good thing: I had no interest in being one with a horse. The time I'd tried it, in summer camp, the counselors lifted me on top of an enormous beast, offering not one phrase of equine instruction, though I think one of them might have said "have fun," fun being the furthest thing from my mind at that point, having been crowded out by thoughts of survival. The horse took off at a trot; I had a vague idea I was supposed to be holding the reins, but to do that I'd have had to let go of the saddle horn, which, as I saw it, was the only thing keeping me from catapulting through the air. The horse jogged up and down, and I jogged down and up, landing—bam—on his back again and again. Nothing I did would slow him down, though I managed to hang on, white-knuckled, for the entire ride.

That said, I admit I was charmed when the author returned from the Wild West with two large boxes for me. One held a pair of cowboy boots, reddish leather tooled with an intricate rope design, lariats circling the enormous heaven of a boot-maker's imagination. The toes pointed toward the sky; the heels toward the earth. The other box held an honest-to-god cowboy hat. Made of suede buckskin, it was tough and soft at the same time.

"Just like you," she said.

"Oh, you think I'm tough, do you?" I plopped the hat onto my head and poked up the front of the brim friendly-like.

"Only a little, on the outside."

I sat down on her flowery couch, yanked off my high-tops, and pulled the boots up over my jeans, and when I stood up, I swaggered a bit. "I guess I'll have to get me one of them bolo ties," I said, "and take you down to the saloon for a little whiskey and dancing. Course, I might have to shoot up the bar a little."

"You do know how to impress a girl, Billie."

Billie was the name of her leading character—the southern belle turned cowpoke in drag. Her real name was Barbara Elizabeth Ashcroft-Wilkes, hyphenated to imply good breeding, but boys who wander around gold-prospecting towns generally have no breeding at all—hence "Billie."

I was up for the game. "Well, Miss Lily," I replied, bestowing on the author the name she'd chosen for the proprietress of the Lost Angel Hotel (and house of ill repute), "I reckon you don't come across the likes of me very often."

"I reckon not," she said, reaching for my belt and pulling me toward her. "Why, Billie, I do believe you're the softest thing I've ever come across. You know you're much too young for me, don't you?"

"Yes ma'am," I said, and swallowed hard.

She'd kicked off her thong sandals and stood barefoot in a gauzy blouse and skirt. In my new boots, I was as tall as she was—taller, if you counted the hat, which sat like a solitary rider atop my head.

"I swear I can smell tumbleweeds, Miss Lily."

She flicked my hat backwards and it flew off, then came to rest against my spine, held there by the knotted lanyard that now tugged against my neck. "Tumbleweeds don't have a smell." She breathed the words into my ear.

"I believe they do," I said, running my hand down the inside of her waistband.

"So you think you're boy enough for me? Perhaps you'd care to prove it."

Her hands blew through my hair like wind on the grasslands. I looked her straight in the eye.

"Miss Lily."

"Yes, Billie?"

"Have you noticed that our names rhyme?"

"That's a rhetorical device, Billie." She turned my head and breathed into my ear. "The writer can make up any names that she wants. The character belongs entirely to her—name, eye color, cowboy boots, the way she blushes when approached by a certain barmaid. You understand, Billie."

I blushed. "Yes ma'am, Miss Lily," I said, and I swear I could feel the open prairie calling to me.

Even after several years of lying side-by-side, face-to-face, back-to-back, spooning, forking, necking, words spoken and answered by the body, even after wearing out every flat surface in every room of her house, I still teetered on the edge of a precipice whenever she opened her mouth to my tongue, scratched her fingernails up the inside of my wrist, exhaled warm air across the hairs on the back of my neck. Sometimes she had only to glance at me across the top of her reading glasses, and I was already lost, already down for the count. Other times I was lost to the scent of her perfume, her lipstick, the suggestion of wine on her breath.

I would play at being a cowboy virgin, or a cowboy virgin who's uncovered as a girl virgin in cowboy's clothing. I would be concubine, odalisque, co-conspirator. Yes, it was about sex, but sex is a complicated emotion. Call it hunger, call it falling off the brink of a question toward something approximating heaven. Call it the thing we tumble out of and into our lives.

I couldn't explain it then. I can't explain it now. It had nothing to do with words, phrases, exposition. It had everything to do with me, and with her, and that nebulous place we called "us." When I left her, when I walked out the door of her well-appointed house and into the door of the studio apartment she'd never visited, it was still there, in the mist I sprayed on my ficus trees, in the dialtone of the phone when I picked it up to call her, even in the cotton sheets I'd shared only with another woman.

Max.

Really, it had nothing to do with Max, either. Max was fine. Max was great. Sex with Max was about sex. I won't say I didn't enjoy it. It had its own complexities and they were interesting enough, but it wasn't labyrinthine, it wasn't a mosaic of sensation and forgetfulness, memory and longing and a comet imploding in the pit of your stomach.

One night Seabird and Augustine tried to explain lesbian sex to me. I'd run into them at the market; they brought me home for dinner.

"You have to enjoy the first couple of years," said Augustine, "because then it just peters out."

"No pun intended," added Seabird. "But really—one day you can't wait to tear each others' clothes off, and the next you're satisfied with a little cuddling, and before you know it, you're looking around for the next thing."

That didn't sound like my experience. But Max had likely filled her roommates in on my situation. Maybe they thought my dalliance with her was filling a need my other lover couldn't meet. Maybe they were right. But it wasn't sex that was lacking.

It was odd to be in that kitchen without Max, who was doing her academic tap dance at some Podunk state college in New Mexico. Gigi made up for the lack of drama in her own way, barging into the kitchen then doing a quick about-face when she saw me sitting there.

"Always good for comic relief," said Augustine as she sliced potatoes for an entrée called The Tubers Karamazov.

"Not to mention sexual tension," added Seabird, who was whipping some sort of white sauce into a frenzy. Then, as an aside: "You have to keep whisking this or it'll burn."

They'd set me up with a couple of enormous hothouse tomatoes, which I was supposed to be chunking into cubes, though what I was actually doing was more like pulverizing. It reminded me of the blender that served mostly as decoration on my kitchen counter. (I'd once considered turning it into a planter, but didn't want to offend Jeff, who'd given it to me as a present after I bemoaned my lack of skill in the culinary arena.) It had five settings—stir, mix, blend, puree, and liquefy—but really they were all the same, only progressively faster. Blending was just picking up the pace on mixing; liquefying was stirring gone absolutely amok. This was a concept I could relate to, a mathematical equation: everything could be accomplished with the same action; the x in the equation was velocity.

Lacks a certain subtlety, don't you think? asked the ancient Greek, just as my too-dull knife sent a splatter of tomato innards into orbit. One glob thwacked against the wallpaper; another landed, unceremoniously, on Seabird's T-shirt.

"Oh, shit, I'm sorry."

"Don't worry about it." She peeled the shirt off over her head and rinsed the stain under the faucet.

"She's happy for any excuse to take off her shirt in front of company," said Augustine, dumping the potato slices into a pot. "And really, a little tomato juice is pretty mild, considering."

"Considering what?" I wanted to know.

"Something volatile always happens whenever we make Tubers Karamazov," Seabird said, wringing her shirt out over the sink.

"Like what?"

"Oh, like Augustine's ex-girlfriend bursting in and demanding the return of her underwear."

"She wasn't my ex-girlfriend." Augustine turned toward me. "I only slept with her once, and I didn't even have her stupid underwear."

"Yes, you did—remember, we found it six months later behind your bookcase."

"Well, okay, I had it, but I didn't intentionally keep it as a trophy, which is what she accused me of."

"In a very loud voice, I might add," Seabird put in.

The corners of Augustine's mouth turned up. "She did have a good set of lungs."

That's when the white sauce, which had been cooking unwhisked for several minutes, took the opportunity to bubble up with a kind of volcanic intensity, spilling over the edges of the pan and down onto the burner.

Seabird and I yelled at the same time, causing Augustine to jump up and tip over backwards in her chair. I got to the pan first, and grabbed the handle without anticipating it might be hot. It was. I let go, and the thing tipped over, spilling whatever hadn't already overflowed onto the gas flame, which leaped into the air with a roar that muffled the sound of the back door opening.

"Hey, I've got great—" And in walked Max.

She stopped mid-sentence and gaped. I was by the stove, shaking my burnt hand, Augustine was hauling herself off the floor, and Seabird stood topless by the sink with a wet T-shirt in her hand.

"Tubers Karamazov, I presume," she said, stepping over Augustine and turning off the burner.

The hardest part about writing things down is resisting the temptation to revise. The author would not consider this a problem. "If it doesn't fit into your overall vision, change it," she would say.

"Change a name, a word, a sentence, a paragraph. Jettison entire chapters if you have to. Hell, change your typewriter ribbon if that's what's keeping you from seeing the plot clearly."

Easy for her to say. She writes fiction. She's not confronted every day with the overwhelming realization that you can't take back words you've actually spoken, you can't combine two imperfect lovers into the consummate composite, and you can't backspace over two dozen years of—what, regret?—to remove the tomato stain on the faded floral wallpaper above the chair where someone sat, spending an entire evening not inviting you to drop your life and move to the Southwest.

When the author talks about revision, of course, she's talking about syntax, detail, character development. The things we learned about in my high school creative writing class. Her themes were always the same: some variation on persistence, will, true love, and good breeding winning out, even if it takes three generations and the destruction of entire families, entire ways of life.

My themes are less grandiose, and much less easy to pin down. Even now, if you ask me What is the message of your life, I could probably blurt out something about kindness and reflection and just being along for the ride, but really, who wants her life to be a series of homilies?

In fact, if I could change anything, it would probably be my intent. Because some things I actually can change and no one would be the wiser. The tomato stain could become a heart-shaped tomato stain, for instance. A little heavy-handed, maybe, and maybe not even emotionally true, but it has a certain impact. Still, I can't change the fact of letting people walk out of my life as easily as I let them walk in. Was that my intent? Call Max "Lucy" or "Judith" or "Goodnight Irene," give her long brown curls and an endearing way of hesitating between phrases, and she still won't ask me to come with her, and I still won't ask her to stay.

We stopped talking, Max and I, in the days before her departure. Or I should say we stopped talking about anything of import, the fact that I was staying and she was leaving. She had things to attend to, the minutiae of moving and the little catastrophes that go along with it. I was one of the catastrophes, and while I pretended to understand the complexities of my own heart, I did not. I spent my days in the inner sanctum of the archives—the climate-controlled cave that held books too valuable or too much in disrepair to read. What if I accidentally touched, say, *A Concise History of the World*, and it crumbled beneath my fingers, turned to dust? These thoughts had nothing to do with Max or with wreaking havoc on civilization, I told myself. I was doing my job, the annual inventory of letters great and not-so-great, but certainly old, certainly ancient.

I was mourning a loss I hadn't yet lost, and part of me wanted her to be already gone so I could go back to my only slightly less complicated life with the author. So I left Max to her packing. I didn't ask her the details of her new job, her new apartment, the four-day journey towing a U-Haul. Still, the nights she came knocking quietly on my door after I'd climbed into bed, I always let her in, and I always let her hands start a lengthy argument with my body, and she was always considerate enough to tiptoe quietly out before I awoke with any expectations that she might still be there.

The night before she left, some two weeks after the volcanic eruption of The Tubers Karamazov, I sat down with the purloined volume on Greek philosophy, which I'd had all good intentions of reading and rereading until the ideas became fully integrated into my own less-than-panoramic imagination. Instead it sat on the back of the toilet, where I'd occasionally pick it up to peruse the sparse details of Socrates's life as presented in the introduction. Now I intended to jump headlong into "The Apologia," Socrates's famous farewell, the words delivered before he kissed the vessel of hemlock and drank it deep. Such a romantic notion—kissing a vessel of hemlock. And in fact, my notions were romantic. A couple of paragraphs in, I recognized that I was more intrigued with the idea of Socrates than with the ideas of Socrates. And I didn't want to read anyone's apology.

So when I stood in the middle of Max's street the next afternoon, watching her Volkswagen chug out of my romanticized little life, I gave Socrates his walking papers too. I'd had enough of questions bounced back at me like errant ping-pong balls.

And what's wrong with questions? Such were his parting words. The minute he was gone, I felt an enormous question mark lodge in my stomach. It occupied the space once held by Max's elaborately named vegetarian concoctions, and as her car turned the corner, I realized I'd neglected to ask for any of the recipes.

PART THREE

HILDEGARD / 1992

CHAPTER 9

It's possible, in literature, to age ten years with the turning of one page. No explanations necessary, though a quick flashback, a gesture or two of regret, a barely perceptible jadedness in tone of voice is helpful to the reader. One can assume a fair amount of change and a fairer amount of stasis. For example, I was now a full-fledged librarian with whatever status and benefits and ugly stereotypes that title conferred. I wore my shoulder-length hair tucked behind my ears. I no longer showed up for work in jeans and T-shirts, and I no longer spent the bulk of my workdays reshelving documents or unpacking cartons. And yet, there I was, in the same archives room, surrounded by the same outdated and mysterious volumes that lined the bookcases the day the author walked in and looked me up and down. Now I was in charge, having stepped in when my former boss retired, just in time to usher in the Information Age. We still had a card catalog, but now it was an artifact, its painstakingly typed bibliography having been painstakingly transferred to hard drive.

"I think I just miss the paper chase," I said to Jeff one night as we shared a beer on the porch. "No one talks about books anymore; it's all data and information. You can find whatever you need without turning a page. I spent most of the morning trying to track down an obscure translation of the Psalms for a cute senior with green hair and a nose ring, and I did it by going into the state library database, then making a handful of phone calls, and voila, the entire passage in question arrives via fax, all nicely imprinted on a long glossy scroll."

"I'll bet green hair was pleased, though."

"Tickled pink."

Jeff looked tired. After eight hours of coordinating schedules, soothing egos, and ordering supplies for the law firm, where he was now office manager, he'd waited for thirty minutes at the drugstore while the pharmacist put together Colin's AZT prescription then stood in another line at the supermarket checkout on his way home.

"How's he doing?" I asked, nodding my head toward Jeff and Colin's half of the house.

"Sleeping, at the moment. But from the looks of the kitchen, he hasn't eaten much all day. I'm going to whip something up with chicken and broccoli, and see if I can coax it into him."

"I thought you were going macrobiotic?"

"He liked the concept, but the flavor left a little to be desired. 'It tastes like dirt,' he said. 'I can get dirt out of our back yard; no need to spend a lot of energy sautéing it.' The problem is he doesn't seem to want to eat anything."

When we first bought the duplex and moved in, me on the left-hand side and the two boys on the right, Colin had taken pity on the two of us and assumed most of the cooking duties. Or perhaps he couldn't bear the thought of pizza and Chinese food every night for the foreseeable future. We were grateful, regardless of his motivation. Colin was one of those people who, faced with a refrigerator containing nothing but a couple of eggs, the remnants of a salad, and half a carton of cottage cheese, could whip up a soufflé worthy of Julia Child. In fact, he was convinced that he was the second coming of Julia Child—a sort of gay male Julia Child who'd been admitted to the bar in three states—and he liked to offer a play-by-play of his cooking techniques in an over-the-top Julia Child falsetto.

"First you select the plumpest, roundest, reddest bosoms—I mean tomatoes," he'd say, holding a couple of juicy ones up to his chest, "then you have just a smidgen of forty-year-old-Scotch"—he'd take a huge gulp of seltzer—"then you slice the tomatoes in delicate wedges, not chunks, mind you, wedges, chunks are not delicate, then you have another smidgen of Scotch—How old did I say that Scotch was?"

I tried to conjure up an image of Julia Child sautéing dirt, but instead I kept getting a picture of the green-haired girl browning her crumpled-up Psalms in a saucepan.

"Chicken and broccoli sounds comforting," I said to Jeff.

"If uninspired. Wanna come?"

"Thanks, but I've got a date to hear the latest chapter of *Conestoga Sisters*."

"Oh, right, the nun story. Still habit-forming?"

I groaned. "Actually, it's rather titillating in parts. All those New Orleans novices crossing the plains in wagons. There's a campy little scene where they rinse out their cotton underthings in a creek."

"Some day your sweetie's going to be the subject of a queer theory course, Lesbian Subtext in Pulp History."

"I could write the subtext."

"Honey, you are the subtext."

"Maybe I'll write it after she's dead."

Jeff flinched.

"God, I'm sorry," I said. "My mouth is way ahead of my brain, as usual."

"It's okay. We're all going to die. Just some of us sooner than others." He lifted his Rolling Rock in a toast. "The best we can hope for is to go out gracefully."

"Or at least wearing clean underthings and reciting the Psalms." I clinked my bottle against his.

"The lord is my laundress?"

"I shall not want."

Funny the things one remembers from childhood. I carry around no home movies in my cerebral cortex, no images of family picnics or schoolyard humiliations or kissing the boy next door out behind the garage. No, what came back to me were sentences and phrases, not my own or those of my family and friends, but the written word, learned, as we say, by heart.

When I walked in the woods, for instance, I thought: "Miles to go before I sleep."

So I was not surprised when the Twenty-third Psalm came back, first in bits and pieces and then full-blown.

I recited it that night for the author, from The lord is my shepherd to the green pastures to the valley of the shadow of death, etc.

She looked charmed but puzzled. "It's always been one of my favorites. But wherever did it come from?" Meaning how did a heathen like me happen to pull that one out of my hat.

"Courtesy of my third-grade Sunday school teacher and a green-haired girl with a penchant for theology." I told her about my Psalm quest, how the punky student had charmed me into spending half the day tracking down a hard copy of the verses she needed so she could meet a deadline—never mind that she'd obviously put this off long past the time a traditional interlibrary loan would work.

"That would take, like, two weeks," the girl had said. "I need to outline this section by Monday?" She was trying hard to look serious and earnest, but I saw procrastinator's panic written all over her face.

Ordinarily in this sort of situation I'd give the student a print-out of the libraries where the sought-after text was on hand, then point her to the pay phone in the lobby. But I knew she'd have a much better chance of getting what she needed if I made the calls. And she was such a bundle of contradictions, with her solemn face ringed in a crown of green spikes, that I'd put aside my project of the morning—weeding out some of the duplicate volumes in the collection to make room for new acquisitions—and got on the telephone myself.

"It's just that my advisor is, you know, really strict? And this is my senior thesis so I can't afford to piss her off so early in the year?"

"Why is it that girls feel the need to turn all of their statements into questions?" the author asked rather crankily during my dramatic re-enactment of the scene in the archives room. "What makes them think that's attractive?"

"I don't think being attractive to sixty-five-year-old women is high on their list of priorities."

"You don't have to rub it in."

"Don't worry. You're still gorgeous, Grandma."

And, in fact, she was.

Rather than aging, the author seemed to grow classier. A few years back, she'd talked her bridge club into skipping their pre-game cocktails and taking brisk walks instead. Now several of them met three or four mornings a week, strapped pink weights to their wrists and ankles, and strode purposefully around the neighborhood. She'd switched to a low-fat diet, and had her hair touched up weekly, adding extra henna to the dark blonde to accentuate its reddish glow.

By contrast, I already sported a few gray hairs. My exercise routine consisted of lifting beer bottles to my open mouth while flopped on the couch next to Jeff and Colin, as Fred and Ginger sashayed in formal dress across the TV screen. Curiously, though we both turned the calendar's page on the same day, we seemed to be getting closer in age, the author and I. Or maybe I had arrived, finally, in my grown-up skin. Its wrinkles seemed to suit me.

And, surprisingly, they suited her as well. It apparently was not so unseemly for an elegant woman of a certain age to dine out or attend the theater with a middle-aged friend, and so she no longer insisted on driving miles out of town for an evening out. I'd even given up parking my car around the corner when I spent the night at her house. One day it just seemed ludicrous, so I claimed the space right next to her walkway. She never mentioned it. What, after all, could the likes of the author and me be doing all night in a nicely landscaped house in the better part of town? I never told. If we missed the allure of the illicit secret, we were happy enough in our private arrangement. I had little energy for anything more in those days of helping Jeff take care of Colin, and it was a relief, sometimes, to go to her and be able to speak the word "death," which Jeff had banned from our house as if not saying it would render it a moot concept.

We'd all pretended, in the first years of the diagnosis, that death could be run out of town like a cattle poacher, that some new medication or vaccine or diet or happy outlook on life would ride in on a white horse just in time for the dramatic climax, and the dénouement would consist of everybody going back to their ordinary lives, but with a new sense of purpose.

The author knew that stories always do turn out well, but only after pestilence, fire, cruelties of fate, and men's inclination for hurting one another. People die along the way. Others don't find happiness until the sequel, or they find it in spite of their bad luck or no luck at all.

So it's not surprising I was so drawn to her current project, with its Mother Superior heroine leading her cast of novices across the untamed panorama of a country still growing into its terrain. Every couple of weeks she'd sit me down in a prim armchair in her living room proper and deliver an oddly formal standing oration of the latest chapter, occasionally glancing down across the rims of her reading glasses to gauge my response.

The chapters had titles like "Charity" and "Hope," "Perseverance" and "Sorrow"; the characters understood from the outset that they shouldn't grow too fond of one another, for it was clear only a handful would make it to the god-forsaken desert town they planned to give over to the kingdom of the lord through acts of faith and conversion and denial of the flesh.

This isn't to say the book was dreary or moralistic. Her readers wouldn't stand for that. In tonight's episode, Sister Ignatius Loyola, a sturdy twenty-two-year-old orphan raised in the convent, fashions a snare from her rosary beads and bags a rabbit for the soup, the first meat the women have consumed since a company of prospectors took pity on them a few chapters back and left an offering of three skinned squirrels.

Mother Superior is equal parts thrilled and dismayed with this display of primal instinct on the part of Sister Ignatius, and after the feast of rabbit soup she leads her to a nearby hillside, takes her hand and offers a novena to the sky, which really is bigger above those rolling fields of prairie grass, so big God seems a genuine possibility, not just something to believe in.

Maybe it was the note of earnestness in her voice, maybe the way the sleeves of her white tunic flapped like wings when she turned a page or gestured for dramatic effect, maybe I was just a sucker for the author's, well, authorness. But sprawled there as casually as humanly possible in that upright chair, listening not so much to the words themselves but the way, coming from her mouth, they sounded like rainfall or maybe a late afternoon breeze, I was struck by the idea not of love, exactly, but of something like reverence. Holding something so dear it takes up permanent residence in your thoughts, your body, the way you carry yourself.

She stopped reading abruptly and took off her glasses. "What are you smiling about so distractedly?"

I grinned. "You do realize," I said fondly, "that you're acting out all of your fantasies in this book."

She looked vaguely annoyed and set down her manuscript on the end table next to my chair. "I act out my fantasies in every book. That's what writers do. Are you just now figuring this out?"

"This time it hits a little closer to home than usual, though, don't you think?" I was quite enjoying this, and kept my voice light so she'd know I was teasing. "The bold and stately Reverend Mother, mysteriously beautiful under her long robes, leads a group of nubile young things hardly out of their teens across the fertile landscape. No men around except the ones who show up right on cue to repair a busted wagon wheel or shoot something for dinner. I'd say your proclivities are hanging out left and right, Miss Famous Writer who likes her lovers young, female, and virginal." Somewhere in the middle of this speech I pulled her onto my lap, and the last sentence I whispered into her ear, thinking of hot wind blowing across a divide.

"Oh, so that's what you think of me?" Her voice dropped so low I had to hold on to it with all my concentration to be able to hear her words. "Perhaps you hadn't noticed that you're not exactly young and virginal anymore."

I knew she was whispering so I wouldn't be able to tell from her voice whether she was upset or just teasing me back. Not that it mattered; we both had edges but we'd learned to use them more as letter openers than weapons. You can reveal or you can wound, and I was happy there were still revelations to be had.

"I may not be young, but I'd still follow you into the desert on some crazy-ass scheme of saving souls." Not exactly a revelation, but it was nice to find that I still believed the words of the love letter I was opening for her.

"We'd have to start with yours." She brushed a wisp of hair from my forehead and gave me a look far more serious than the conversation warranted.

I pulled back a little to try to read what was in her eyes. "Am I so bad?"

Her face relaxed. "You're not half bad. But you're going to need strength to get through the next months. Colin's not going to get better. He's going to need more and more care, and you're going to have to be strong not just for him but for Jeff. You'll need something larger than yourself to fall back on."

I considered this. It was true; lately much of my energy had gone into being cheerful for the two of them, doing my best to keep their spirits up. It was hard work, and a slip of the tongue or an innocuous statement taken the wrong way would send either or both into their own inaccessible closets of retreat. If I had such a closet, it was inaccessible even to me. "But I have you," I said to her.

"I'm not larger than yourself," she said, something I didn't believe for a second, "and we both know I can't give you everything you need. That's not what I'm talking about. You know I'm here whenever you need me. I'm talking about belief, conviction, some sense that things will work out as they should, even when there's no logical way to see through to that."

Nothing could convince me that a vibrant forty-year-old man turning steadily into a stick figure could ever be described as things working out as they should. "Is that what your religion teaches you, to blindly follow some clichéd proverb about happy endings?"

"I didn't say anything about things ending happily. I said things happen as they should." She spoke patiently, as if explaining something to a child, a tone that struck me as vaguely absurd given she was sitting on my lap.

"So after something lousy happens, you Catholics can all sit around and say, 'Hey, it's okay, really, because this lousy thing was *supposed* to happen.' "

"Faith is not a Catholic idea. Every religion on earth subscribes to it. That says something. I happen to be attached to Catholicism, probably because of some character flaw or maybe due to the huge crush I had on Hildegard of Bingen when I was a kid, but you don't have to belong to any organized creed or even believe in God per se to have faith. It's just something you arrive at—I can't explain it any better than that—and it really helps."

"Hildegard? Doesn't sound very sexy." "Oh, but she was, you know. Hildegard of Bingen was a Benedictine nun who had visions and founded a couple of convents in pre-Renaissance Germany. Sister Hildegard, my ninth-grade English teacher, was named for her."

"So which one were you crushed out on, the saint or the sister?"

"Both. By high school I allowed myself to fall madly in love with any nun who didn't whack my hand with a ruler or make me stand in the closet for hours."

I'd heard some of these Catholic school horror stories before, and I knew part of her was still waiting in that dark storage closet at the rear of the third-grade classroom, breathing in chalk and paper dust and listening to the muffled sounds of her classmates being released for recess and then later for lunch. The offense was long since forgotten, but it probably had something to do with being smart, she'd told me, a quality to be discouraged in Catholic schoolgirls. The author couldn't help herself. She had a smart mouth, a smart attitude, the nuns said. "Don't be so smart," they'd tell her.

"It's amazing you have any faith at all after what they put you through."

"It wasn't so bad. There was Sister Hildegard, after all."

"Now I'm jealous of some eighty-year-old nun."

"Actually, I still think of her as twenty-six, looking out from a dark habit with her moon-pie face." She took my hand and described the shape of Sister Hildegard's face with her finger on my palm. "This was back in the days when nuns covered up from head to toe, so their faces were really all you could see, and hers was so animated we were all absolutely riveted to it. She was nuts about Shakespeare, especially the historical dramas, which she'd make us act out at the front of the room while she stood on a chair motioning us around and shouting 'Emote, emote, remember, this really happened!'"

"Well, that explains a lot."

"Yes, I guess it does, doesn't it." We sat quietly for a moment, her finger still looping around my hand.

"I love the part where Sister Ignatius snares a rabbit with her rosary beads," I told her after a while.

"Thank you. There's more than one way to snare a rabbit, as they say."

"Or words to that effect."

"Yes, exactly."

I thought about faith a few mornings later in the library, wondering how the same thing you might just arrive at could also reach out and snare you with its rosary beads and then plop, you're in the soup. This was prompted by an impromptu visit from the girl with green hair, who stuck her head in the door to thank me for producing the Psalm she needed, only this time her hair was blue.

"I was so paranoid about not having something to show my professor, and afterwards I thought, Oh, wow, I never told the librarian how cool it was that she helped me out."

"No problem," I said. And then, as she was ducking back out, I shouted, "Hey, have you ever heard of Hildegard of Bingen?"

"Who hasn't?"

"Me. What's with the blue?"

She poked her cerulean head back in. "I was feeling sad," she said happily, and loped off toward the staircase.

Such a marvelous thing, to reflect your inner world so perfectly on the outside, I thought. Though that wasn't really right; the green-blue-haired girl may have been sad when she did the dye job, but she didn't look very sad now. Even blue hair can be deceptive. She also didn't look like the kind of student who usually came into the archives room. I presided over a library subculture, one walled off from the hustle and bustle of general circulation. One couldn't wander through here on the way to somewhere else, snapping gum and calling loudly to a friend across the room. There was one door in; the same door went out, and the door stayed closed, always, unless someone was passing from one side to the other.

The archives had its own climate—one I thought of as summer in the Rockies—cool enough that you want long sleeves or a light cotton sweater, moist enough that you never get parched, dry enough that you never get soaked. Then there were a couple of sub-climates. A vault in the back held books too fragile to open, too fragile even to touch, and too valuable to keep anywhere but under combination lock. It was a good twenty degrees colder in there, and pitch black. The lights, when I turned them on once a month to check inventory or add another crumbling tome, were dim and diffuse. We had, in the outer sanctum of the archives, carefully made reproductions of many of the books that spent their lives in the vault. There were companies that specialized in such things: preserving the essence of the past on reprographic paper so history itself can turn slowly into a mound of dust. Or, in this case, sit alone in the dark, like a bad light-bulb-changing joke.

There were also a couple of cabinets kept at the appropriate temperatures for their contents and fronted with tinted glass that filtered out any harmful effects of fluorescence or the sun.

I liked to think of my library domain as its own closed ecosystem, since the books under my aegis weren't allowed to circulate in the usual sense. Students could come in, spend entire afternoons reading at the oak table or in the wing chair I'd installed near a tall, arched window. They could jot down notes, even photocopy pages from certain of the volumes. But they could not check the books out with their student IDs, couldn't carry them outside to read on the sloping lawn or in their dorm rooms or ratty off-campus apartments, couldn't even take them into the lobby of the library.

And, in fact, not many students were interested in the quiet, cool place where I spent my days. They preferred the flurry of the lobby, with its rows of computers, or the long, sleek lines of the stacks, or the spirited whispering of the reading room, where an entire wall was devoted to contemporary thought, fictional and otherwise. The young people who ventured into the archives tended to be studious and smart and a little apart from the river of students that flowed through the rest of the library, which had been, in fact, designed for pedestrian flow, unlike the pool of the archives. Most of my patrons were faculty members or people affiliated with other schools who were interested in some particular item in our collection.

How did I get started on this line of thought? Oh, yes, faith and the green-haired girl, a good title for Helen Gurley Brown. I wished, that first day she came in, that I'd asked her more about her project. What did she want from the Bible? I was not well versed in the so-called "good book," but I knew enough to get the idea that its premises were good and its particulars could do great harm. Why did people need stories to believe in? If I needed a mythology to believe in, I'd create my own, thank you.

Even so, I swiveled around to the computer, saved and clicked off the quarterly report I was halfway through, and called up the card catalog search. "Hildegard of Bingen," I typed in, and she typed back "seventeen entries." And I swear, from somewhere outside of my own thoughts I heard these words:

O ye of little faith.

CHAPTER 10

What is it about the unexpected that compresses time? A young woman meets someone she likes and within minutes she's picturing the house in the suburbs, the two precocious kids. All right, perhaps this is a bad example, coming from someone who grew up to have a duplex in the city and two precocious gay men. And I'm really talking about the accordioning of the past: you play a little music and time folds like a Japanese fan. Or in this case like a mixed metaphor, since I don't think the Japanese have a tradition involving organ grinding or the polka.

But, in fact, there I was, listening on my car radio to an NPR story about the resurgence of the polka in a little Pennsylvania town, where residents from three counties showed up at the VFW hall to set a record for longest continuous polka, a song and dance that had been going on for seventy-eight hours at last count. The tune itself never ended, but new dancers and musicians cycled in without missing a beat or a twirl.

The song was still going when I pulled into my driveway, tapping away on the clutch, and nearly drove into a motorcycle that was parked in my space. Jeff had told me that AIDS Services was sending over a home health aide for Colin, who wasn't doing well on his own all day while we were at work. Mostly he needed someone to keep him company and lift his spirits. He could still get around with a cane, remember to take his medication, and fix himself a sandwich, but was sometimes too depressed to want to do those things.

I wasn't sure what an AIDS aide would look like, but I'd been picturing a cross between Florence Nightingale and the doctor in the Village People—if there was a doctor in the Village People, which I was pretty sure was not the case. Something like Marcus Welby in a white dress, or better yet, his young assistant, played by James Brolin. That would keep Colin's heart beating.

I grabbed my groceries from the back seat and Colin's prescription from the front, and hauled them up the steps of the duplex, taking a good look at the motorcycle along the way. Pretty hard to ride that thing in a dress. My hands were full so I leaned on Jeff and Colin's doorbell with my elbow rather than letting myself in, which I usually did. We had the run of each other's houses.

As it turned out, the aide was not James Brolin or Marcus Welby, or anybody in a dress, for that matter. The aide was a solidly built butch with slicked back hair, ripped Levis, a black leather vest, and a delicate gold loop piercing her left eyebrow. Something was familiar about her, but I couldn't quite put my finger on it. She opened the door, I opened my mouth to speak, and a loud pop came from the kitchen.

"Oh, shit," she said, turning and running away from me and toward what I hoped was only a culinary disaster.

That's how I recognized her, watching her fleeing the room.

"Gigi!" I called out.

I ditched the groceries and followed her to the kitchen, where I found Colin sitting at the table, a hand of cards splayed out in front of him, laughing hysterically. Gigi was picking the lid of the pressure cooker off the floor while a small geyser erupted in a pot on the stove.

"Don't tell me," I said. "Tubers Karamazov?"

"It would have been if I'd locked the lid on that damn contraption correctly."

"It's my fault," said Colin, whose giggling fit was transforming into a coughing fit. "I told her it'd cook faster under pressure."

He looked surprisingly good, considering he was doubled over, hacking like a life-long smoker. I looked suspiciously at Gigi, who was now wiping splatters from the countertop. "What have you been up to?"

"Oh, playing poker, watching soaps, whipping up explosives," she said.

"That's not what I meant." I suddenly realized I was standing with my hands on my hips like some crazed 1950s housewife. When

I tried to adjust my body language, I ended up with my hands folded over my chest instead. That would upgrade me to 1960s beehive-wearing mom status. "I mean, how are you?" I asked lamely.

Gigi rose to her full height, which bested mine by four or five inches, and took up a proprietary stance in my kitchen—or at least in my neighbors' kitchen—setting her feet apart and rocking back and forth on her motorcycle boots.

Colin had recovered, and was looking from me to her and back to me again. "Do you two know each other?"

"We used to run into each other years ago," I said after a minute, fighting the urge to back the hell out of there.

"Oh. O-o-oh," said Colin, shuffling the cards loosely in his hands

"Not 'Oh.' We were both hung up on the same woman, and she won," Gigi said. "I just didn't take it very well." She shot me an embarrassed grin, picked up the offending pot, and gingerly set it in the sink. "So much for dinner."

They both looked at me as if they were expecting some grand pronouncement. "Take-out Chinese?" I offered.

Apparently, that was grand enough. The two of them started babbling like old cronies.

"Okay, but tell them no MSG."

"And get some of those little tofu dumplings."

"Not pork?"

"I'm a vegetarian."

"You never told me that."

"I've only known you six hours. You want my whole biography?"

"I already know you shared an itch with my best girl over there." He gestured toward me with the king of hearts, the one that's sticking a knife into his head.

I sighed and picked up the phone. I knew the number by heart. We always ordered from the same restaurant, even though it was across town and the food was mediocre at best, because who could resist the House of Woo? Certainly not me.

❧

Colin and Gigi got along like a house afire, which is to say they required occasional dousing. One day I came home to find a litter box in my bathroom, a bowl of Purina in the kitchen, and the scraggliest alley cat you've ever seen cowering in the living room behind the tallest ficus.

I was not charmed. "You can't just deposit pets in people's houses when they're not looking. I haven't got time to deal with a cat. Look at it—it's probably got fleas or mange or something."

Colin looked stricken; Gigi looked annoyed.

"He needs a home," Colin pleaded.

"And you've got one," Gigi said, as if that were that.

"Well, yeah, but—" This would have been the perfect opportunity for pointing out that they both had homes, too, and I didn't see them taking in strays. Or that I have never felt the need to bond with four-legged creatures, domesticated or otherwise, and this particular four-legged creature clearly appeared otherwise. But then I eyed the two of them. Colin looked like a frail bird in his yellow running suit, the jacket zipped all the way up to his neck. (How odd that the sick wear athletic clothing, as if they're just taking a short break between the bicycling and swimming legs of the decathlon.) Gigi was stocky in her uniform jeans and black leather. I imagined them ambling slowly through the park, Colin a wobbly tripod of legs and cane, Gigi bouncy and swaggering. Perhaps they'd stopped at a bench for Colin to catch his breath, and the cat just came up to them, rubbed its matted fur against Colin's leg. Or maybe it darted across their path, maybe Gigi carefully led Colin to a bench and settled him there before chasing down the scruffy thing.

"It looks so, so—"

"Adorable?" Colin suggested. "Sweet? Cuddly?"

I took another look. The creature was all black, with long skanky hair that I was already picturing floating about the house and clinging to my work clothes. I peered around the plant. It lifted its back and hissed at me, revealing two fanglike canines—or would that be two fanglike felines?—and two crazy-in-the-wild-sense yellow eyes.

Menacing was the word that came to mind, but I opted for "unhousebroken."

"He looks unhousebroken. And is he a he?"

Gigi shifted her weight. "Do you know a thing about cats? You just plop them in the litter box and they get the idea. And he might be a he. Or he might be a she. It's a little hard to tell through all that fur."

"We'll just say he's flexibly gendered," Colin suggested. "Give him a name like Chris or Leslie and he can go either way." He was talking fast, like a carnival barker who needs to hustle his marks in to see the bearded lady and the married midgets before they can put their money back in their pockets. I thought about a story I'd once heard, that Barnum, or maybe it was Bailey, had put up a sign to keep people moving through the sideshow. It said "This way to Egress," with an arrow pointing to the door. A nice thought, but my egress was blocked by a big dyke and her scrawny, immuno-suppressed sidekick.

"He's a gift," said Gigi. "You needed a cat. We got you one. Say thank you."

Colin shrugged his shoulders, as if he were helpless in the entire matter.

From somewhere inside my head, I could hear a voice saying *Thank you*, but it wasn't my voice. "Okay, but this one is it. I'm not going to be a home for wandering cats."

So now I had a cat. Gigi and Colin took him to the clinic, had him wormed and vaccinated and given the once-over. Like expectant parents in some bizarre parallel universe, they asked the vet to make sure the cat had been appropriately neutered, but forbade her from revealing his gender. We always referred to him as "he," a pronoun I counteracted by naming him Betty.

Betty and I were like polite roommates—we occupied the same house but gave each other a wide berth.

"Doesn't Betty ever sit on your lap?" Jeff asked once, noticing the cat skulking around the edges of the room to avoid passing between us.

"He believes in personal space."

"He sits on Colin's lap."

This was true; he did sit on Colin's lap. "But Colin's so, I don't know, kind of fuzzy." Who wouldn't sit on Colin's lap?

Illness had brought out something sweet in Jeff's lover. I'd liked the original Colin, the sharp-edged, caustically funny defense lawyer, the kind of guy who'd describe himself in a personal ad as "straight-acting"; the kind of guy who could get a serial murderer off on a technicality and then order shrimp cocktail for dinner. But the new Colin I loved. He'd softened, as if his own vulnerability could slow the earth's spin on its axis. I knew one day he'd be so blurred he'd no longer exist, and all that sweetness would dissolve like sugar in a glass of iced tea. That's why I put up with Betty, I think; because I knew Colin felt I would need him, somehow. And if Colin were changing into someone who could sit all afternoon dishing about soap operas with a big-boned motorcycle-riding gal, then maybe I could become one of those people who coo over their pets, keep their pictures in their wallets in the slots where pictures of children should go, and serve up organic gourmet cat food at a dollar-fifty a can. God, I hoped not.

Here are a few interesting pieces of information on Hildegard of Bingen: She had no formal education in writing, though she was taught to read and sing the Psalms in Latin. She had visions, beginning in her youth and continuing throughout her life. At about the age of forty—this would have been in the year 1138—she began to document the visions. She did so by relating them to a monk named Volmar, who served as her scribe.

I'd been dabbling in research on Hildegard ever since the blue-green-haired girl showed up again one morning. I say blue-green because she'd apparently reached some sort of compromise—blue near the roots, green at the tips.

"So you're feeling sad and envious?"

"No, just goofy," she said, tossing me the kind of apologetic smile that young people give the older generation. Oh, God—was I the older generation? Apparently so, because here she was, giving me that smile. "I brought this for you," she said, handing over a sheet of paper. On it was typed this:

Ave Maria

Hail Mary,
O, you root of life
who restored salvation,
mystified death
and crushed the serpent
whom Eve sought,
her neck raised,
inflated with pride.
You have trampled the serpent
by bringing forth from heaven the son of God,

who was breathed into you
by the spirit of God.

O dearest,
O most loving mother
who gave the world
your son issued from heaven,

who was breathed into you
by the spirit of God.

Glory to the Father and Son
and holy Spirit,

who was breathed into you
by the spirit of God.

"It's by Hildegard von Bingen," Constance said.

"Oh, I didn't realize she wrote poems."

"Not poems; songs. Words and music. She also wrote plays and visionary treatises and stuff like that? Plus guidelines for using plants as medicine. She was pretty cool for a twelfth-century nun."

"I'll say." No wonder the author was so taken with her in the ninth grade. Those 1940s Catholic schoolgirls were big on ascetic passions.

"But why are you so interested in all this theological stuff?"

"Oh, just trying to figure out what gets lost in the translation." She tilted her blue-green head. "I'm trying to go back to the original texts, you know, in the original languages? To see how close the modern versions are, and to trace all the steps in between what was first written and what we call gospel now."

She looked so young and earnest that I almost grinned. But I didn't. "That sounds like a lot of work."

"Yeah, and it's actually work that's been done before, by 'real' scholars"—here she made little quote marks in the air with her fingers—"but I kind of want to see it for myself and make my own conclusions. I'm just taking a few passages here and there, mostly from the New Testament but also a couple Psalms because I think they're beautiful and because I'm guessing they've been changed less than some of the other stuff."

"Pretty ambitious for a kid with blue-green hair," I said, wondering what particular ways the Bible had been used against her in childhood that would lead her on this quest. "Does this mean you speak, what, Greek?"

"Greek for the parts I'm looking at, but the Old Testament is mostly ancient Hebrew and some Aramaic. I'm lining up people to help with the translations. And hopefully some nice librarians to help me track some stuff down?"

Now I did grin. "We're all nice, didn't you know?"

After Constance left (that was her name, poor kid, Constance; no wonder she had to dye her hair outrageous colors to offset that), I took another look at Hildegard's lyrics. So Mary, through the act of giving birth to Jesus, redeemed womankind after Eve's notorious fall into the spell of the serpent. That certainly explained her appeal, at least to half the population. Still, who would genuinely want a world without serpents, without knowledge, without the darker sides of pleasure? And what, exactly, did God breathe into Hildegard that she should transfer her visions into words on paper, into clear tones wafting through the damp of the abbey, things that would outlast flesh, miracles, beliefs?

Autumn came slowly that year, like a wagon train of nuns edging its way toward the horizon. Or, to be more precise, autumn came episodically, like a bedtime story about a wagon train full of nuns edging its way toward the horizon. That is to say, the days came alternately warm and cool, punctuated by occasional overnight freezes and regular installments of the saga of Mother Superior and Sister Ignatius Loyola, et al., plodding toward the endless sunset.

"Are they ever going to make it to Santa Fe?" I asked, circumnavigating the author's left nipple with my tongue.

"Not if you keep doing that."

"Just circling the wagons." I reached over to offer her right nipple the same treatment with my index finger. "Did you want me to stop?"

"Did you want to hear the rest of the chapter?"

"Oh, yes. But I thought we should maybe act out the characters' fantasies, since nineteenth-century nuns were probably not well versed in the pleasures of the body." Plus I was wet myself from the sisters' ritual ablutions, performed knee-deep in a river in full vestments and highlighted by the removal of the head cloth, the freeing of the hair and the brisk dumping of a bucket of water over the head. And it was her idea to read this chapter in bed, propped up naked against a pile of downy pillows like characters in a cheesy lesbian romance.

"Perhaps a brief interlude would be in order," she said in her expansive author voice, tossing the manuscript to one side.

Had I mentioned that I was floating in those days? That sex, like everything else, failed to anchor me to anything resembling ordinary life? Curious, too, because I spent more time than I ever had before going through the most basic motions of living: picking up groceries, chopping Chinese herbs, stroking Colin's back while he knelt before the toilet, vomiting. Sometimes I felt like the people on the *Ripley's Believe It or Not* TV series, the ones who die on the operating table and float awhile above their own bodies, watching calmly while simulated doctors and nurses work frantically on their now vacant flesh and bones, only to be hauled back, unwillingly, perhaps, by that pesky little blip of a heartbeat. But I wasn't dying, and instead of undergoing medical heroics I was taking out the trash, watering the ficus jungle, standing in line at the Pharmorama while my consciousness drifted about like an apparition.

And did I confess that I was hearing voices? Or, to be more precise, a voice. That fiery voice. Hildegard of Bingen had taken up residency in my thoughts and seemed to be spending a fair amount of time kneeling on my left shoulder, from whence she could whisper directives directly into my ear.

She's very sweet with you.

Don't watch this! You're practically a saint! What do you know about sex?

I know about love. You should be more attentive.

The author stopped doing whatever she was doing to my inner thighs with her fingertips. "You seem distracted."

"No. Just trying to get out of my head and into my body." I batted at the saintly air above my shoulder blade. Nothing there.

"Maybe this will help," she said, and plunged in.

She was awfully sweet those days, the author, as if she'd quietly set her sense of irony aside for a while. There's a trite saying about adversity bringing out the best in people, but I think actually it subdues the worst. If ever there were a time for bitterness, this would be it, yet those in my immediate orbit had backed away from the cynicism that had become a conversational default. Even Jeff, who surely had a right (and some would have said a responsibility) to be angry, who had the most to lose and would indeed be losing the most, could, in moments of clarity, express gratefulness for what he had.

"You know, I was going to break up with him," he confided one Saturday morning while we cleaned out the garage. A one-bay outbuilding that stood to the back of the yard, it had turned into a receptacle for various broken items we'd hung on to out of sentiment or laziness. No one ever parked in there; its barn doors were too unwieldy to deal with on a daily basis. But Colin had become increasingly worried lately about his car, a red Mercedes convertible left over from his hotshot lawyer days. A man who once kept his appointment book entirely in his head, Colin now kept lists. Lists of books to read, lists of doctors' appointments, lists of food he wanted to try, places he wished he'd visited. And lists, long ones, of his possessions and the people he intended to leave them to. Jeff would be getting Colin's retirement package, a portfolio of mutual funds already waiting in a dedicated trust. He'd told Colin to give the car to someone else, a friend or one of his nephews, that he was more of a Toyota Tercel guy. That was true—dear, goofy Jeff was not exactly a Mercedes person. Now that Colin couldn't safely drive anymore—his eyesight was failing and his reflexes shot—he didn't want the convertible sitting in the driveway. I suspected it made him too sad to look out the window and see it parked there, as if waiting to take him to the courthouse or the next fabulous party.

So we were emptying the garage of one set of mechanical ghosts to replace them with another. Jeff had purchased a pre-fab aluminum storage shed, and after he and I spent a failed afternoon attempting to assemble it, Gigi took pity on us and whipped it together in an hour. We'd already moved the lawnmower, barbecue grill, and patio furniture into the shed; everything else needed to be carted to the sidewalk for the trash collectors to pick up.

Jeff was chucking a busted toaster oven into a box when he mentioned that he'd once been close to dropping Colin. It was news to me. "Really? I thought you were crazy about him right from the beginning."

"It's not that I didn't love him. It's just that he was too much sometimes. Too beautiful, too witty, too successful."

Too pleased with himself, I thought, but didn't say.

"It was hard to compete with all that. Some days I just wanted a regular guy in sweatpants with smelly feet."

I thought of Colin, safely tucked into his reclining chair in front of a Packers game. "Be careful what you wish for."

Jeff tossed a couple of empty bottles into the box. He turned his baseball cap backwards and gave me a sad smile. "Yeah, that's the crazy thing. I was working up to dumping him—can you imagine, me dumping a guy like Colin?—when his test came back positive. So I kept putting it off and putting it off. I didn't tell you because I was afraid you'd think I was breaking up with him because he was sick. And maybe that was part of it, too. But, I don't know, after all that putting it off, something changed. I changed, he changed."

"He turned into the person you wanted him to be."

"Well, I didn't want him to get sick, and I don't want him to die." He looked at me with some urgency. "You don't think I'm one of those sickbed martyrs, do you? Who get their jollies out of denying their own needs and taking care of other people?"

"Saint Jeff? I don't think so."

I heard a faint chuckling. Hildegard. *Look up at that shelf in the back*, she whispered. It looked like all the other shelves—packed with cartons and random junk.

"Yeah, but I have to admit, it's kind of nice to feel I have something to offer him." He followed my gaze to the back shelf. "Hey! Is that what I think it is?"

"That depends on what you think it is," I said, wondering how a figment of my imagination, granted a saintly one, could see inside boxes. "What do you think it is?"

Jeff grabbed a wooden stepladder that lay on its side along one wall, a process that required relocating several earthenware pots still cradling their long-dead, root-bound occupants, and set it up in the back. It teetered dangerously, one leg resting on the lid of a paint can and another propped inside an empty box that had held the programmable coffee maker I couldn't figure out how to program. I held on to the ladder while he climbed, skipping the second step, which had rotted through. He grabbed the box in question and carried it down the rungs and directly out the side door, setting it down on the picnic table.

"What, what?" I said. "The suspense is killing me."

He pulled a little folding knife from his pocket and slit the seal on the box, then yanked open the flaps and began tossing wadded newspaper up in the air, giggling like a kid at his own birthday party.

I batted at the balled-up paper. "What are we celebrating?"

"It's my movie equipment!" He pulled an old 16-millimeter camera out of the box and squinted at me through its lens.

I put my hands up. "Don't shoot. I'm only the piano player."

"Smile when you say that." He set the camera on the table and gave it a good look-over, opening little doors where batteries and film would go. "Is this cool? It looks like everything's still in working order." Lifting it back to his eye, he aimed at my feet. "Dance," he said.

"Why do I have the feeling you're going to be dangerous with that thing?" I asked, twirling around the lawn.

It's funny how you can forget things about people. About your own best friend, even. Jeff had put away his camera about the same time he took the job at the law firm. The whole point of waiting tables at night had been to free himself up during the day for working on short films. But he hadn't had, what, the drive, the focus? So he'd wrapped it all up, his camera, his editing equipment, and the beginnings of a screenplay or two, put it all aside and never mentioned it again. I felt terrible, suddenly, for letting it slide into the recesses of my own memory. All those years and I'd never asked about his dreams, his passions. He surely hadn't forgotten. Imagine going to an office every day and keeping things running like clockwork (admittedly by flirting shamelessly with everyone on staff, male and female alike, plus a goodly number of the clients, plus every messenger and delivery guy to walk through the door . . .) so a bunch of overpaid egos could achieve their goals of becoming more overpaid and more egotistical. And all the while the lens through which you prefer to see the world is wrapped in newspaper in a box at the back of a garage.

"We're not putting that out on the street," I said.

"Okay."

"And we're not giving it away."

"Okay." He really didn't need any encouragement from me. He was happily taking filmless home movies of the house, the yard, and Betty, who eyed him skeptically from a perch on the porch railing.

I finished clearing out the garage myself, ending with a little Ginger Rogers number with the broom while Jeff followed me around with his camera. At the end of the day, before we moved the Mercedes in, disconnected the battery, and covered it with a tarp, we had a little ceremony. We put the top down on the car, then went in to our respective duplexes and got cleaned up. I waited on the porch in a little sundress and denim jacket, thinking about Hildegard and the lists she kept of maladies and medicinal plants. Finding the cure was simply a matter of lining up the right illness with the right herb.

After a few minutes, Colin came out, leaning on Jeff's arm. He looked all serious and sweet, like a kid trying to be grown up, the tails of a too-large white dress shirt hanging outside his running pants. He'd put on a tie, too, a campy thing with little Marilyn Monroes all over it. I was startled to realize it was his own shirt hanging limply over his shoulders like a becalmed sail. Jeff, dapper in chinos, T-shirt, and clip-on bow tie, offered me his other arm, and we drifted slowly down the stairs and to the driveway, where the Mercedes awaited us. As designated chauffeur, Jeff helped the two of us into the back seat, then hopped in front and started the engine. No one spoke. It wasn't that kind of occasion. Jeff made a couple of slow circles around the city while Colin and I looked from side to side like beauty queens in their final parade. After an hour or so, Colin leaned against my shoulder and nodded off, but Jeff kept driving through the spiraling dark.

CHAPTER 11

There have always been people willing to die for God. In the Middle Ages, some men and women—mostly women—chose a kind of living death, a life so shut off from life it was like being dead to the world. Called "anchorites" and "anchoresses," they were walled up in rooms attached to churches, with only a small window through which to receive meals, pass out refuse, bodily and otherwise, and listen to Mass. Before their interment, they were given last rites and funeral services, during which they lay on biers as if about to be buried.

Jutta of Disibodenberg was one such anchoress, though her cell had a door through which the daughters of nobility, a dozen or so during the course of her confinement, could enter for religious instruction. Hildegard was one of them. Sent in 1106, at the age of eight, she had been promised to the church by her parents, a common practice in those days.

By then, she'd already begun her career as a mystic, though she initially kept her visions to herself after discovering her talents were not "normal." Everyone did not close their eyes to see bright light. Everyone did not fall prey to temporary blindness as black as the sun is white. Everyone did not stare into the present to find the future staring back at her.

"It's like, truth is relative." Constance stood with her arms out like an airplane, balanced on her right leg while her left foot snaked around it, a demonstration of a pose she'd learned in body movement class that morning. "If you write something down, does that make it true? Now you try."

"This isn't really my sort of thing," I said, obediently stepping out of my loafers and doing my best to contort myself into her posture.

"I'm thinking I look like a giant corkscrew."

"Don't think, just feel."

"I feel like a giant corkscrew."

She deftly pulled out of the pose and tried to rearrange my limbs as I tottered, Tower-of-Pisa-like, toward the oak table.

"But really, what happens to fables when people write them down? Do they become more true or less true?"

I disentangled myself from myself and tried to focus on the verbal rather than the physical conversation. "I don't know if I'd even use the word 'true.' I'd just say it is. A moment in time captured at another moment in time."

"Okay, think of it like, oh, you tell a funny story about something that happened to you. You go home tonight and you call up your friend and you tell her about the nutty student with purple hair who made you twist your body into the shape of a corkscrew, you know, exaggerating here and there to make the story funnier, maybe mentioning that the student's hair is a different color every week, and she calls a friend and embellishes a little, and she calls a friend who embellishes a little more, and three hundred years later there are entire communities of people who dye their hair bright colors and do bizarre poses every day and hang enormous corkscrews at the fronts of their churches. And I'm, like, the great prophet, and my picture is on votive candles and prayer cards and painted by number on velvet."

Constance was cute, all worked up under the purple dye job. "You'd look great on velvet," I told her, "and the truth is, maybe you are a great prophet for the cause of body movement. You got me to try it."

She hopped up to sit on the table. "The truth is, I'm taking this class because I need a phys ed credit. But the truth also is that exercise of any sort is good for you, and that could be a good truth to send into the world."

She was right about that. And I had to admit, I wouldn't mind belonging to a religion that worshipped Constance and movement. "So where does writing things down come into all this?"

"Because, see, somewhere along the way, at some stage of the story, somebody put it on paper that in order to be a true adherent, you have to have red hair or blue hair. And it isn't enough to just practice body movement, you have to do it every day at a certain time on a certain color mat, and you have to shun people who don't hang little corkscrews in their bedrooms, and all this would be attributed to me, like any of it was my idea."

I laughed. "It must be rough being a prophet. I hope you at least get to drink a lot of wine in your religion."

"Oh, tons of it. In gigantic bottles."

I spent the rest of the afternoon amusing myself with images of hundreds of Constance clones with rainbow-colored hair, nose rings, and baggy pants waving their arms like synchronized windmills in a field of poppies, like Up with People on acid. In my world of primary, secondary, and tertiary sources, writing things down could only freeze a moment in time. Here's one way to look at a myth; here's another. The truth, if there is any, lies between the lines. "What writers do," the author once told me, "is line up one big fat lie after another, in the hope of approximating something like life."

At the time I wondered if that was what I was living—something like life, for I have not infrequently felt my existence as something proximate, on the margins of what life should be.

Now I was thinking of myself instead as being descended from an elaborate fiction, the luminous vision of a twelfth-century nun with an overactive imagination.

Vision and imagination aren't necessarily separate things, said the figment of my imagination currently taking roost atop my left shoulder.

And how are they the same?

Ah, she said.

Great answer. What was the use of having imagination if it didn't get you what you wanted?

"And what is it that you want?" Colin asked that night when I stopped by to check in on him. Gigi had just left, and Jeff wasn't due home for another hour. Colin was the only person I'd told about my otherworldly visitations, about Hildegard and her childhood and her writings, and then only recently, as he'd begun to seem otherworldly himself. Propped on the couch with a blanket over his lap, even though the temperature still hadn't caught up with the season, he looked vaguely luminous under the halo of his reading lamp.

"Do you believe in God?" I asked him.

"You're not answering my question."

"If I knew the answer I would tell you."

"I could say the same."

"I didn't ask you whether God exists. Just whether you believe."

Colin looked tired, or exasperated, or maybe both. "But if I believed then he'd exist, no?"

"No." I wasn't interested in getting into a discussion on rhetoric or philosophy, which often struck me as the same thing. "I could believe the world is going to end tomorrow, but that doesn't mean it will happen."

"You could get hit by a bus tomorrow."

"I realize how central my existence is to the general functioning of the cosmos, but I still think the world would go on as usual should I be hit by a bus."

"But the world *as you know it* would cease to exist."

"Yeah, yeah, yeah. Just tell me, what do you think?" Now he looked annoyed. "Why is it that people think you suddenly get wiser when you're dying? Or that you spend all your time contemplating the nature of life?"

I guess this was a fair response, if somewhat unnerving. For years, we'd been performing the verbal equivalent of tiptoeing around the idea of Colin's death; now, as it came nearer, he'd begun to speak of it more openly, as if death were a character waiting in the wings to come onstage. I know this was probably a healthy thing, but hadn't we all been happy in our denial? I looked at my hands and thought of dirt. "Sorry," I said. "I guess I was hoping that at some point in life, we gain some understanding of the big secrets."

"You'd better get introspective fast, if you're planning to be hit by a bus tomorrow."

"No such luck. But really, do you not wonder? About an afterlife, the soul, God, that kind of stuff?"

"Why? So I'd have someone to be angry with for my premature demise? Or so I'd have someone to be thankful to for having you and Jeff and that crazy biker chick in my life? I don't need AIDS to be a little cell where I'm walled in with a bowl of porridge and a view of the altar. I'd rather be angry and thankful, enjoy the time I have, and let the rest of you get philosophical about it. I'm going to die. That's not theory, that's fact. I'm doing my best to live with that information."

Loose ends. That's how my life felt in those days, like the fringe on a cotton rug or bits of moth-eaten yarn at the edges of a hole in an old cardigan—comfortable enough but ready to unravel in any number of directions. I had a much older lover whom I could never, in honesty, call partner; the boy next door was gradually slipping over some threshold I couldn't begin to understand; I had for a pet a scraggly cat named Betty who stared down at me like a vulture from his perch atop the bookcase; and a twelfth-century mystic had taken up residence in my thoughts. I'd been reading Hildegard's verses; she liked to begin them with "O." "O flower," "O branch," "O dawn," "O Mary, worthy of praise." I liked that O, the round mouth of the letter about to start singing. Not a sigh, not the "oh" of surprise or derision, no, something sacred, assured, O of praise, O of prayer.

You should try it, Hildegard said, *prayer. It helps.*

I don't know how to pray; I don't know who to pray to.

Stop thinking so much. Stop analyzing. Stop wisecracking. Just feel what you're feeling.

That's pretty touchy-feely for a cloistered ascetic . . .

Be quiet and listen, she told me, *you're having a crisis of faith,* and I knew it was true, even though it seemed one ought to actually have faith in order for it to be tested.

Is it a crisis not to have faith? The author's nuns were still making their way across the wilderness, a journey that went on for chapter after chapter, and so far, a good third of them had died of various hardships along the way. They certainly had an overabundance of faith, and see what happened to them? And that's not even counting the one who was initially killed off by savage Indians, until I told the author that wouldn't do in these times of enlightened multiculturalism, so now she runs off on her own accord to marry a long-haired brave who can fell a buffalo with one well-aimed arrow to the heart.

Even at work I couldn't escape the pull of the prophets. Constance had taken to studying afternoons in the archives, having found that most students avoided my room full of written antiquities like the plague. She was one of the rare twenty-year-olds who had an interest in anything more than one generation old. In her most recent incarnation, her hair was dyed bright orange and she'd taken to wearing mostly black—black tunics over black leggings—so that she looked vaguely like a giant matchstick that had just been struck.

Not a bad metaphor for a kid who was taking on the Bible for her senior project, one verse at a time coming up through Latin and Greek and English and the hip '70s-speak in the version I was given in my fifteenth year, the one in which Jesus said "Hey, man, dig in," to his twelve disciples as they sat down to eat the Last Supper. That was okay; I could picture Jesus as a sort of gentle hippie. It all fit in with the long wavy hair and the beard. But it made me wonder whether he was now being fed to teenagers as an aging punk or worse, a surfer dude, carting around scrolls in his messenger bag and making a nuisance of himself on the sidewalk with his skateboard.

Colin had spoken of not wanting to be an anchor like Hildegard's teacher, but in fact he was an anchor of another sort. His dying kept all of us—me, Jeff, Gigi—riveted not exactly to the house, but to the space dying takes up.

Would we all drift off when he finally took his leave? Or would his death simply tie up one of my loose ends?

Some days suck, some days don't suck. That was how Colin had taken to answering the question "How are you?" It was apt enough.

On one of the no-suck days, while watching Martha Stewart hand-weave placemats from birch bark and convert an old birdbath into a centerpiece, he had an idea. "We're hosting a dinner party," he announced.

The rest of us were game, especially since Colin didn't get excited about things very often any more, and since the no-suck days were fewer all the time. The planning, which went on for weeks while Jeff and I were at work, was shrouded in secrecy. We were told to "invite some fun people," but were otherwise not privy to the flurry of whispering that passed from Colin to Gigi and back again.

"Sounds like a big production," the author said as we walked around her block.

"Enormous, apparently," I said, breathing hard. "Yesterday I found cookbooks spread out all over their kitchen table, and Gigi keeps showing up with mysterious bags strapped to the back of her motorcycle."

"Food nourishes in many ways."

"I hope so, because considering Colin's lack of appetite, he'll probably just pick at it. Hey, how 'bout slowing down a little? This isn't the Indy 500."

"Well, I missed the power walk with the girls this morning because my agent called, so I have some catching up to do."

I let out a laugh—I would call it a chortle but I think people chortle only in books, not in real life. Let's just say it was a derisive little harumph, as in "Harumph, I'm the one trying to catch up here." Or at least catch my breath. But then, people don't harumph in real life either, do they?

In any case, the author showed no sympathy for her poor huffing-and-puffing lover. "Darling, we need to walk at a clip in order to maximize the aerobic benefit. Surely you can keep up with a little old lady like me."

Watch out, Hildegard whispered. As if I needed a dead Benedictine to tell me to mind my manners.

I harumphed again, wishing I had put on my sneakers or at least a pair of decent shoes. I had to stop every couple of minutes to shake little pebbles out of my clogs. At least she had the good graces not to point out that she was outwalking me even with small weights strapped to her wrists and ankles. I had the good graces not to mention that she looked like an aging cheerleader in her pink jogging suit and matching headband.

"What do you and the girls talk about when you're power walking?" I really was curious about this, though I couldn't resist teasing her. "Sex, drugs, rock 'n' roll?" I picked up speed, passed her, then swung around and jogged backwards so I could face her as she walked.

She stopped. "Don't be fresh. It's not becoming."

I was having none of that. "Neither is being smug," I said, still pedaling away from her, in reverse.

Watch out!

That sounded urgent. But it was too late. My heel had already snagged a crack in the sidewalk and I was doomed, going down backwards. In the movies, these things happen in slow motion, affording the victim an opportunity to review her life, to rue her bad attitude, to watch a quick slideshow of friends and family in chronological order of their appearance in her life.

Of course, I wasn't falling off a cliff, only a flat-soled clog, so perhaps all that drama wasn't necessary. I remember thinking: "Oh!" And then my vision went bright yellow and then black. I couldn't have been out long, for when I came to, the author had just reached me and was kneeling at my side, having the good manners, finally, to be out of breath and vaguely panicky.

"Don't move," she said. "No, maybe you should move. Can you move? Does anything hurt?"

I opened my mouth tentatively. "My skull." The words sounded like mush, like I was speaking through a mouthful of mashed potatoes.

"Your soul? Your soul hurts? What does that mean? Do you mean your sole?" She prodded gently at first my left, then my right foot.

That did it. I let out the kind of noise usually associated with animals being led to the slaughterhouse and sat bolt upright. Big mistake. My foot may have been throbbing painfully, but something akin to an earthquake was measuring 6.5 on my brain's Richter scale. This time I saw orange and had the presence of mind to keel forward instead of back.

"Oh God, you're bleeding." The sound of her voice hurt. Is that possible? She took off her pink headband, laid it against the back of my head, and gently lowered me back down. "Will you be okay for a couple of minutes?"

She raced off while I was still trying to shape my mouth around the word "no." Clearly some tectonic shift was under way and the best I could do was ratchet out my right hand to brace myself against the onslaught. That was presuming that the sidewalk would not open up and swallow me whole. It's no use power walking backwards into the future, I thought absurdly. Colin is going to die anyway. The nuns won't make it to Santa Fe in time to give him his last rites, and even if they could, their King James Bible is locked in the vault in the archives room. Plus, the sun was setting, though I couldn't tell if that was inside or outside my head.

Funny how epiphany looks like confusion. Or was I confusing a concussion with enlightenment? I'm sure the earth moved. Maybe I was confusing epiphany with sexual ecstasy. The sun was such a brilliant noise; who could hear the voice of God through all this racket? But I could hear something, sounds coming through water, or something thicker, lava. O, the whole note of Hildegard filling with music, the sun expanding to fill the entire sky. O. O of orange, O of orbit, O of ocean and opal and orchestra. How do I explain this? The earth held me in her palm. The earth held me up to the wind and the wind carried me in its vast sigh. Birds were singing, weren't they? Or chanting. The steady O of the mourning dove. O. O-o. Sad and round. O. Let go.

Is this what it feels like to die, warm and quiet, lying in the faultline of the earth's palm? Or is this how it feels to live?

Stop thinking in questions. So said Hildegard. *Stop thinking in words. Just feel.* Hmm. That's what Constance said, too, after she twined me into a corkscrew.

Then Colin's voice: *You have to find your own way.*

My own way. My own way? Way in or way out? Questions again. Don't think. Don't think. Just feel. Until I was so far inside my body I felt its horizons blurring, becoming indistinct. I floated like this for what seemed hours, the sun hot and bright around me, and I realized I was inside a prayer and a prayer was inside me.

Something tugged me back, a hand on my face, words turning me solid. "Come back, please, come back now," and the earth beneath me hardened into concrete and my head started up a slow and steady pounding. She came into focus, the author, kneeling beside me on the sidewalk on the west side of the small city where I'd been doing her bidding for some fifteen years.

It was clear, then, what I had to do.

The author had run back to her house, grabbed the car keys and an old towel to spread on the back seat so I wouldn't bleed all over her Volvo. Now she was back, with the car, and she was saying my name over and over. "Come on, sweetie, let's get you to the emergency room."

I know this because she told me later. While the author had shifted into emergency mode, coping quite competently with my little accident, I was swimming through the geology of consciousness—intrepid terrain, in my case. Apparently I let out some sort of a cry as she was helping me slowly from the pavement. O?

"It felt, I don't know, reverent," I said to her a few hours later while my foot swelled and the topical anesthetic prickled at the back of my head. One broken ankle, one concussion, five stitches.

"What felt reverent?" Now that the immediate crisis was over, she paced distractedly around the examining room. I could tell she was trying hard to focus on me instead of worrying that someone she knew might see us together there.

"Everything. Life. My life. Plate tectonics." It was hard to look like someone who'd had a momentary grasp on profundity while wearing a hospital gown that was open at the back, but I pretended it was the sort of thing a philosopher might sport while sitting on a cold metal table doped up with codeine.

She looked at me skeptically. "I think you were probably hallucinating."

Maybe, but something was still beckoning from inside my thoughts, which were less ideas and more a dull throbbing, like tribal drumming bouncing around the atmosphere. Or was the weather just different on the underside of reality?

Twelfth-century Catholics knew that Hildegard's visions were a gift from God. The contemporary neuroscientific opinion is that she suffered debilitating migraines. Which is true?

Why do you have to choose?

I left the hospital with a bottle of painkillers, a pair of crutches, and something incomprehensible scribbled on a prescription pad. We agreed Jeff and Gigi had enough to do without taking care of me, so the author took me back to her house and settled me in on the couch, propping a pillow under my leg.

"I guess this means I'm sleeping alone?"

"You can hardly climb the stairs with a broken foot. And the doctor said no excitement, remember?" She wagged her finger at me.

I groaned. "This maternal instinct is most unbecoming," I said, my head pounding away in Morse code.

The humans in my life were mostly amused by what Colin called my "mystical mishap," once they'd ascertained that, other than a little cosmic juggling of the brain cells, I was okay. Betty, though, was practically awestruck by my misfortune. I don't know—maybe he missed me during the three days I spent convalescing in front of the author's TV, alternating between *The Hunger* and *The Trouble with Angels* until she threatened to cut the cord to the VCR.

"Nuns and vampires," I said to Betty, plugging *The Hunger* into my own video player. "Who wouldn't love 'em?"

Betty indicated his agreement by jumping up on the footstool and sniffing at my toes, which stuck out of the cast like five fat little piggies who tripped and fell on their way to market. My immobility must have made me more approachable from a feline perspective. Who'd be threatened by a lump in an easy chair, lolling about in the near dark and tossing out caustic comments? Apparently not Betty, who was happy to go along with all of my pronouncements and appreciated my taste in movies. For instance, he was as mesmerized as I by Catherine Deneuve; he didn't mind watching her seduce Susan Sarandon over and over while the videotape racked up late fees. Secretly, I think we both wanted to be Susan Sarandon, if only to be able to stand in an airy parlor while Deneuve teased a sonata from the grand piano.

Every now and then Gigi or Jeff checked in on me. We'd talk for a few minutes until the effort of moving my tongue around in my mouth became overwhelming, after which the cat and I would be left to our own devices, those devices being remote controls—one for pausing and rewinding, one for turning off the sound. After a while, we pretty much knew all the dialogue, so there was no point in filling our heads with unnecessary noise. "You'll make some crazy nun," I mouthed along with June Harding shortly before the credits began to roll on *The Trouble with Angels.*

"Ack," said Betty, which, roughly translated, meant "No, let's break out of this teenage flick and establish a lesbian separatist colony in the woods of Vermont."

"But maybe Betty's a boy, and he'd rather run off to Soho to manage a fitness center," Jeff suggested when I reported on our conversation. He'd arrived with a bowl of dried-up tuna casserole that had been reheated three or four times already. "Sorry about this. Gigi's spending all her time helping Colin plan his dinner party, so we're all stuck with my cooking."

"Even if Betty is a boy, he's still a cat, so I'm sure he'd much rather be in the woods with a bunch of lesbians than watching pretty boys oil their chests." I attempted a bite of casserole, which was actually quite tasty despite its unintended crunch.

"If Betty were a lesbian, she wouldn't want to leave the convent."

I granted him that point. Take them out of their habits and nuns look a lot like lesbians, what with their bad haircuts and sensible shoes.

"All right, Betty, we'll stay in the nunnery if you want. But don't expect me to be on my knees at 4:00 a.m. in some cold chapel."

Betty shot me a patronizing/matronizing look then jumped into my lap and stuck his face in my tuna. "Ack," he said.

I looked at Jeff. "Ack," I said.

Is it possible to orchestrate one's own hallucinations? Because really, that's what I was doing—taking advantage of a concussion and a broken foot to coax myself into an altered state. It required a few props—shades for the window, a little bottle of codeine, the suggestion of lusty vampires and teenage novices. All I had to do was wait. Hildegard's migraines brought on visitations, otherworldly music, the word of God revealed through a monk's quill. I had the headache, but it was leading me nowhere. I couldn't get back to Hildegard's O.

"I was starting to figure out a few things," I said to Colin. Gigi had set us up in lawn chairs on the porch, then draped blankets over our laps. We looked like a couple of hipster invalids in our dark glasses and backwards baseball caps, my crutches and his cane propped up against the railing.

"Things about her?" He said the author's name.

"Things about me. Things I sort of wish I hadn't figured out. But Hildegard, she had a headache and she saw God."

"Hildegard was a drama queen."

"You think?"

Colin's measured breathing filled the space between us. "Well, look at what you know about her. Her parents donated her to the church. Talk about guilt-free child neglect. Brownie points for them, a palette to sleep on and gruel to eat for her. Not to mention a life of quiet contemplation. What do you do when you're bored silly in a nunnery?"

I thought of the young troublemakers in the movie, and of the author's flock bushwhacking cross-country like outlaws. "Hmm.

See a few apparitions, stir things up a bit?"

"What else?"

Interesting theory, though I'd read that Hildegard's visions began long before she was deposited with the nuns. She was so young, in fact, when first overtaken by the illusory world, that she assumed everyone had visions.

"When I passed out, I was praying, in an odd sort of way; I was part of a prayer, but now I've forgotten how I got there," I said.

"I know what you mean about forgetting. As it turns out, actually, dying involves pretty much forgetting everything you've ever known."

I was tired of death. "Don't do that."

"Don't do what?"

"Don't make everything about dying."

"Everything is about dying." He sounded fatigued. "Do you know I can't walk more than ten steps without Jeff or Gigi holding me up? I wake up every night drowning in my own sweat. I'm wearing fucking diapers underneath this lovely ensemble." He spread his arms in a sitting-down curtsy. "I am dying."

"Just not today, please."

"Yes, today, and tomorrow, and the next day, and the next day, until I'm finished."

I felt very foolish all of a sudden, with my delusions of mysticism and my delight at being the center of attention for a change. It wasn't Colin's fault that he was sick. He must have been even more tired of it than the rest of us.

"I'm sorry," I said. And then: "How do you figure?"

"Well, eventually I'm going to get it right."

"No, I mean how do you figure that dying is about forgetting? I'd think you'd be remembering every interesting person you ever met and every interesting thing that ever happened to you."

He leaned his head back and closed his eyes. "I do. Or, I should say, I have been. But then I let them go."

"The people and things, or the memories?"

"Both, I guess. It's an interesting process, like being born in reverse. I think I'm reverting to being just a body, no ties, no history, no needs except for the immediate physical ones: breathing, shitting, drinking, eating."

I thought about how he was already forgetting to eat, and pulled my blanket up over my chest. "Just don't forget about me, okay?"

"Not a chance."

I forgave him for lying. Dying was another matter.

The nuns were in a predicament. Winter was coming on, provisions were low, and two of the sweetest, youngest ones, two who'd only just taken their vows, Mary Pius and Mary Joseph, had taken sick with consumption. The group was holed up in a frontier town that was right out of *Little House on the Prairie*, still weeks from their destination and totally dependent on the kindness of strangers.

"Oh, you can't kill off the two Marys," I said when the author finished reading the chapter. I'd recovered enough to go back to work, and was getting around in my car by using one of Colin's canes to push in the clutch. It was a bit tricky, given that I had to completely release my grip on the steering wheel to change gears since I needed one hand to maneuver the cane and the other to operate the stick shift, but after stalling a few times and discovering it was best not to attempt shifting mid-turn, I found I could navigate the city fairly well.

"I'm afraid the Marys are dispensable," she said, coming to sit beside me on her couch.

"But I like them," I insisted. "They represent innocence, purity, the whole future of a young country stretched out in front of them."

"That's very sweet," she said, stroking the scarf I'd tied around my head to cover up the shaved spot where the doctor had stitched up the gash that Jeff said looked like a lopsided gull in flight. "I'll be sure to have you write the critical analysis."

"Consumption seems so, I don't know, consuming. Couldn't you give them something they'll recover from, like bad colds or broken legs? Just amend your outline a little. Be flexible."

"Actually, I'm afraid I've already fallen off my outline."

I had a momentary image of the author stepping from a ladder of headings and sub-headings and free falling into a blank white sky. "Really?" I twisted my body so I could look at her, swinging my leg around and setting the cast in her lap. I'd never known her to stray from a plan in her writing.

"The story's gone a little wonky since your accident." She petted my cast distractedly. "Everything seemed to be going fine, and then suddenly the nuns are totally off course, out of Catholic territory entirely, and they ought to have arrived at their destination by now."

"At the risk of sounding like a new-age greeting card, maybe they're just where they're supposed to be. Maybe this book is about the journey."

She considered that for a moment. "The oddest thing happened. Sister Ignatius lost her rosary beads. You know, the ones she used to snare the rabbit?"

I nodded. I often pictured Ignatius rigging a trap in the pioneer outback, crossing herself a time or two and then waiting behind a large rock for God to send along a small animal. Did she flinch as she smashed its head with a stone? Did she understand the irony of taking a life for Christ? But that's a contemporary notion, that animals and people are on the same footing. Like Hildegard, Ignatius would have believed that plants, animals, air, everything was put on earth by God for the use of humanity. Still, might she have been pleased by her own ability to take life from the rabbit and give it to her sisters?

"I love that chapter," I said to the author. "All that proto-feminist consciousness."

"Proto-feminist my foot." She knocked on my cast. "Ignatius Loyola is sheer nerve, bolstered by faith. So when she reached into her vestments for the beads and they weren't there, well, I guess it put both of us at a loss. I can't even understand where they've got to. They were tied up in a little pouch she kept wrapped around her waist, next to her skin, so she could get at them only through the tear in the seam of her robe. But the pouch wasn't missing, only the rosary."

"Perhaps the Mother Superior snagged them during one of their off-the-page trysts?" I was convinced the two were going at it hot and heavy while the narrative was focused elsewhere, even if the author insisted nothing of the kind was going on.

"Only in your imagination. The problem is, she wasn't supposed to lose the beads. She was supposed to reach in and pull them out and say a couple of Hail Marys. But honestly, they just weren't there and now we're both a little off-kilter."

"Both" meant the author and Sister Ignatius, I realized, but it occurred to me that pretty much everyone I knew was a tad out of whack right then. "It's your novel. Can't you just write your way back into kilter?"

"That's what I was trying to do, and now instead I've got the Marys on their deathbeds and the rest of the poor girls at the mercy of a bunch of Lutherans."

"Maybe Sister Ignatius is trying to tell you that she's going to do what she's going to do no matter what you had in mind."

"Or die trying."

"Don't even think about that. I might be convinced to let go of Mary Pius and Mary Joseph, if only for the sake of wringing a few extra tears out of your devoted readers, but Ignatius is a major character. The whole plot would fall apart if she went under." My adamance surprised me, though it shouldn't have: death, even of fictional characters, wasn't a capricious thing for me those days.

The author sensed that, and softened her voice. "Okay. I'll take good care of Ignatius Loyola for you. Maybe she'll even find her rosary, someplace where she least expects it."

"Or maybe she'll convert to Lutheranism and give up the rosary in favor of short, practical prayers. 'Please lord, make it rain on my cornfield.' 'Jesus, don't let my dumb lout of a husband squander all our money on whiskey.' That sort of thing."

"I suspect not."

"No."

CHAPTER 12

Hildegard showed up again as I hobbled through the baking goods aisle of the supermarket. My orthopedist said I should begin putting pressure on my foot. There was also some discussion of the tibia, or the fibula, or some such thing, but the upshot was, I was supposed to walk on it and it would hurt like hell for a while, after which it would only hurt like heck.

I'd been dispatched with a list. "As long as you have to torture yourself, you may as well pick up some ingredients," Gigi told me. Then she took away my crutches, pointed across the room to where the list waited, pinned to the refrigerator by a Carmen Miranda magnet.

"You don't have to enjoy this quite so much." I half hopped, half dragged myself across the linoleum, grabbing at the backs of chairs and the countertop whenever possible and wincing all the way.

"You want to get better, don't you?"

"Yes, Nurse Ratched."

Poor Gigi, I thought as I examined bottles of olive oil. She was probably just happy having a patient who would recover. Virgin, virgin light, pure virgin, extra virgin. I clearly didn't understand the labeling. Virgin I got. Virgin light? Okay, so maybe you slipped just once, at the drive-in, in the back seat of a '59 Chevy. But pure virgin? Extra virgin? Sounded redundant.

Enter Hildegard. *It has to do with processing, and the quality of the oil, of course, and marketing. The more qualifiers in the name, the more you can charge.*

"You disappear for a week and a half and then show up to dispense wisdom on the marketing of olive oil? You're a twelfth-century nun, for God's sake. What do you know from marketing?" I didn't realize I was talking out loud until I noticed the only other shopper in the aisle, a middle-aged woman who was disposed toward Hamburger Helper and Kraft Macaroni & Cheese, was now making a great show of examining Jell-O boxes while she eyed me from behind a display of artificial sweeteners.

"It's the olive oil," I shouted to her, taking license from my fiberglass-encased appendage to play unbalanced. "It's too pure. I can't corrupt it with my jalapeños."

She dumped about six boxes of lime green into her cart and backed slowly away, as if I might chuck a bottle of extra virgin at her if she turned her back to me.

Be nice, Hildegard warned.

The woman had Wonder Bread and Cheez Whiz in her shopping cart.

And you have avocados and party hats.

Well, so far, but I'm going to get . . . I fished the list out of my pocket. Five-alarm salsa, Twinkies, toilet paper with lotion, the *National Enquirer* . . . Okay. Point taken. I'll try to act normal.

Normal isn't necessary. But a little kindness goes a long way.

Is that what you came to tell me? Because, really, I'm a very decent person, other than the occasional flare-up in the supermarket. I think I get fluorescence poisoning.

Hold on to the sunlight, she said. *And I'd go with the extra virgin. Couldn't hurt.*

I really was trying to hold on to the sunlight, but autumn had arrived with a sudden vengeance and blanched the light of its color. The days were getting noticeably shorter. Usually I was moved by the chill in the air and the early dark, but that year they signaled an approaching claustrophobia.

"Hold on to the sunlight," I said to Gigi as I limped in and deposited the groceries on the table and myself in a chair.

"What's that, some new dish soap?" She rummaged through the bag.

"Just something somebody said to me at the supermarket."

She looked puzzled for a moment, then left the kitchen,

returning with my crutches. "Sorry I took these. I get carried away sometimes."

"It's okay. You were just trying to help." Gigi looked more tired than I felt. "How are you?"

"It's been a long day. We spent the morning at the hospital nailing down the exact number of T-cells Colin's lost during the last month, then I gave him a bath, then made lunch. After you went for groceries he just had to see this Hitchcock movie, *The Birds*, so I called all over town until I found it at a video store in the shopping center out by the highway, and by the time I got back with it he was fast asleep."

"So did you at least watch the movie yourself?" I asked Gigi.

"I plugged it in and caught bits and pieces of it. I had no idea Suzanne Pleshette was such a babe before she married Bob Newhart."

"No kidding?"

We were both quiet for a while, then I had to ask. "Do you ever hear from her?"

"Suzanne Pleshette?"

"You know who I mean. Max."

"Never. How about you?"

"The same. But I hear she's an associate professor now, with tenure and an anthropologist girlfriend." I hadn't thought about Max in a long time. It had been a few years, in fact, since I'd gone to bed with anyone other than the author. My life was complicated enough.

"She really liked you, you know. I hope I didn't screw things up, running away every time I saw you. It wasn't personal."

"Oh, I know. If anyone screwed things up, it was me. I didn't have room in my life for her. Maybe I should have made room." I was feeling claustrophobic again, a feeling I realized was coming from my foot, which was sweaty and itching like crazy. I grabbed a fork from the table and stuck it inside the cast.

"Be careful. Your skin's probably pretty raw in there." Gigi came around the table to keep an eye on my scratching.

The fork was no match for my itch, an organic thing that started in the bones and emanated outward. "This is gross; I'm sorry. It's been a little ticklish all along, but now it's really unbearable all of a sudden."

"The epidermis has nowhere to go." Gigi fished around in the junk drawer and came out with a knitting needle. "Try this."

I stuck the needle in the space between my leg and the cast. It was longer than the fork, but clearly not designed for scratching. "Epidermis? Sounds like something that should be extinct."

"It's the outer layer of skin. Your body's trying to shed it, but it's trapped in there."

"Oh. You sound like you know what you're talking about."

"Well, I am a nurse."

"You're a nurse?"

"What did you think, I was some sort of glorified orderly?"

As a matter of fact, that is what I thought, but I knew enough not to say so. "Wouldn't you make more money working at a hospital or in a doctor's office?"

"Maybe that didn't work for me."

Our little attempt at bonding seemed to be going awry. "But I'll bet you looked cute in a white cap," I said, in a lame attempt to bring it back on track, shaking my foot in some crazy epidermal dance. "Do you have any duct tape?"

She eyed me suspiciously, then pulled a roll from the drawer where she'd found the knitting needle. I ripped off a small piece and used it to tape the fork to the needle, which I then immediately plunged inside the cast. It was a tight squeeze, but it at least gave the illusion of scratching at the outside of my foot. The inside was another matter.

"Whew. I thought I was a goner."

"Don't lose that fork in there; we'd have to operate to get it out." Gigi lifted her motorcycle keys from the rack beside the door, grabbed her leather jacket off its peg and walked out the back.

"Tomorrow," she said.

I sat there scratching myself until Jeff came home.

Two mornings later, I woke to church bells, brought close by unusual gusts from the southwest. I thought of the young Hildegard, rising from her straw bed and placing her feet resolutely on the stone floor while bells clattered through the broken air. No wonder she wrote music that sounded like the sighing of the wind, something to shush the ugly approximations man made of heaven. Constance had brought me a cassette of Hildegard's songs, performed by a women's chorus, that she'd picked up in a second-hand bookstore in town. I played it in my car on the way to and from work. Sometimes, to spice things up, I sang along in mimicked medieval Latin, adding a country twang to my voice. Mostly I just let the songs fill up the gaping canyon in my head.

The church bells, muted and carried along on the breeze like a sailboat, made rather a lovely transition out of sleep. I'd always felt, on waking, that I was surfacing from the underside of my own life, rising from a Grimms' fairy tale into something more resembling Dr. Seuss, but recently I hadn't been dreaming at all, except for perhaps a swimming through the dark waters of a long-abandoned quarry.

Well? You know what you have to do . . .

Don't rush me. I'm not ready.

And then I was lulled back into sleep by the sighing of angels.

Not for long, though. What seemed like only a few moments later, a body much too large to be Betty came slamming down next to me.

"What would you like to share with our viewers on the auspicious morning of Colin's dinner party?"

I opened one skeptical eye to find the eye of Jeff's camera staring back at me. I pushed it aside. "Go away! I'm not sharing my bed with your nonexistent audience."

"I'll bet you wouldn't treat Stephen Spielberg that way."

"Yes, I would, if Stephen Spielberg crashed my bed on a Sunday morning. Get that thing out of my face."

Jeff was sprawled on the passenger side of my double mattress, aiming the 16-millimeter directly at my bed-head. "Smile, sweetie."

The camera made a purring sound.

"Is that thing loaded? I thought it was broken."

"Picked it up at the shop yesterday. It's lubed and focused and rarin' to go. Wanna stroke the zoom lens?"

"Get out of here! Go home."

Jeff put down the camera and sat up cross-legged. "Sorry, can't. I've been banished while Colin and Gigi get ready for the big event."

"They're still keeping the menu a secret?"

"I think they're actually stocking certain items just to throw me off track. I opened the cupboard last night and found SpaghettiOs and Marshmallow Fluff next to the falafel mix and rice pilaf."

"That would explain the Twinkies on my shopping list. You know, I'm going to be sorry when this is over. I've been enjoying the mystery."

Jeff put the camera back to his face and aimed it at Betty, who was watching from the top of the bureau with a bemused look on his face. "Colin's been looking forward to this for weeks. I'm afraid he's going to be lost afterwards."

I sat up, took the camera and turned it on Jeff, remembering my thoughts in the moments between sleep and wakefulness. "What will you do when he's gone?"

"I guess I'll be lost too." He looked so directly at me that I had to move the lens away. I trained it on Betty, as if a cat might have something more instinctive to offer on the finer points of sorrow.

"Ack," Betty said.

"Me, too," I said. "What an excuse for finding ourselves."

Jeff stood up. "I'm supposed to get cigars. Wanna come?"

"I dunno, Dr. Freud. Real cigars, or Get-you-out-of-the-house cigars?"

"Both."

"Give me a minute to do something with this mess." I ran my fingers over the bruised spot on my head, which was sprouting a soft fur some half-inch long.

"I have an even better idea," he said, tossing me a fishing hat that lived on top of my seldom-used iron.

Jeff's better idea, it turned out, wasn't so bad. He took me to Kwik Cuts and, over my protestations that I didn't want anyone who couldn't distinguish between a Q and a K coming near me with scissors, instructed the boy stylist to "Make the rest of her hair look like this fuzzy spot in back."

"I'm a librarian, for God's sake. I'm supposed to look like a grownup. I'm supposed to wear my hair in a goddamn bun." I groused, but I let the young man, who looked fresh from a six-week hairdressing certificate program, lead me first to the shampoo sink and then to a chair in front of a floor-to-ceiling mirror.

Sometimes it's better not to watch. I closed my eyes and grabbed tight to the armrests, feeling a bit like Captain Kirk frozen in a Vulcan death grip.

Jeff, oblivious to my distress, issued directives.

"A little more on the left. We want it the same length all over, like a cat."

Great. I was trapped in a bad science fiction hairdo fantasy, and now I was going to look like a cat. But when it was over and I tentatively rejoined the rational world, lifting one eyelid at a time, I had to admit it looked pretty good. Not out loud, of course. "Are we done?" I said to Jeff's camera. "We still have to buy cigars."

While he was paying the boy wonder with a twenty-dollar bill for the cut and another ten for a tip, I ran my fingers through my new mane, then shook my head the way Betty does when he's just come in from a drizzle. I felt a little lightheaded and rested my weight against the cane that had replaced my crutches.

"You look ten years younger," said the receptionist, who wasn't even close to being born when I was ten years old and who sported a Pebbles Flintstone bone and pigtail atop her head.

"You do look luscious, darling," Jeff said, taking my free arm and helping me through the door.

"All right, it's pretty cute," I allowed. "But now I'm going to need new earrings and probably a necklace or two."

As it turned out, we both bought new earrings (only one for Jeff, a tiny silver crucifix that dangled just below his right earlobe), I bought a skimpy little black dress with spaghetti straps, Jeff bought a tuxedo jacket complete with tails, and, as the pièce de resistance, we both got tattoos.

Oh—and somewhere in the middle of all that, we each devoured a tall stack of blueberry pancakes at the IHOP, which Jeff insisted we patronize given the state of my mobility.

"Not a bad way to kill a few hours, eh?" Jeff said as we drove back to our neighborhood.

"I have a feeling they're going to be sorry they threw us out."

"Not us, me. But you are the best friend in the world for indulging me."

"Ack," I said.

CHAPTER 13

We had to park in the street, as some of the guests had already arrived and usurped the driveway. We ducked into my duplex for a quick change. I put on the new dress, and Jeff arranged his tuxedo coat over the T-shirt and painter's pants he'd been wearing all day. As an afterthought, he knotted the bowtie that came with the jacket around the base of his camera, then picked out a cherry red lipstick from the medicine cabinet and drew a huge pair of lips on my cast. Thus fortified with accessories, we walked/hobbled the few steps from my front door to Jeff's and rang the bell, ready for our grand entrance.

Gigi opened the door dressed nattily in black jeans, white oxford shirt and skinny tie.

"About time you showed up," she said, patently ignoring my new look. "And keep that thing away from me." She pointed at Jeff's camera, which was peeking around her and down the hallway.

Once past the bouncer, Jeff bounded over to kiss Colin messily on the cheek. He was seated regally in the reclining chair, wearing a cardboard tiara and gesturing with a scepter.

Colin's sister Judy and her husband, Bill, sat awkwardly to one end of the couch, looking decidedly uncomfortable and Midwestern. "We didn't know this was a costume party," she said when I introduced myself.

It's not, honey. "You two look great," I said. "Just like you're on your way to church." I'd heard the story of how Judy was the only member of the family to stand up for Colin when he passed the bar and came out of the closet, and now she'd driven two hundred miles to come to his dinner party. I welcomed them warmly, hoping some responsible librarian vibes would leak out through the little dress and littler haircut.

And Gigi had invited Seabird and Augustine, whom I hadn't seen since they'd found sitting me on the sidewalk in front of their house the night Max drove away. "You two haven't changed at all," I marveled.

"Well, neither have you," Augustine said, pulling me in for a hug, and I remembered the cropped haircut and sundresses I'd sported a decade earlier.

"Actually, I have. It's a long story." One I didn't go into as I was distracted by the arrival of a new guest: the author.

"You came," I said.

"Don't you look adorable!" And she actually took my face in her slender hands and kissed me right on the mouth, the kind of kiss that could be interpreted any number of ways. She wore a gauzy white wrap that made me think, absurdly, of the netting around the bed where the vampiress Catherine Deneuve seduced Susan Sarandon. "Did you think I wouldn't come?"

Of course I thought she wouldn't come. She'd never been to my house, let alone been there in the presence of strangers. Even when I needed a ride home from my period of recuperation on her couch, Jeff had come over on the bus and driven me and my car back to the duplex.

"I'm glad you're here," I said, reaching up to rub the scar on the back of my head, which had started to throb, faintly, like background noise.

"What's this on your arm? Did you hurt yourself again?" She laid her hand gingerly on the large Band-Aid at the top of my left biceps.

"It's a secret. I'll show you later."

All in all, when the doorbell stopped ringing, we were a couple shy of a baker's dozen: Colin, Jeff, Gigi, the author, Bill and Judy, Seabird and Augustine, Constance, who showed up with a scraggly beanpole of a boyfriend in tow, and me. We made for an unlikely but congenial crew: Colin had decided he didn't want the party to turn into a premature wake, so other than Jeff and Gigi and I, he asked only that his sister be invited and that we three bring along some interesting people who didn't know him. Gigi had asked

Seabird and Augustine, I'd snagged Constance, tempting her with stories of eccentric grownups, and Jeff, with my permission, had sent an invitation to the author.

"Colin really wants to meet her," he said.

"Okay," I responded, "but don't tell him you've asked her, because she probably won't show up."

As I was the only guest who knew everyone, if you count a two-minute conversation with Judy and Bill knowing them, I was asked to make the introductions. Jeff followed me around behind the lens of his camera, which had turned him into a cross between Marlin Perkins, the Mutual of Omaha guy, and a game show host. As I said each person's name, he panned the room then zoomed in on his prey.

"Tell us a little something about yourself," he'd say. "Ever been arrested? Do you like your job? What's your favorite color? What do you think of the art of Andy Warhol?"

Seabird was up to it. "Purple, yes, no, and it's highly overrated," she ticked off, "not necessarily in that order."

Jeff was actually quite good at interviewing. He could sense who it was okay to tease, who would throw something shocking right back at him, and who should be treated gently. When the camera landed on Judy, he backed up, angling for a wide shot that would include Colin at the edge of the picture. "Tell us a story about your brother as a boy," he said to her.

She cocked her blond head. "Colin was so smart and so charming, you know. He could get away with anything."

"Like what?" Jeff prompted.

"Oh, little things. Stealing cookies. Cutting up our mother's best panty hose to make a slingshot. Swimming naked in church."

Jeff perked up. "Swimming naked in church? He swam naked in church?"

"Oh, don't tell that story," Colin protested.

But the rest of us would have none of it. "Tell, tell," we shouted.

"Our mother played the organ for Sunday services," Judy continued, "and she'd take us along on Saturday afternoons when she did a run-through. We usually sat in the Sunday school room and did our homework or read the pamphlets on Jesus and John the Baptist."

"So one day we get bored," Colin jumped in.

"You got bored," Judy corrected. "This was your idea, even if it got us both in trouble."

"Poor Judy," Colin said. "She was supposed to be taking care of her little brother, and I was always dragging her into some mischief or other."

"Swimming," Jeff reminded them, pantomiming a crawl with his free hand.

"So Colin gets bored, and starts poking around the back corners of this big old church while I follow him around like a good girl saying 'No, Colin, don't touch that, don't go in there.'"

"And the whole time the hymns are booming so loudly I can barely hear myself think, let alone hear Judy nagging at me, you know, all that wrath of God coming through my mother's fingers and pouring out of the organ pipes and into the sanctuary. Naturally, it occurred to me that we could fill up the baptismal and no one would hear it."

"This is a Baptist church, remember," said Judy, "so the baptismal was like a huge tub, chest deep when you waded into it, and it was hidden behind a velvet curtain at the rear of the altar. The curtain was kept closed unless someone was being dunked, which only happened once a year or so."

"You have to admit, it was a brilliant idea."

"Oh, right. 'Come on, Judy, no one will find out.' " She lifted her voice in approximation of a preadolescent boy.

"Well, we did manage to fill the thing with water without being detected."

It wasn't hard to picture Colin as a boy; he'd become so boy-like in the last couple of years. Not just physically, though he'd lost his bulk and his muscle tone along with the patch of curly hair on his chest. It had more to do with a delight in small things, like matching me up with Betty, or riding around the block at ten miles per hour on the back of Gigi's motorcycle, or planning this dinner down to the subtlest of spices.

So it was easy enough to envision the music stopping, the curtain opening, and the members of the Ladies' Guild standing there open-mouthed and laden with decorative garland as a buck naked eight-year-old cannonballed into the baptismal.

"The worst of it was," Judy said, "after they got over their surprise, the ladies decided it was a hoot! I was the one who got scolded for letting him do it, as if I had any say in the matter whatsoever."

After Judy's story, the rest of the introductions were mostly anticlimactic, though Constance's guitarist boyfriend, whose name was Frog or Fog, I couldn't tell which, barked out, at Jeff's request, a little piece of a ditty he'd composed that afternoon. The lyrics were, like his name, mostly unintelligible, but the words "wombat" and "peanut butter" figured prominently.

And the author, of course, was dazzling.

"Let's hear about the status of your work-in-progress," Jeff said, zeroing in on her. "What are those crazy nuns up to?"

"The nuns have completely run amok," said the author, as if this were the most delightful thing that could possibly happen. "They can't decide if they're cowboys or Indians, and now the main character is considering abandoning the Mother Superior entirely."

This was news to me. The last I'd heard, Sister Ignatius was still looking for her rosary beads.

"Everything happens for a reason in fiction," said Jeff in his best Door number 1, Door number 2, or Door number 3 voice.

"That's what I'm told, but certain of my characters insist on doing as they please, regardless of reason."

When Judy had talked, people relaxed in their chairs, as if leaning back into her story. But the author had the opposite effect: Colin, Constance, Judy and Bill, Seabird and Augustine all tilted toward her. Even Gigi poked her head out of the kitchen and tipped an expectant ear in the author's direction. It wasn't what she said, or the way she said it, exactly; rather it had to do with intimacy—the sense that she was sharing something private and special. This was the seduction scene she pulled over and over again at mall bookstores, on regional morning talk shows, in editors' offices. No wonder everyone was taken in. Hell, it was the same seduction scene she'd pulled in my archives room fifteen years earlier.

"You can't imagine how trying it is when one's characters attempt to escape from historical accuracy," she was saying. "And now I'm certain they're going to want to cannonball naked into the Colorado."

I was veering between the smug satisfaction of going steady with the most popular girl and slight embarrassment at her over-the-top performance. Why did she have to act like such a celebrity? But that wasn't fair. First of all, she *was* a celebrity. And second of all, she didn't act like a celebrity around me. This was almost enough to make me glad I'd been spared the book tours and the New York City publishing parties.

I left Jeff to finish with the introductions and pushed my way past Gigi into the kitchen. "What the hell have you got cooking in here?" I asked, rummaging through the junk drawer for aspirin. Pots bubbled on every burner, the counters were covered with foil-topped casserole dishes, and the table held a hodge-podge of salads, starting at the bottom of the gourmet chain with tiny marshmallows trapped in lemon Jell-O and progressing up to a bowl of the kind of leafy greens that are discussed on public television cooking shows.

"We're calling it 'The Supper of Earthly Delights,' " she said, a bit defensively. Colin's title, no doubt. Gigi was more of a "Blue Plate Special" kind of gal. "It's a buffet."

"So I see." I popped two extra-strength Tylenols, swallowed them with water scooped from the faucet, then, thinking of the author sitting out there on Jeff's couch, downed a third.

"I told Colin about all the crazy dishes we used to make, and he wanted to serve them all at once."

I peeked under some tin foil. "Hey! Vegetables Psychosis!" Then I raised my eyebrows. "You didn't . . . "

"Nope, no Tubers Karamazov. I told him I would quit before I made that for a houseful of his weird friends." She grinned. "Hey, your girlfriend's totally cool. You should bring her around more."

I helped Gigi finish up the last of the stirring and steaming and broiling, and we arranged the dishes on the table and countertops so the guests could file through and help themselves, then carry their plates into the dining room. Colin had hand-lettered, in shaky script, the names of the entrees and side dishes on colored index cards, which we matched to the appropriate bowls and pans.

"Filing through" was perhaps not the best choice of words for what ensued, which was more of a giddy free-for-all, something you might see at Denny's on all-you-can-eat night. Seabird and Augustine were in nostalgia heaven. "Look, Collective Onions Consciousness," Augustine squealed. "I love this stuff. Where's that sauce we used to put on it?"

"Peanuts Envy? Right over here," said Seabird, holding up a gravy boat.

"What's this?" asked Constance, pointing to the marshmallow-gelatin salad. "It doesn't have a sign."

"Oh, you have to ask that one what it's called," said Gigi in a moment of uncharacteristic gregariousness.

Constance looked confused. "I don't get it."

Gigi, Seabird, Augustine, and I put our heads together. "Jell-O, I love you, won't you tell me your name?" we sang.

"I'm sorry I asked," Constance said, scooping up a huge wiggly spoonful of the stuff.

Even Bill, who heretofore had said about two sentences, and those only because he was pressed by Jeff, got into the spirit of things, kidding with Frog-Fog about the "Bagelian Dialectic."

Colin was already seated at the center of the table, so he could be as close as possible to everyone and wouldn't miss any of the conversation. Jeff had fixed him a plate with a spoonful of everything. He looked radiant but wobbly, and I was glad his chair had armrests to shore him up a bit. Once everyone was seated and the water and wineglasses filled, we all turned instinctively to him.

He held up his glass of Chablis. "Ladies and gentlemen of the jury," he said, "my love," he tipped his glass shakily toward Jeff, "my family," he tipped it toward Judy and Bill and then me, "my partner in culinary and other sorts of crime" (Gigi), "my friends old and new, I've decided not to make a closing argument. It turns out—and I know you'll be surprised to hear this, Jeff—that I don't need to have the last word. I just want to be part of an ongoing conversation, maybe even have a dish named after me. The whole time I was planning this dinner party, making my duplex mates so crazy one of them retreated into a concussion and the other into celluloid, I imagined myself saying something profound, because people expect that from you when you're dying, some words from the gangplank, as it were, but actually it's me who wants to hear your words and voices carrying across the water as I head out on my bon voyage, the next leg of the journey, and maybe you would all wave a little and shade your eyes with your hand to keep out the glare while you're watching my ship sail out to sea."

My eyes were rapidly filling with salt water, and through the blur I saw tears escaping from behind the view finder of Jeff's camera. Colin was losing his train of thought, and the guests who hadn't met him before, who'd been laughing along with his dramatic monologue, were now looking either at their plates or at their laps.

The author, seated to Colin's right, rescued us all by raising her wine glass. "Bon voyage," she said.

"Bon voyage" came from all around the table, and soon everyone was happily eating and bumping elbows, which was unavoidable given the size of the table and the number of guests seated around it. I was wedged between Jeff and Constance, my plate wobbling on the seam where a card table had been pushed up against the dining room table. Jeff was useless as a conversation partner, being more interested in spying on other people's conversations with his camera. I was a little annoyed with him for neglecting Colin, but then I realized the camera was trained on Colin more often than not.

"I love your hair," Constance said shyly, as if she really wanted to run her fingers through it but was constrained by the student-librarian nature of our relationship. No one else seemed so constrained, however; people had been cooing and playing with my fuzz all evening, as if I'd left in the morning as an old fuddy-duddy and returned as the sort of person people felt compelled to touch.

"I love the bird on your cast, too," Constance added.

"It's lips," I said.

She looked baffled. "The bird? Oh, the cast. That can't be good for your foot."

She thought I'd said "it slips," I realized. I tried again. "It's lips. It's not a bird, it's a giant set of lips."

Across the table, the author regaled Colin and his sister, who was a big fan, with her standard response to the "Where do you get your ideas" question.

"Actually, if you read my critics, you know that they're all the same story," she said conspiratorially. "I simply take my last book, change all the names, dress the characters up in different uniforms and airlift them to a new locale."

Judy, whom I was coming to like more and more, protested. "Those critics would give their writing arms to have your kind of success. No, really. Your books may not be considered serious literature, but they're dramatic and sexy and they have a great sense of pacing. You're a natural storyteller."

"Colin, I just love your sister," the author said. "We've got to get her a job on the *New York Times Book Review* so I can get a mention every now and then."

Actually, she was mentioned quite regularly in the *Times*, sometimes in snide commentaries by literary types but more often on the paperback best-seller list.

"Thanks," said a clearly flattered Judy, "but I don't think I'd enjoy books if I had to spend a lot of energy figuring out which theoretical paradigm they fit into. Sometimes, it's enough just to be entertained." She took a huge swig of wine, looking as surprised as the rest of us at pulling the phrase "theoretical paradigm" out of her conversational hat.

"Yeah." Fog/Frog swallowed a mouthful of The Communist Manicotti. "But, like, you can't escape it. Even anarchy starts to fit into a pattern after a while."

Seabird, who I'd learned managed one of those new age-y shops that smell like burning mildew and sell crystals and self-help books and recordings that sound like they're descended from dentist office and elevator music, waved around a forkful of Lady Endiva. "Everything is connected," she agreed. "Everything happens for a reason."

"Oh, fall off of your limb, Shirley MacLaine." This from Augustine, who was angled into a corner at the opposite end of the table. "Some things are just random. Some things just suck."

Then the table got quiet again for a little while, until Bill, bless his heart, asked which dish everyone liked best.

"The food, or the name?" Constance asked.

"Oh, I think we can vote on both," said Colin. "But remember, I get to be Miss Congeniality."

I swallowed a mouthful of Spaghetti with Philosophy, picked up my plate, and ducked out as unobtrusively as I could, given my fiberglass-encased foot. Jeff and Gigi were in the kitchen, arguing about how long they should allow the party to go on. Their discussion was complicated by the fact that every time Gigi tried to make a point, Jeff picked up his camera and caught her in the crosshatches.

"He looks really tired," she said, draping a dishtowel over the lens. "He's going to want to go to bed soon."

"He looks happy to me. This is the last party he'll ever go to. It won't hurt him to stay up a little late."

Colin belonged as much to Gigi now as he did to Jeff, I realized. Still, I was in favor of anarchy. "Why not let him slip quietly up the stairs when he's ready, and let the party go on without him?"

Which is exactly what happened. An hour or so later, after we'd all adjourned to the living room, Colin gestured me over to his recliner. "Help me up the stairs, will you?"

For the last few weeks, he'd been sleeping in a hospital bed in the dining room so he wouldn't have to climb to the second floor. Jeff slept beside him on a cot. But for the party, they'd rolled the cot and the bed onto the back porch and pulled the table out from the corner.

"Do you want to say good night first?"

"No. I'll see Judy and Bill in the morning before they drive home. I'll let you and Jeff say goodbye to everyone else for me."

A few minutes later, having discovered that my foot could now take not only my weight but Colin's as well, I had him settled in the bedroom, in an armchair by a window that looked out over the backyard. "Do you need me to help you get changed?"

"No. Give me a half hour to enjoy the sounds of my party, then send up Gigi. She'll be happy for an excuse to get away from all the socializing."

I leaned in the doorway. "It's a terrific party. Best one I've ever been to."

"That's the idea." He shifted his weight a little, then took off the paper crown he'd been wearing all night. "Listen, don't be so afraid of change. Sometimes it's just what you need."

"Oh, *now* you're going to get philosophical on me." I blew him a kiss. "Sweet dreams, sweetie." I propped the door with a cast iron cat, which incidentally looked remarkably like Betty, so he could hear the strains of Janis Joplin asking the lord for a night on the town.

"Hey," Colin called as I clumped down the hall, "I like your bird."

Downstairs, people were getting chummy. Jeff had taken over the dining room and was bringing the party guests in for filmed commentary, one by one, escorting them to the seat they'd occupied at dinner. He did his best to grab them after they'd had a couple of drinks but before they'd had too many, "so they'll be loosened up but not stupid," he whispered as he beckoned Constance.

"This is it, your fifteen minutes of fame," he told her.

I found Gigi and the author in the kitchen, loading the dishwasher and laughing at some joke they clearly did not intend to share with me. The author tossed me a questioning look, and I heard Hildegard's voice saying *What are you waiting for?* I grabbed a Rolling Rock from the fridge and backed out into the living room. Colin's chair was empty, but it didn't seem right to sit in it, so I ended up in the middle of the couch, at the vortex of two conversations.

Augustine and Bill had discovered they were both natives of New England and were rehashing a seven-year-old World Series in which some poor schmuck first baseman had blown it for the Red Sox by letting an easy grounder roll through his legs. Seabird, Judy, and Frog/Fog were debating the future of the former Soviet Union, now that the big green wall had come down. Or maybe I was confusing the two discussions. I got up and slipped into the dining room, taking a seat by the door where I wouldn't distract either Jeff or Constance.

"I hate this," a magenta-headed Constance was saying to Jeff's camera. "I only just met Colin and I'm already losing him. It's not fair, you know?"

"I know," he said. "It sucks. I've known him for ten years and it stills sucks. It absolutely sucks."

I hated it too, and now my headache had relocated to the pit of my stomach. "I think we should dance," I said when Jeff swung the camera toward me. I stood up and pulled Constance from her seat, and soon we were a whole conga line of dancers, me in front, then Constance, the Red Sox fans, the Soviet Union deconstructionists, and Gigi and the author, whom we picked up while snaking through the kitchen and out the back door into the floodlit yard. I made Jeff put his camera down and join us at the end of the line. Then I circled around and grabbed his hand and thought about Colin sitting upstairs and watching us through the window, his cast of misfit disciples spinning like a full sun under the sickle moon.

"Thanks for helping clean up," I said to the author. Everyone else had gone home; Jeff was upstairs getting into bed. "Are you okay to drive?"

She hesitated. "I was hoping to spend the night."

And so, for the first time ever, some twenty minutes later, I looked at her across my very own pillow.

"The party wasn't exactly what I was expecting," she said.

What was she expecting, a demure cocktail hour? "Well, we're not exactly New York City sophisticates."

"I'm not explaining very well. I meant, the party was what I expected, but I didn't expect to have such a good time. I liked all your friends, even that 'Dog' character."

"You should go slumming more often," I said, irritated. Now that I had her in my bed, I was feeling territorial. Even so, her perfume, the wine I'd drunk, the wine on her breath conspired to undo me. I lifted her nightshirt roughly and took one nipple between my teeth. She cried out a little, but she didn't say Stop, and she let me pin her wrists over her head with my left hand while the right went searching. There was a sense of urgency, and it was over quickly. Afterwards she held me for a long time while I sobbed without making any sound.

"I want to show you something." I carefully peeled the bandage from my arm. Underneath, the tattoo was swollen and black and blue, but she could tell what it was.

"A sun," she said. "It's beautiful."

"It's for Colin. I got this to remember him by."

"Jeff, too?" She'd noticed the edge of the Band-Aid peeking out from the back of his collar.

"Jeff got a moon on his shoulder blade, to cover the hours when the sun isn't up." I switched off the light and pulled the covers up. The author wrapped her arms around me from behind, and I lay there for a long while, looking at the blackness outside the window and listening to her breath.

When I was certain she was asleep, I whispered: "I think I have to leave you, and I don't want to."

"I know," she whispered back.

PART FOUR

SUZANNE PLESHETTE / 2002

CHAPTER 14

Mostly I was quite happy in my bright office in the library's sleek new wing, a pointy-topped glass-and-steel box we referred to as the Bow-wow-haus, or strolling among the banks of computers in the busy lobby. But there were entire days, weeks, when I longed to be back in the archives room, in charge of something quiet and immutable. The light was different there, charged with antiquity and filtered through leaded glass. It didn't fill the room, as it did in my new office; rather, it fell in curious trapezoids and parallelograms across the oak table and wide floorboards. I'd come to see nostalgia as loss dressed up in vintage clothing. The smell of must, music from the 1970s—why do we want to be reminded of these things when there are so many new things to think about, so many things we'll have to let go of one day?

It could be argued I accepted this new job—Library Director, Queen Bee of the Whole Shebang—in order to cut my losses. Why else would an archivist take on the absurdities of e-books, of staff management, let alone the maintenance of a gawky, hybrid building? I was in charge of the pipes, the furnaces, the third-floor men's room where the urinal overflowed almost daily. Books were an abstraction, something to acquire, to catalog, to purge.

Some days I just wanted to curl up with a simple story.

"There are no simple stories," Jeff said. "Face it, you're a grownup. Everything is complicated."

Easy for him to say. While I'd gone steadily professional, exchanging my baggy flax trousers for tailored suits and my canvas bookbag for a leather briefcase, he'd done the reverse, trading in his job at the law firm for a grant-to-mouth existence as a documentary filmmaker. After his first movie, *Colin's Dinner Party*, made a respectable splash on the film-festival circuit, he'd quit his job and spent Colin's life insurance on new equipment and converting the garage into a studio. Constance, who'd quickly grasped the potential of film for her own particular brand of proselytizing, had talked him into taking her on, first as an unpaid intern and then, after she graduated, as a cameraperson/editor/script writer/jack-of-all-trades. Now she was in film school in New York City, doing her thesis project on none other than Hildegard of Bingen.

And Jeff got to wear jeans and a baseball cap every day, and drive around in a junker of a van held together by bumper stickers.

Moon Tattoo Productions made a name for itself with up-close portraits of ordinary people who, for one reason or another, had become extraordinary. The Colin film was followed by a piece on a Salvadorian au pair who'd baked a loaf of bread that contained the image of the Virgin Mary on every slice, including the end pieces. Jeff filmed most of *The Virgin of the Marbled Rye* in Chicago, where the miracle loaf attracted pilgrimages from the devout as well as considerable media attention. To complete the filming, he and Constance flew to San Salvador, where the au pair was living after the publicity brought her to the attention of the INS.

Later, Moon Tattoo did a couple of shorts focusing on children: an eight-year-old girl on the autism scale who composed symphonies on her mother's upright piano; a nerdy junior high kid who made it to the finals of the national math bee.

I mention these to make absolutely clear the inappropriateness of the idea Jeff broached over supper one night, as if just having the idea wasn't inappropriate enough.

"You can say no," he said. "I won't do it if it doesn't feel right to you, but please think about it before you dismiss it out of hand."

I frowned. "This sounds serious."

"It's about my next film." Then he said her name. The author's.

"No."

Jeff pushed back from the table and got a beer from the refrigerator. My table, my refrigerator, my beer, I might add. "I knew you would do this. Just listen, please. This could be really important to my career."

I let him open the screw cap then took the beer away from him and used it to wash down the panic rising in my throat. "As if she'd ever agree to such a thing."

"I was hoping you might help me talk her into it."

"I haven't seen her in eight years." My voice shook; I covered the shaking by upping the volume. "Besides, why would you even want to do her story? I thought you were interested in regular people. She's not regular people. There's nothing regular about her."

"Aren't I allowed to change and grow as a filmmaker? What if Woody Allen kept making the same movie over and over again? Okay, bad example. But really, aren't I allowed to try out new subject matter?"

"And aren't I allowed to leave my past in the past, rather than have my best friend drag it out all over the big screen?" I handed the beer back to him.

"This is about her, not you." He took a swig, then set the bottle in front of me.

"Oh, don't tell me you think you can do justice to her story without bringing me into it. You're going to have to interview me. And do you really think she's going to sit back and let you yank her out of the closet?"

"That's why I need you to talk to her. She's what, around seventy-five now? I'll bet she's ready to tell the real story. And you—you'd be brilliant. You know how cute you looked in *Colin's Dinner Party*, getting your hair buzzed off and showing off your tattoo."

He reached over and fluffed my fuzzy head, my last stand against the establishment. The tattoo was still around too, of course, but usually I kept it hidden under my sleeve. "Please, please help me. You know I'm so co-dependent I can't even drink my own beer."

I got him his own beer. "I'll think about it," I said, but what I was thinking was: Not in your wildest dreams.

Like all good lesbians, the author and I had taken some two years to break up. Then there were a couple more years of checking in with each other by phone once a month or so for post-traumatic processing and the occasional bitter recrimination. By the time I met Sadie, we were both pretty tired of our shared train wreck and I was relieved to be moving on to something less complicated, or at least complicated in ways that hadn't yet revealed themselves.

Later, I told myself it wasn't about our age difference, and I wasn't acting out some Freudian adolescent drama. The author was nobody's mother, and certainly not mine; I had a perfectly good mother living two states away whom I visited on holidays and occasional weekends. And it wasn't about her closeted life, or the fact that the secret was no longer thrilling for me. It wasn't even about living apart: in one moment of late-night desperation, she had offered to let me move in. After sixteen years of not letting myself hope for such a thing, I realized that I didn't even want it. And I knew she didn't really mean it. Even middle-aged, even conservatively dressed, I would be hard to explain to her bridge gals. Especially since I'd long since given up explaining myself to anybody.

Really, I think I was just exhausted from the weight of my own life. And so, I left the author and the archives room at about the same time, and took up office in a bright, windowed place. I told myself I was leaving her there, where she'd found me, among yellowing diaries and maps of the flat, rectangular world.

For the most part, she stayed there, safely in the past. She came back to me in brief bursts, when I ran across her name on a book-review page or in a library journal, for instance, or came face-to-face with her latest trilogy while trapped in the check-out line at the Ready-Mart.

"Aren't you even curious about her?" Jeff asked a few nights after trying to rope me into his scheme.

I was curious. I did wonder how the author was making out, alone in her brick house in the affluent end of town. I'd been thinking of her more often in the six months since Sadie moved out, after breaking every dish in the cupboard as well as a couple of windows that got in their trajectory. I wasn't at all sorry to see Sadie leave, and while I fumed about the dinner plates, I rather admired her ability to enact such a physical manifestation of our shared life then walk straight out the door without turning back. The relationship was worth it just for the performance art, I told Jeff as we swept up shards of broken china from the kitchen floor, pleased with my clean get-away.

The author was another story. No roomful of glass and pottery shards would ever be enough to sum up our years together, let alone negate them. And I didn't want to live in the houseful of glass that I knew would accumulate should Jeff train his lens on the author. I wouldn't mind running into her in the present. A phone conversation, maybe a light-hearted lunch at some neutral café to say hello, catch up on the latest novel-in-progress—that would be fine. The past could stay where it was, thank you.

But the past, being complicated, does not want to stay where it is. Just the mention, aloud, of the author's name, just the idea of her image flitting grainily across Jeff's editing screen, primed me for seeing her wherever I went. There she was sitting at the oak table in the archives room when I went to take a look at the vault's overheated cooling system. No—it wasn't her. The woman at the table was barely older than me, I saw upon second look. Or she ducked into the back row at the theater, after the lights went down, and ducked out again while the credits rolled. But maybe that was just a shadow? I hardly knew. Every Volvo that drove by—wasn't that her behind the wheel? Hadn't she just stepped into the ladies room at the Mediterranean restaurant? Wasn't that her strolling briskly through the park?

When I got into bed I remembered the only night she'd slept there, and how tenderly she had held me while I wept. When I got into my car I imagined it heading to her neighborhood of its own accord, while I sat uselessly pumping the brakes. I expected her to be everywhere and found her nowhere.

"My existence is so damned spectral," I said to Betty.

"Ack," said Betty, who was still prone to philosophizing but rarely shared his thoughts.

Finally, I decided to put an end to it. I told Jeff flat out, in the no-nonsense voice I'd developed for the library director job, that I would have no part of any movie about the author, and furthermore, that any movie about the author would have to be filmed over my dead body.

It worked. Jeff backed off and started developing a script about a man who won $73 million in the tri-state lottery and gave it all away. And the author receded into memory, a small note on the inside back page accompanied by an even smaller photo.

So I was confused when I heard her name on the phone, and a little panicked. The film is not happening, I thought. This can't be right. I said, "Pardon me?"

The person on the other end was impatient. "You're listed as her next of kin. She's at the hospital; we need you to come down and sign some papers."

No, I thought absurdly. It's one in the afternoon. She's at her dining room table making notes on index cards. The tea water is brewing.

"You are her next of kin?"

"Oh—yes. I'll be right there." How could I be her next of kin? I couldn't legally sign anything. I didn't even know whom to call. Did the author even have a next of kin? And why couldn't she sign the papers herself?

"She's not—" I hesitated. "I mean, she hasn't . . . "

Miss phone-side manners sighed. "They've taken her for some tests. You'll have to ask the doctors anything else."

The nurse hung up, but I couldn't put the phone back in the cradle on my desk. I sat there shaking, then dialed Jeff on his cell phone.

"She's not dead is she?" he asked as delicately as one can while shouting over the racket of a jackhammer.

"They said not, but apparently she's not able to sign her own admission papers. Where are you?"

"Stuck in construction, about ten miles out of town. I'll meet you at the hospital as soon as I can get out of this mess."

I thought of Colin's last weeks at the hospital, and of Jeff spending every waking hour at his side.

"Jeff, I can handle this." I tried to sound sure of myself. "You don't need to come."

"You're going to need me to help you through all the bureaucracy. First off, whatever you do, tell them you're a relative, otherwise they won't let you see her."

"They think I'm next of kin."

"Good, let them think that. Now breathe. You're going to be fine. I'll be there within an hour."

Whose idea was it to make hospitals so imposing? Not just the building; the people inside, too. They acted like anyone who wasn't sick had no right to be there. When I gave the receptionist the author's name, saying loudly, "I'm her next of kin," just to get used to saying it, she first told me that no such patient existed, and if she did, she hadn't been entered into the computer.

"She might show up, if you want to come back in a while," the woman said, dismissing me.

I cleared my throat and tried to sound authoritative. "The hospital called me and told me to come right away."

She looked skeptical. "Who called you? Which department?"

"I don't know. Someone who rates right up there with you on the rudeness scale who wants me to sign some papers." Really smart. Just insult the woman, and she'll tell you whatever you want to know.

She tapped her pencil eraser on the desk three times then punched a few numbers into her telephone. She said the author's name, then said it again, grunted, and hung up. "Go through the double doors and turn right." She said all that without once looking at me, and I understood that I was lucky to get any information at all. I headed through the doors.

At the end of the hall was Admitting. I pictured bright lights aimed at my face, maybe a thumbscrew or two lurking on the table, and me blurting out: "I admit it! We're not related. I had sex with her twice a week for fifteen years, even though she's old enough to be my mother. Then I dumped her and didn't visit for eight years."

I stopped in front of the door and breathed in. I'm her next of kin; I'm her next of kin. Please tell me what's wrong with her.

Fortunately, the man who escorted me to a cubbyhole office was not interested in anything I had to admit, other than the author. He had a form already typed up, and there was my name, under Next of Kin.

"I'm sorry I can't tell you anything about her condition," he said, "but the doctor will fill you in on the way to Intensive Care."

Intensive Care didn't sound good. Oh, God, please don't let her die when I'm so close to seeing her again. "Who filled out this form?" I asked as casually as I could while I signed in triplicate on four different dotted lines.

"The ER nurses get the information from the patients, and then we type it up."

That sounded more hopeful. The author had at least been able to supply her name and address, and tell the nurses how to find me. That meant she was conscious and cognizant, even if she couldn't sign her own name.

When I was done signing mine, the doctor was waiting for me. She looked about twelve.

"Your aunt had a stroke," she said. "We've done some tests, and we're waiting for the results. Right now she's lost most of the movement in her right side, but we're hoping that's only temporary. We'll know more tomorrow."

We walked down a set of hallways and up one staircase and down another set of hallways and around two corners until I was near tears, clearly the intended Pavlovian response for this maze. "I'm her next of kin," I said like an idiot.

The doctor, apparently used to people acting like idiots under these circumstances, touched my shoulder to steer me around a nurses' station. "We're doing everything we can for her. She's stable right now, but don't expect her to seem like herself. She lost muscle control on one side of her face, and her speech may be difficult to understand."

I was cautioned to visit for no more than five minutes, then ushered into a room with safety glass in the door. The author looked terrible, rigged up to machines with an IV in her left arm and a tube pumping oxygen into her nostrils. Her face, lopsided, sagged to the left, unable to hold up its own weight. She blinked at me, but I couldn't tell if she was being playful or if she couldn't quite place who I was.

I did my best to be cheerful, hoping I didn't sound too phony. "Couldn't you have made me your second cousin?" I asked. I thought I ought to take her hand, but one of them looked useless and the other was occupied by the intravenous drip, so I leaned awkwardly over the bed railings and kissed her sagging cheek. It felt rubbery. "That would be slightly less incestuous."

She said something that sounded like a cross between "ingénue" and the name of a Japanese art film I'd recently seen. I smiled and nodded foolishly, then realized she was making a joke. "Once removed."

"Not too far removed. I'm here, see? You just rest and get better. I'll take care of everything." That was what next of kin did, wasn't it? Offer meaningless comfort and sign on the dotted line?

She was exhausted from the effort of assembling two words and spitting them out at me. And now a little stream of drool trickled out of the lopsided side of her mouth. I was doing my best to pretend it wasn't the author, my author, lying there damaged in the ICU, which wasn't hard. Something about her was changed, something more than just the evident symptoms of the stroke. During the several years in which I hadn't seen her, the author had grown old. Yes, just like an ordinary mortal. She lay there looking like an advertisement for modern medical science, all the efficient machines doing their efficient jobs, while she stared out from behind her own eyes doing the deer-in-the-headlights thing. Oddly enough, this made me feel not exactly better, but at least capable of taking care of the things I needed to take care of. Still, when my five minutes were up and

I was expelled from the toxic air of her room into the slightly less toxic air of the hallway, I was happy to fall into the arms of Jeff, who was waiting outside the door.

"Oh, God, I hate being a grownup."

Jeff and I spent the rest of the day at the hospital, navigating and circumnavigating the particular bureaucracy of the health-care system, which differs from other bureaucracies only in that it is accompanied by a vague sense of panic. We talked to three doctors, all of whom offered a wait-and-see diagnosis, one insurance processor, and a social worker who asked me questions about how I was prepared to deal with long-term care issues. I bolted from the last interview, held in a small windowless room—the sort of place where I imagined police interrogations taking place—and let Jeff collect the pamphlets about rehab centers, nursing homes, visiting nurses and the like.

In between those sorts of dread-inducing episodes were hourly five-minute visits with the author, which created their own brand of dread.

"I think I'm seesawing between red tape and a black hole," I said to Jeff, slumping in a plastic chair in the ICU lounge, which consisted of a horseshoe of said chairs, two vending machines and seven No Smoking signs. I understood why the signs were there: long bouts of anxious waiting could conjure up a desire for a cigarette in even the most fanatical of health fanatics. I myself was beginning to feel a desperate craving to do something, anything, to negate the reason for being there. If someone had handed me a cigarette, I would have taken it, and probably only because the No Smoking signs made me think of tobacco, and the way holding a cigarette while smoke curls into the air can provide a sense, if fleeting, of purpose.

When I confessed my craving to Jeff, he said, "If they sold them in the gift shop, I would get you a pack."

"I don't want a whole pack. I'd only smoke 'em. Just one would be plenty, so I could breathe something other than hospital air into my lungs."

"We could go down to the parking lot and inhale exhaust fumes."

"I'm exhausted enough already, thanks."

Then it was time for the last five-minute visit. I sat by the author's good side and watched her sleep. Funny how many times I'd done that—in the early days with a kind of raw amazement that she'd invited me into her bed; in the later days, wanting to wake her up so we'd have an excuse to argue. But I never did wake her up. What was it about sleep that turned everyone childlike, vulnerable? There were times I would lie awake beside her, put my hand on her back or her belly, and will myself into her dreams. Then, in the morning when she opened her eyes, I'd ask, "Did you dream about me?" and she'd always murmur, "Yes, yes, you are the girl of my dreams," which was not exactly the same thing, but was maybe even better.

When the hospital finally ejected me into its parking lot, I found Jeff perched cross-legged on a stone wall, eyes closed, leaning back into the colorless March dusk. I hopped up beside him, choosing a dry spot between the crusty piles of snow left over from a less-than-enthusiastic winter.

"If you meet the Buddha in the hospital parking lot," I said.

He opened his eyes slowly, but didn't turn his head to look at me. "How is the old girl?"

"Lopsided. Still sleeping. I did this stupid thing, you know, sitting there with my hand on her arm like a faith healer." I let out an involuntary sob.

Jeff put his hand on my back. "Doesn't sound stupid at all. I used to do that sort of thing for Colin, you know, filling the room with happy energy, fine-tuning our chakras, whatever they are, laying my ear on his solar plexus."

"Did you hear the ocean?"

"The ocean, the desert, you name it." He fished around in his pocket, came up with a handkerchief, and blew his nose. "Oh, God, I'm sorry. This isn't about Colin, or me."

Great. Now we were both crying. "Well, hell. How could you not think about Colin after being shut up in that hospital all afternoon? I thought about him too, in between pretending to be next of kin and fantasizing about lighting up."

"Oh!" Jeff brightened and reached inside his jacket. "Look what I found!" He came out with two cigarettes and a book of matches.

I whooped it up like Columbus being handed his first stogie. "Hey! Who'd you have to sweet-talk to get these?"

"Pharmacy clerk." He lit one, handed it to me, then lit the other for himself. I'd never been much of a smoker, but this one tasted good, in the way that harsh things taste good at the end of a lousy day. We sat there smoking, letting the March evening settle into our hospital-weary bones. I tried to do what all the self-help books say you should do in such circumstances: let myself feel what I was feeling. The problem was, I didn't really know what I was feeling, other than a generic panic that came and went like a crazy, speeded-up tide. What had possessed her to speak my name in the emergency room? Was I, as she'd said in those last weeks of our relationship, not the great love of her life, but the happiest? Was she the great love of mine? Probably. And the great passion, and the great regret. Did I regret my time with her? No. Had I stayed, would I have regretted staying? Possibly.

Over the course of the day, I'd managed to piece together what had happened. The author was in the park power-walking when she was, as the hospital staff put it, "stricken." I thought of lightning, a surprise bolt on a warm, late-winter morning, months before the season for electricity in the atmosphere. Then I thought, inspiration. Stricken with inspiration, with an idea so powerful it shoots right to the central nervous system.

No, the doctor said. It probably started as a twinge and a feeling of faintness, something that made her sit down on the ground beside the path. And then she couldn't get up. A jogger found her there and called an ambulance on his cell phone. He stopped by in the late afternoon to see how she was, and the ICU nurse pointed him in my direction. When I said her name, his face registered nothing. To him, she was just an old lady; all of her accomplishments disappeared when she was hit by something that wasn't lightning and wasn't an idea—or if it was, it was a very bad idea.

"I'm just glad I was there to help your aunt," the jogger said when I thanked him. He was sweet, really, taking my hand between his as I got up for the next five-minute visit. He turned to Jeff. "Tell your wife not to worry too much."

"I will," Jeff said.

So the author's power walking had saved her life, even if not in the prescribed manner. Had she taken sick in her house, it might have been days before anyone found her. I made a mental note to sign her up for one of those medic-alert buttons and to get her a cell phone.

You want to know what I was feeling? I'll admit it, I was annoyed. I don't hear from her in years, she goes and has a stroke, and the next thing you know I'm her favorite niece, stuck with dealing with pesky insurance clerks and possibly weeks of rehabilitation and physical therapy and home health care. I didn't need this; I had my own life—not that there was anything pressing in it at the moment besides a job that was far more grown up than I was, a cat who insisted on watching videos every night and a duplex-mate who got by between grants by mooching off me.

"This sucks," I said.

"Maybe you shouldn't inhale."

"Not the cigarette. The cigarette is probably the best thing about the whole day. And you." I inhaled again, then poked the stub into a little mound of snow.

"Funny how one's past returns to haunt one."

"Funnier when 'one' is somebody other than me. What did she mean, giving them my name?"

"Are you sorry she did?"

"Yes. No. Hell. You started all this, you know, with your film idea. It had been so long since I'd thought about her, really thought about her, you know, and then all of a sudden she's all over my thoughts, and now she's manifested herself right back into my life. Only the manifestation isn't quite whole, it isn't quite her. And I'm supposed to piece her back into someone I don't even know anymore. Why would she ask me to do this?"

"Probably because she knew you could handle it. And remember, she asked you to make arrangements, not to nurse her back to health on your own."

I wasn't so sure about that, and I wasn't so sure the author thought I could handle much of anything. But it was true, I could be done with this whole mess with a handful of phone calls. I'd certainly managed logistical crises at the library that way, by reminding myself that my job was problem solving and oversight, not reshelving books from Fiction into Autobiography. Tomorrow we would know more; the author would be less sedated and better able to speak and move, if all went well, or, as doctor No. 3 put it, "as best as can be expected."

"Pizza and a movie?" Jeff asked, and it was just the anticlimax I needed, a reason to climb into my car and drive home.

CHAPTER 15

Later, I came to associate the author's stroke with an invasion of seagulls, crows, sparrows, and the image of Suzanne Pleshette, tragic and sultry and splayed out on the walkway to her house beside the schoolyard, a victim of randomness.

"Even dead, she has way more personality than Tippi Hedron," Jeff observed, handing me a paper napkin. He'd made a detour on the way home and shown up with a pepperoni-mushroom and *The Birds*, following the theory that other people's troubles made one's own troubles seem manageable, even when the other people aren't real.

I imagined Suzanne brooding down from an afterlife that included sashaying through Bob Newhart's Danish-modern Chicago apartment in paisley bellbottoms. Eventually, the birds would get everyone—when it's your time, it's your time, no matter how dark and steamy you are, no matter that you're only important as a foil for the main character.

The author's stroke fell into the "could have been better, could have been worse" category. She wasn't one of those patients who were back to normal in a week, with only a slight change in memory or personality—a certain imprecision in naming people and things or an uncharacteristic abandonment of tact, of niceties. Nor would she be relegated to a confused existence in a wheelchair, unable to line up her thoughts with the words that corresponded to them. No, she'd be slowed down for a while, would go from the hospital to a rehab facility where she'd learn work-arounds for the nerves and synapses that no longer functioned as intended. She could be pretty much back to normal, whatever that meant, within a few months, according to the prognosis. Still, I knew the birds could come back at any time, and they had the capability of bursting through the chimney, pecking through a boarded-up window. They could fill your living room with feathers, your attic with wind. They attacked children; they killed Suzanne Pleshette.

Well, yes, but I got better.

In a manner of speaking. Are you allowed to be visiting me like this? I mean, you're not even dead.

My point exactly.

So what are you saying? There's life after birds?

Oh, I'm not giving anything away. This is your plotline. You'll have to wait and see where it takes you.

Easy for her to say. She got all her scripts in advance. She had Alfred fucking Hitchcock sending her into the raven-infested schoolyard. I, meanwhile, had no other choice but to wait around to see where my plot went. So far, I seemed to be on a bizarre pretzel-shaped flight plan, with my past twisting around to meet my current trajectory. With mustard and a bit too much salt for my taste, I might add. And maybe the Mobius-pretzel-strip theory of existence wasn't all that far off: our undersides do connect to our conscious life in an infinite ribbon of sorts. Or at least mine felt like they did. I'd always been better at asking questions than coming up with answers, and if you ask enough questions you end up where you started. In my case that was right back in the drama that had always surrounded the author, and still did, even when orchestrated from a hospital bed where she lay groping for words. The scared old lady routine didn't last long—by her second day in the regular ward she had me phoning publicists and editors, filling them in on her condition so they could send appropriately gaudy and overblown flower arrangements. Next thing you know, all the nurses and even a couple of the doctors were reading her latest saga.

She was herself and not-herself, for the wiring of the brain is a complicated matter. Things could short-circuit and you would not even know it, except for a sudden dislike for olives, say, or the inability to pretend to be civil to a grating acquaintance.

It was too early to put my finger on exactly what was her and what was not-her, except for the most obvious thing: her voice. It had slowed to a crawl, as if it were the sounds of the words that were important and not their meaning. Her clipped staccato had lengthened into a lolling river.

"I hate to tell you this," I said to her as I pushed her wheelchair into the parking lot for the ride to the rehab hospital, where she'd spend four weeks relearning how to walk and talk, "but you've gone southern on me."

This elicited a jerk of the head and a one-sided snicker. "Chahming, isn't it," she said, and the phrase rolled out in front of us like a carpet.

"Huh. It still works." I turned my key and pushed tentatively on the author's auspicious front door. It resisted for a moment, then glided in an arc across the top of the carpet.

"Did you think she would have the locks changed after you split up?" Jeff stepped gingerly into the hallway, his voice suddenly quiet. "Why do I feel like I'm not supposed to be here?"

"I felt like that every single time, the whole fifteen years. What's really weird is that I'm still carrying this key around on my key chain." I let it swing hypnotically in front of my eyes for a moment, then followed him in.

The house was dark, even though it was mid-afternoon. The author had gone for her walk before her morning ritual of tugging gently on each shade until it snapped to attention. We crept from one room to the next, spelunkers who might suddenly tumble into a mineshaft or uproot an extended family of bats.

"Hey, is this where she writes?" Jeff was exploring the dining room. His voice echoed back to me as if from a great distance, though I was right behind him, moving out of the living room. Once in, I whacked the dimmer switch on the wall, which was set low so the room wasn't so much a room but a cavern set aglow by lamplight.

"This is where she gets her plots straight," I said. "She's got an office upstairs where she does the actual writing." I went around and yanked on the shades, which did not pop open nicely for me but instead hopped jerkily upwards in a grudging sort of way, some of them stopping at half mast and refusing to go farther. It was like the room was watching us with half-closed eyelids.

I mentioned this to Jeff, who said, "Actually, I think someone's squinting rather dubiously at us."

"That would be the omniscient narrator." I picked up what looked like the early draft of an outline from the table. "I don't think we were intended to be in this part of the story."

As if to prove my point, the outline stared back at me, incomplete. The author had been sketching out an idea that appeared to involve the daughter of a railroad tycoon and a traveling Baptist revival meeting. There was a scene in which the railroad daughter returns home from a finishing tour in Europe, with her childhood played out in subcategorical flashbacks. There was a scene in which the Baptist preacher passes the hat not once, not twice, but three times during the course of a sweltering, hours-long service in a field outside Fredericksburg. Then another in which the preacher, counting his money and smoking a fat cigar, chugs toward the town where the tycoon's family lives. After that, a few cross-outs and a big question mark that appeared to have been scrawled in a moment of frustration, or perhaps after a long afternoon of passing the hat around the entire circle of muses of historical drama and coming up empty.

It looked as though, after getting stuck on the plot, she'd attempted to come at the book from another angle. Fanned out neatly on the table were a pile of character descriptions for the preacher, the tycoon, the daughter, and a handful of assorted folks who had yet to reveal how major or minor their parts might be.

The other end of the table was taken up with galley proofs of what must have been the next-book-in-print. It was lined up next to her original typescript, so she could compare the two to see what travesties the copy editor might have performed.

"Got quite a little factory going here, doesn't she?" Jeff was still speaking in hushed tones—his awe of the author had not abated even through all these years of knowing me. "I wish I were this disciplined."

"You don't want to be this disciplined. She can't even start writing until she knows how the story's going to end. Let's open up in here. This place is like a vault."

Something was different about the house, but I couldn't put my finger on it. I pushed through the swinging door into the kitchen, where I fluted out the venetian blinds and switched on the overhead fluorescents. Everything looked the same here. Same table, same chairs, same pots hanging from the ceiling. She still had the picture of me from our first vacation, the one where I stood by the falls trying to look like I wasn't mad at her. It was on the refrigerator, in a mix of photos of friends and actual relatives, the ones she didn't call when something burst inside her brain.

A couple of African violets drooped into their pots over the sink. I'd let Jeff take care of them, and all the other plants. I'd reached a truce with my own ficuses and assorted greenery; in return, they'd adjusted to my haphazard care and didn't ask for more via dramatic displays of leaf-dropping or communal fungus parties. But other people's plants I left alone. Nurturing was not part of my makeup. I knew this because Sadie told me so a couple dozen times a day in the weeks before she moved out. I couldn't remember the author taking issue with my nurturing abilities, but then I couldn't remember the author ever needing to be taken care of, either.

Until now, of course.

Which jolted me back to the reason for our trip to the author's house. We had a rented hospital bed in Jeff's van, along with an assortment of other sickroom items like a raised toilet seat and a stool for sitting on in the shower—things I didn't particularly want to think about, but would soon be dutifully installing like a good next of kin. Our mission was not archaeological, no matter how much I felt I was looking at the relics of an earlier civilization. We were here to prepare for the author's not-quite-so-bold new future, one in which, for at least the next few months, she'd need to adjust to one-story living.

I made a pot of coffee and set about hauling her computer, piece by piece, down the stairs and into the dining room while Jeff shoved furniture around in the den, making way for the rental bed.

She was still using the same IBM I'd helped her pick out more than a decade earlier, which only added to the feeling of being in a time warp. I couldn't imagine her editors were happy with that, but given her sales, they'd probably be content to receive manuscripts scrawled on the backs of cocktail napkins like a postmodern Picasso. I was tempted to lug the thing out to the sidewalk and start her over with a new system—something with usable word processing software and an internet connection. And why not? I set down the hard drive in the middle of the staircase and posed my brilliant idea to Jeff.

"Brilliant, maybe, but also lousy," he replied. "A computer is a very intimate thing. You don't just toss out a computer and replace it without asking. That would be like throwing away someone's underthings and buying a different brand. Or throwing out their porn collection and replacing it with *People* magazine or *Family Circle*. Or . . ."

"Okay, I get it. I won't touch her computer or her pornography collection."

"Well, we should at least rifle through the porn," he said, shoving the leather couch into a corner and plopping down on it. "Just don't throw it away."

In the end, I compromised. I lugged *computer obsoleticus* back upstairs, plugged the cables back in and booted it up to make sure no connections were crossed. I grabbed one of the five-inch floppies from a case on top of her desk and fed it into the slot, just to be certain everything still worked. An early version of Word Perfect kicked in, all white letters drifting across a blue sky. At the top was a working title: *Conestoga Sisters*. It was the nun book—the only story that'd ever stymied the author mid-plot. She'd put it aside to go back to the old formula—three wealthy sisters, four suitors; one of them unsuitable.

There were no suitable suitors for nuns, of course, and maybe that was the problem. Maybe that was why she'd decided the sisters would have to be left undone.

I scrolled to the bottom of the file, a process that took a few minutes as I couldn't figure out a command that would jump me to the last page. Instead, I pushed the down arrow and watched it do a freefall through the screen, with the author's sentences rushing up to meet it. When it finally stopped, it landed on two words: "The End."

Huh. So she'd finished the nuns but never published them. That was interesting. So interesting I switched on the printer, which commenced clattering and was soon kicking out a copy on one long, multi-hinged sheet of paper.

Downstairs, Jeff had carried in the hospital bed and was now prone on the bare mattress, remote control in hand, raising alternately his head and his feet.

"Here's my favorite," he said, punching a button that made the bed squiggle into a sideways Z, so his head and knees were lifted. "Perfect for perusing pornography."

"I'll be sure to mention that," I said, picturing the author reclining there with a copy of *On Our Backs*, the lesbian erotica magazine.

I left him there with the bedding and a couple of safety bars to install in the bathroom, then took the van across town to an office supply store, where I purchased a laptop, complete with CD and DVD drives, internal modem, the most recent version of Word, and a couple dozen extraneous software programs littering the desktop. I talked them into throwing in a four-color inkjet printer, a ream of paper, and a box of disks. By nightfall, the author had a handicap-accessible bedroom and bathroom and a new work area at the dining room table boasting a state-of-the-art laptop with internet access and an email account.

And I had a bootleg copy of *Conestoga Sisters*. It seemed like a fair trade.

Was it possible the author had become mysterious to me in the not-quite-decade since I'd seen her? Or had she simply become one-sided in the way of the brain-injured—in her right mind and her left body? It was easy enough, I admit, while she was hospitalized and then as she huffed and stretched her way through rehab, to think of her more as an ailment, a condition, than a person whose spine I'd once tickled with my fingers. A condition for whom words and the objects or actions they represented no longer matched up. The author, of course, put her own twist on everything: the brochures I read said to expect the patient to confuse people's names with names from the past—for instance, a person who's had a stroke might refer to her son by her brother's name. The author wasn't about to do anything by the book. Yes, she had trouble dredging my name from the spongy cerebellum where it resided, so she simply substituted "Billie," the name of the boyish heroine in the cross-dressing Western she'd penned during the early years of our affair. Taking her lead, I'd begun calling her "Miss Lily," the woman who ran the saloon in the same book. It seemed a fitting way to christen our reconstituted relationship.

Other words were trickier, though. It was one thing to call your former lover "Billie," quite another to call a table an "eating" or a banana a "peeler," as if the thing had been replaced by its requisite action. Her physical therapist recommended that we play word games to help her recover her verbal dexterity, and we'd fallen easily back into our long-ago answers-and-questions routine.

"Genius," she'd say. "Good luck. Fortune."

It was a double conundrum for me, as I first had to decipher the words through her slurred speech and then figure out the pattern they made.

"Oh—kinds of strokes!" I'd say, like a contestant on Jeopardy who'd forgotten to phrase her answer in the form of a question. Clearly, she hadn't lost her sense of irony.

Out of some actual stroke of fortune or just the circuitous wiring of her brain, she did better putting words on paper. Saying them out loud, she'd been reduced, temporarily, to single utterances or short phrases, all of them delivered with the sense of urgency of one who doesn't have any language to spare. But give her a pen and a legal pad, and she could get out whole sentences in her new, shaky left-handed scrawl, sometimes leaving blanks that she'd go back and fill in after a time delay.

Now she was almost ready to come home—or come back to her own house as modified by me and Jeff. Funny how any room—an elegant parlor, a comfortable den—becomes frumpy and alien when you roll in a hospital bed. I did my best to prepare her, and she knew she wouldn't be climbing stairs anytime soon; still, I knew this rearrangement of her first story would be as frustrating to her as the recircuiting of her brain, and I was as sad that she wouldn't be able to express that frustration with her earlier verbal vigor as I was about the bed, the walker, the stool in the bathroom.

Go with that feeling, said Suzanne Pleshette, who'd been making cameo appearances in my consciousness every now and then since I plugged *The Birds* into my VCR.

What do you know about my feelings?

I played a psychologist's wife on TV, she said, affronted.

His patients never got better, of course. They're still whining about their mothers in syndication.

I wasn't particularly interested in wallowing in sadness, and I'd had enough of being scared lately, so when I stopped at the video store on my way home from the author's house, I bypassed birds and went straight for comedy.

When I got back to the duplex, Jeff had already showered and was plopped in front of the television with Betty, who preferred films but didn't mind watching the evening news.

"Ack," said Betty.

"Ack," said Jeff.

"Look," I said, holding up three videos and a carton of pad Thai. "It's a Suzanne Pleshette film festival!"

Betty perked up his ears. I admit it, I'd grown obscenely fond of that cat, and had indeed turned into one of those people who bestow insipid nicknames on their pets, names like "Whisker Boy" and "Mr. Scraggly," and make absurd cooing sounds when calling them in for supper. Betty even had his own chair—the most comfortable in the room, naturally. Jeff was in the recliner, so I plopped myself down on the lumpy couch and scooped noodles onto paper plates while the previews ran.

It turned out Suzanne's performances weren't all tragic, clouded with so many crows you knew no one would get out alive. But Jeff and I agreed that her outfits were across-the-board comically tragic, starting with her Mrs. Bob Newhart paisley bellbottoms and moving backwards through her Disney period and her over-the-top tomboy gunslinger in an unfortunate Western she made with James Garner.

"Oh, she's so earnest," marveled Jeff as he watched her campaigning for Dean Jones, to whom she was married in *The Shaggy D.A.*

"You'd be earnest, too, if your husband kept turning into a sheepdog."

"Even so, I don't think I'd wear white shoes with that culotte number. Sensible blue pumps would be better for a district attorney's wife."

Suzanne didn't have much of a part in the film, and really, who could compete with a dog, a cute kid, and a bumbling ice cream salesman? Still, I could sense something dark and brooding behind the perky wife-and-mother routine.

"She's clearly a symbol for the subjugation of women in mainstream '60s and '70s filmmaking," I observed.

"Yeah, in a neo-retro-pomo-homo-feminist-revisionist sort of way," Jeff agreed.

"Ack," said Betty, who was really quite savvy about such things.

The phone rang. I hit the pause button, right in the middle of the fur-raising scene where Dean-the-dog and the ice cream man teeter across a pipe a hundred or so feet up in the air, and picked up the receiver.

"Please," said the voice that stopped my feminist movie critic in her tracks. "Please." It was the author's voice, spitting out its one word over and over.

CHAPTER 16

I didn't blame her for her occasional panic attacks. I was prone, myself, to panicky insomnia—bouts of anxiety cupped in sleep's parentheses. I understood how fear comingles with regret, how time backward and forward can roll into one long list of personal transgressions. I was as afraid of not finding love as of finding it, just as I imagined the author was as afraid of living as of dying.

In comparison to my own life, keeping the planet of the library spinning at the appropriate tilt seemed easy. It was a microcosm, I knew, so many facts and fictions filling up an imposing edifice. A microcosm for what, exactly, I wasn't sure—my life, perhaps (less the imposing edifice); an entire body of literature and knowledge; lies and truth. I spent days dwelling among stories that were not my own, nights acting out my part in my own story. Is that right? Are we all simply characters in our own autobiographies? Or was I merely a character in someone else's story—the author's, perhaps, Jeff's, Colin's?

Don't confuse living and acting, said Suzanne Pleshette, a person I knew only as a series of characters. *No one's going to tell you what your motivation should be in life. No one's going to write your script.*

Still, characters could come alive. Wasn't I bereft every time I closed the final chapter of a novel or watched the credits roll in a darkened cinema?

I could use some help, I saw, with the plotting of my autobiography. It certainly hadn't followed any happily-ever-after scenario, though I couldn't say I wasn't happy—just prey to the nagging doubts that make us human. For someone who wasn't a character, I had my share of character flaws, not the least of which was a tendency to see the world as a theater of the absurd and the concomitant tendency to take things either too seriously or not seriously enough.

It seemed the author's re-entry into my universe precipitated a crisis of some sort. Maybe it was time for one in the outline I'd never written. Maybe I was becoming aware of changes in my own body—changes not as radical as the ones she had undergone, but signaling as vehemently a path that led toward old age as opposed to one leading away from youth. My doctor called it perimenopause; I called it getting creaky and forgetful.

In any case, the hieroglyphics of the body were as mysterious as they were insistent, and when I got the author's phone call I translated her words as if they'd come from my own tossed and anxious nights. I couldn't simply modify her house, pick her up from the rehabilitation hospital, and drop her off at the curb. Neither could I pack a suitcase and move into her guest room. The irony would have been too much for either of us to bear, after all those years when I was welcome to stay overnight but not to leave behind so much as a toothbrush or a T-shirt to sleep in.

Still, I knew I couldn't leave her alone, so I picked up the phone and called the only person I could think of.

> The nuns sweltered during the day and froze at night in the desert, the landscape of the change-of-life. The wheels of their one remaining wagon sank into the heavy sand, a kind of dry, gritty muck that clung to anything moist—the corners of the novices' eyes, the spaces between their toes. Though they'd found their geographical compass, and were plodding toward their initial destination, the north-south of their inner compasses still swung wildly. The Mother Superior felt her thoughts slowly giving over to coarse dust. She'd lost her resolve when the wind began blowing from every direction at once, something she may have taken as a sign from God only a week earlier, but that now seemed designed to torment her, as if one's soul could be tossed around in so much bluster.
>
> Now, thirst of the basest sort kept her going. The barrels in the back of the wagon held enough water for two or three days for the Mother Superior, the five remaining novices, and the two remaining horses. They'd had to let the others go: four horses cut loose in the great prairie; a couple of novices who'd jumped wagon at small settlements where an east-bound stagecoach would come through

every few days; and the one who was presumably a native now, married to a brave and calling on who knows what false gods to make the crops grow or conjure up buffalo for the great hunt. The others lay in the wake of the one wagon, the two Marys with sturdy oaks for headstones and moss for blankets; another swallowed in swampland; two more covered by this impossible hourglass of sand.

The Mother Superior said a few words each time, then turned them over to the hands of God. That's what she'd called the holes where they'd carefully laid their sisters-in-Christ, "the hands of God," and now when she thought of that phrase she wanted to stomp all over the shifting sand that was all they had for ground.

Sister Ignatius Loyola, the tomboy nun, was still without her rosary, so now she kept the whole coven of nuns fed with rabbits and squirrels picked out of the air through the grace of a musket, for which she'd swapped a trapper two bolts of coarse cotton fabric and which she loaded one bullet at a time. She kept the wagons heading southwest, toward anything other than despair. The Mother Superior had left off feeling responsible for anyone and let herself be ushered along by the younger woman.

Nuns' habits serve only as padding against ordinariness, Mother Superior thought, and one evening at what she imagined was the exact moment that night backs into day, she removed all of her clothing, every robe and veil and undergarment and stiff woolen stocking, and she knew she was doing this to spite God. Or maybe she was trying, like an errant daughter, to get his attention. The wind feels hot and cold, she thought, then she thought: that can't be right. But somehow it was, and she was feeling it on her bare skin as if for the first time, as if she'd been born full-grown and middle-aged into a world that still might have something in it for her that could be described as joy.

When Sister Ignatius found her like this, rapt and caught in the dim glow of the slender moon, her robes a black puddle on the ground beside her, she said nothing, only took the older woman in her ample bosom and let her weep from something other than the wrath of God's love.

A week later, I settled the author into her modified digs. After a month of physical therapy, she looked surprisingly good for someone who'd thrown a blood clot into the nerve center of her brain. She wore the same pink sweat suit she'd had on when the jogger found her in the park, lying on her side and muttering incoherently. Now, she was coherent, and if her sentences had been clipped into phrases and single words, she made up for that with her new drawl, which dragged even the shortest of utterances into long slides down a slippery roadway. Her body was the reverse: it looked graceful, even muscular, after weeks of hauling it along a treadmill and slogging down the lanes of the therapy pool, a daily regimen she called "underwater cripple ballet." Arranged in a chair, she looked like an older version of the woman I'd fallen in love with. But once she pulled herself up, clutched her walker and made her way across the room, it was clear her body now had a mind of its own. My elegant author, so skilled at making an entrance, moved with awkward, jerky motions, like a robot from a bad 1960s' movie.

I gave her a tour of the changes Jeff and I had made—the downstairs bathroom now had a raised toilet seat and metal bars on the walls, the den was now a bedroom, the swinging door between the dining room and the kitchen had been removed. I got her comfortable in an armchair in the living room, as if she were a guest in her own home.

I should have known, though, that she wasn't about to sit quietly like a good guest. She turned the tables on the situation by putting me in the role of servant.

"Lunch, Billie," she ordered.

"Yes ma'am, Miss Lily." I bowed with an exaggerated flourish and went out to the kitchen, which I'd stocked with frozen dinners and sandwich supplies. I slapped together a couple of tunas-on-rye, making a mental note to pick up a new jar of mayonnaise—the one I'd found in the back of the refrigerator was nearly out of date. I cut off the crusts, chopped the sandwiches into four triangles each, and carried them out on a tray. We were just getting started when the doorbell rang.

The author started. "Who's?" The question rose up in the air and disappeared.

I looked out the window and saw Colin's convertible parked out front. The top was down, even though it couldn't have been warmer than fifty degrees.

"A surprise," I said.

I opened the door to Gigi, who balanced a duffel atop one shoulder. She dropped it and gave me a hug that lifted me off my feet.

"Wow, do you look great," I said—and in fact, she did. There was something about a fifty-year-old woman in a leather jacket and black boots that put twenty-five-year-old women in leather jackets and black boots to shame. Maybe it was the silver streaking through her brush cut; maybe she'd just grown into who she was. Or maybe it was the goofy grin she was giving me.

"No motorcycle?"

"Not with luggage. Had to put the top down to get the wind-blown effect."

One insistent word drifted in from the living room. "What?"

"Come in and say hello to the old gal, then I'll show you your room," I told Gigi. "Really, you're just saving my life here."

"Aw, shucks," she said.

I had a feeling the two of them would get along fine, the newly monosyllabic author and the verbally reticent middle-aged motorcycle-riding butch nurse. Either that, or they'd kill each other.

Gigi set her bag down in the hallway and followed me into the living room.

"You remember Gigi," I said to the author. "She took care of Colin."

"Yes," she said, looking Gigi up and down with her head a bit askew. "Isn't she something?"

Which pretty much summed it up.

> "Dear Ignatius, I fear I've quite lost myself." The Mother Superior looked into the green pools of the young nun's eyes, then quickly looked away. She'd been kneeling in the desert for hours, fingering her beads and saying the litany that had been her salvation all these many years, "Hail Mary, full of grace." But now the words failed to release her from want. Yes, there were things she wanted more than grace, bodily things, water, shade, relief from the relentless sun. She thought she wanted to be touched, but when Ignatius reached over and laid a cool palm across her forehead, she nearly collapsed.

"You're burning with fever, Mother," Ignatius said, alarmed. She helped the older woman to her feet and into her robes, and then, wrapping a sturdy arm around her waist, led her back along their two sets of footprints toward the wagon.

In the absence of rain, a pond, or a trickle of river, the heat made the landscape shimmer, turning it into a watercolor painting, though one whose artist had a limited palette. The horizon line divided browns and reddish browns from the sky's cobalt blue, which was dulled into submission by a white-hot sun. Had an Indian scout or a ranch hand been watching from a distance, from the vantage point of a hill or the back of a mustang, he would have seen two other colors moving across the canvas: the black of the Mother Superior's habit and the white of Sister Ignatius's.

But there was no one, only the two women and the four novices who awaited them, anxiously crossing themselves and stroking the heavy pewter crosses that hung from lanyards around their necks.

"It's no use, Ignatius," the elder nun said, stumbling through the sand. "I can see now that faith has been wasted on me. You see it too: I pray and pray and still nothing comes to relieve me."

"I have come, Mother, and you are not forsaken. You are ill, is all. You need water and rest and then we will all pray for you." The Mother Superior was not heavy; indeed, the trials of the journey had cost all the nuns what little plumpness they enjoyed. Still, Sister Ignatius felt the weight of responsibility leaning into her as they leaned into the hot wind. She was not prone to panic, and she knew she could lead the group to their destination should the Mother Superior become seriously ill or die. Ignatius had no reason to question her own faith: she'd grown up in the convent and faith was just something that was, like the air she breathed. But if she'd had any illusions about a merciful God, they were long gone, buried with her sisters; and while she knew God was too much a part of her to leave behind, she was coming to understand that should they make their way safely to the settlement, she would have to leave the church, even if it meant leaving the Mother Superior.

It's an uneasy moment when history collides with the present tense. Or maybe I just didn't like the sense that I was some accumulation of past events, a timeline on a family tree that included blood relatives only peripherally. It was tempting to ask Jeff to make a documentary of my life, just so I'd have something on film to point to. But I had little to recommend myself as fodder for filmdom, other than an odd predilection for obsessing about historical and not-so-historical characters, none of whom, I was certain, would agree to appear on camera. Besides, Jeff was busy these days with his own project.

I'd heard that people who develop Alzheimer's sometimes lose the valve in the brain that regulates inhibition and the "What would the neighbors think" response. One mother who'd always disapproved of her daughter's lesbian relationship became suddenly warm and loving to her daughter's long-term partner. True, she was slowly losing her mind, but it didn't seem like a bad trade-off to the daughter, who'd thought she'd lost all possibility of closeness with her mother.

The author wasn't losing her mind; in fact, she seemed to be going through reverse dementia—every day regaining words and phrases and movements and becoming less frustrated. She was moving toward something that was whole, but not exactly the same whole she'd been before the stroke. No, the post-stroke author was out. So far out, you'd think her closet never existed. As her words came back, she strung them together into stories told languidly around the gas log, like an old cowpoke looking back on a lifetime on the range. These were stories she'd never told me, and they usually involved some young woman whose name she couldn't quite put her tongue on, though she'd clearly had no reticence about putting her tongue on various parts of said young woman's anatomy.

Jeff and Gigi were her willing audience and, after a while, Jeff quietly took out his hand-held camera and began filming her as she talked. She raised her left eyebrow a bit, but continued with her halting storytelling, only perhaps embellishing a bit more than she'd already been doing and directing her comments more pointedly toward the camera. After a couple of days of that, Jeff started coming over every morning with a tripod and full-size camera, with a list of questions tucked in his pocket.

Much of this went on during the day while I was troubleshooting whatever trouble came up at the library. And even when I was around for one of the author's command performances, I usually got up and left the room. Maybe it was her past I didn't want colliding with my present; maybe I didn't want to think about how different my life may have been had she shed her pretenses long ago. Maybe I didn't want to be a character in her life.

No. That wasn't true. I would play whatever part was open to me, just as I'd always done.

While we were together, the author wanted to know nothing of my minor flirtations with other women, let alone the handful of brief affairs that took me out of her arms and into something even less certain. But now that we were, as she liked to say, old lovers, she seemed to relish quizzing me with her new, halting voice, about my latest failed relationship.

"I don't want to talk about it," I'd say. "It's already been processed into Cheez Whiz."

"Yes, that's what I want to hear about. Cheez Whiz. What wine for supper? What side of the bed? What color roses?"

"Oh, you think details will explain everything?"

She nodded. Smugly, I might add, but it was an earned smugness. She'd written her way into supermarket book racks on the strength of brass buttons embossed with family crests—a whole life described in a piece of utilitarian decoration. And it was her own life she was describing these days, one detail at a time, into Jeff's microphone.

"She wore boxer shorts and a white T-shirt to bed," I told her. "She insisted that her toothbrushes be extra soft and I once drove two hours in a rainstorm to find a drugstore that carried them and bought enough to last her three years. She left me notes addressed to 'My forever girl,' asking me to pick up milk or beer. I wore her camisole under my work clothes so I could spend the day remembering how naked I was underneath it all. When she drove, she was distracted by everything—other cars, hawks above the treeline, yard sales. Is that what you wanted to know? Or did you want to know how I considered cheating on her, how she made a scene in my office, yelling at the top of her lungs while the workers outside the glass window tried to pretend they couldn't hear anything? Or how about this: the day she moved out, she threw every one of my grandmother's plates at the kitchen wall. Is that a telling detail? Can you build a good scene around that one?"

Somewhere in the middle of this rant I'd begun pacing back and forth. I was upset not only because I'd revealed my own indiscretions and embarrassments, but also because the author seemed moved not one iota by my tirade. She sat in her flowered armchair, tilting a bit to the left, listening intently as if I were telling a made-up story and hadn't yet reached its punch line.

"Yes, yes," she said. "Good. What else?"

"What else? We threw plates at each other. Isn't that enough?" But of course it wasn't.

"What did the plates look like, sound like?"

"Who cares what the plates looked like? They're broken. They're in the landfill."

"Oh, don't be so exasperated with me, Billie." It took her a long time to say this, working her brain and then her mouth around the word "exasperated." "I'm just an old lady with a misfiring whats-it."

A misfiring personality, no doubt. Or a misfiring sense of tact or appropriateness. There were times I was willing to fill in the blanks in her speech, but this wasn't one of them. I'd had enough of filling her in on the blanks of my life, too. Sadie and I had started out by being very good to each other and ended by being not very good to each other, until we were so not good we couldn't picture a way back to anything resembling civility. I know it was mostly my fault: I wanted her to be exactly like the author and to be the exact opposite of the author. Both of those were impossible tasks, although the author herself seemed to be doing a good job with them right now.

I sat down. "Oh, go ahead and misfire. I just don't want my life turned into a bad story."

"Why not? Mine's being turned into a bad movie." She grinned lopsidedly.

"Don't let Jeff hear you say that."

Jeff wasn't within earshot. He was home in his studio, presumably splicing the author's ramblings into something coherent. I was planning on waiting for the initial cut before viewing any of it, maybe because I had a substantial part. Jeff had asked me to do voice-over, reading selected sections of the author's novels into his microphone. It wasn't immediately clear why he'd chosen some of the selections that he did. A handful of them were obviously brimming with lesbian innuendo, mostly taken from the Billie and Miss Lily book. Others were selected, I suspect, because they were such good examples of an overblown genre. Jeff knew his audience. The Midwestern housewives who read the author's books were not likely to attend film festivals and one-time showings at independent theaters. No, this was a coming out story, complete with high drama and low camp. I was a big player in this one, like it or not, and I understood he'd asked me to do the narration as a way to warm me up for an interview in which I would tell my story. Or at least my story as it related to the author's story. I hadn't agreed to anything yet, and while I was as out as one could be without slathering rainbow stickers all over my body, I was not interested in tabloid celebrity.

Even so, there was that nagging murmur in my ear.

What are you ashamed of? It's your life. It's not as though you have to go down in history as the babe wife of a dorky psychologist. What's wrong with being the younger woman on the arm of the classy dame?

Nothing, really. And it's not as though I had regrets—I'd let go of the idea of a lifetime partnership years ago, and I'd let go of it easily. But my life was more than an accumulation of scenes with the author, and I wasn't sure I was happy about the idea of being a character in her documentary.

Oh, get over yourself. Character is a social construct. We all play different parts in different people's lives. Hell, we all play different parts in our own lives.

It would be easier to discount Suzanne Pleshette's theories, except that I happened to know that she had played not only a psychologist's wife but also a psychology professor in *Blackbeard's Ghost*, a 1968 Disney flick laden with low-budget special effects. She spent most of that movie trying to convince Dean Jones he had not seen a ghost when, in fact, he had.

Still, my ghosts were my own, and not necessarily for public consumption. But I grudgingly provided narration for Jeff's tour-de-centrifugal-force, knowing full well his documentary would clear a space for the author in the annals of lesbian history. No doubt she would become the subject of any number of tedious PhD dissertations, her books picked apart for knowing glances between female leads and for ever-so-slightly effeminate gentlemen. I would read aloud from her books, but I wasn't about to explicate them, or her life for that matter. And I certainly had no interest in explicating my own life. Living it was quite enough, thank you.

> Ignatius Loyola struggled with the flint while the enormous sky soured into orange and then red-orange before her. Usually she approached fire-making as a ritual, gathering dried grass for kindling then piling it into a little bed over which she would tent small scrub and twigs and whatever wood was available, most often these days the planks from abandoned wagons. Like so many stations of the cross, she thought, then she thought that if the cross of the crucifixion were there beside her in the desert, she'd have more wood to chop up and burn in the fire.
>
> If she could get the fire to catch. If she could coax something like a spark from the pieces of stone and metal that she kept, now, in the pouch once occupied by her rosary beads. Ignatius struck and struck again. The air smelled burnt.
>
> Mother Superior lay a few feet away on a tattered wool blanket, tended by Sisters Evangeline, Bernadette, Abélard, and Jeanne D'Arc. Her breathing was heavy but regular, and even in sleep she fidgeted in her robes. Ignatius had removed the older nun's black head cloth, and then removed her own white one and tore from it a strip of fabric. Jeanne D'Arc was using it to sponge water onto Mother Superior's forehead and wrists.
>
> This time of evening, the temperature did a free-fall; when the sun dropped away, so did the heat. Day was one unbearable season and night another. Most nights the nuns made do with no fire, rationing their wood and huddling together in the wagon for warmth. But Ignatius knew the Mother Superior's fever would soon turn to chills from which she could not hope to dispossess her with the meager stock of blankets and her own body heat. She could

> not fail with the fire tonight. She had a duty, one she'd accepted the evening she took the Mother Superior into her arms, naked and sobbing and looking for deliverance.
>
> Bernadette, prone to histrionics, had been sobbing herself all afternoon, and as she watched Ignatius fail again and again at lighting the fire, she began to wail. "She's going to die," she cried out into the encroaching darkness. "We're all going to die."
>
> "Nonsense. God will not allow that to happen," Ignatius said sharply, though really she had no idea what God would and would not allow.

I called the author on a Saturday night and told her I'd be by to pick her up the next morning. When I arrived, she was dressed in a tan wool pantsuit with a red and orange scarf flung about her neck, sitting slightly askew like a piece of abstract art. The walker that she used to get around the house was on one side of her chair. Strapped to it was a canvas carrier bag, in which was lodged a glass holding the remnants of last night's Merlot. On the other side of the chair stood a metal cane that branched into four legs at the bottom, a spider with an unsightly protuberance. She held her bad hand with her good.

"You look like you've been ready for hours," I said, offering my arm as leverage.

"I have. Gigi went out early, had me dressed and fed by eight." She pulled herself awkwardly to her feet and grabbed the cane. "Where are you taking me?"

I realized it was the first time I'd seen her in anything other than a bathrobe or sweat suit since she'd come home from rehab. It was also the first time she'd ventured out of the house.

"It's Sunday," I said. "I thought you'd like to go to Mass."

She dropped abruptly back into the chair. "Don't go to church anymore," she said, emphasizing every syllable. "Gave it up. Long time ago."

I thought immediately of the Mother Superior standing naked in the desert dark, waiting for the wind to give her direction.

That's what was different about her house. She'd never been the kind of Catholic who hung framed pictures of Jesus on the kitchen wall or posted psalms on the bulletin board, but there had been a small, discrete crucifix in the bedroom—not above the bed, thank God, but arranged among some photos over her bureau. And, on the bedside table, a small soapstone bowl held three or four rosaries. I couldn't remember seeing either of them in my reorganization of her house, and now I wondered if even her family Bible was still in its place on the bookshelf.

I sat down, too, on a footstool I dragged from across the room. "Why?"

"I'm old. I can do what I want." She gestured with her good hand, a dismissal of my question. I resisted the urge to run outside and see whether the Buddha with the glued-on nose still presided over the back garden.

"You'll have to take me someplace else," she said. "I'm all dressed up." She lifted her feet with some difficulty and clicked them together in a seated, mid-air tap-dance move.

I missed the old author, the sophisticated grand dame of not-so-grand letters, someone who would never wear a red-and-orange scarf with a tan suit in late April or perform goofy dances in her armchair. But I had to admit, the new one was a hoot.

Still, I was disappointed about the church trip—I'd been looking forward to sitting in the dusty light that passes through stained glass, to the sound of liturgy echoing off the granite walls, if not the liturgical words themselves. I needed some kind of blessing, it seemed.

So I bundled her into my car and headed across town. If I couldn't have the sermon, the sacrificial wine, the musk of incense rising in the damp air, I could still seek out the quiet, the hushed voices, the sense of higher purpose. The college art museum was featuring a show of self-portraits by local artists, and I knew the author would enjoy delineating art from artifice, even if she couldn't find the words for it.

As it turned out, her make-do words were quite appropriate. For some reason, she wanted to describe the self-portraits, most of which were curiously abstract, with nouns rather than adjectives.

The museum kept a wheelchair for patrons who had trouble

getting around, so I borrowed it to skate her through the exhibit space. The hall did have the feel of an ice rink, and its buffed white floor provided plenty of room for one moderately uncoordinated person to perform double and triple axels at the helm of a wheelchair carrying a slightly damaged prima donna.

Thus seated and somewhat turned around from our wheelchair Olympics, the author was at a bit of a disadvantage, seeing that the paintings were hung at a standing person's eye level. That may have explained why, faced by an oil painting that was nothing more than thick globs of multicolored paint piled haphazardly on a flat board, like an overused, dried-up palette, I made pompous pronouncements about color and texture and the recesses of the mind while she took a quick look and declared: "Bird."

At first I thought she was still reeling from our wheelchair flight of fancy. "Bird? What do you mean, bird?" I squinted, trying to blur the shapes into recognizable wings, a beak, a few stray feathers.

"No, bird," she insisted. Her capacity for stringing together phrases and sentences diminished at times, particularly when she was tired or overstimulated.

"Do you mean 'bold'?" I suggested, peering at the artist's statement.

"During the weeks that I pondered what form my self-portrait would take, I had a recurring dream of flying," I read aloud. "When I looked down from my flight, I saw not my house, not the city streets, but a neighborhood of color that I took to be my self, as if I could fly around inside my own soul."

"Hah!" said the author. "Bird!"

The statement was typed in small print and hanging above the painting; she couldn't have read it from her vantage point. "How did you do that?"

"Makes me think of you," she said pointedly.

"Me? Why?"

But by then she was pointing across the room at a huge metal sculpture. Apparently her wheelchair wanted to bond with it. I spun her around slowly and pulled her away backwards, so we could watch the flight through the soul recede, something that reminded me of the way dreams elude me as I'm waking and grasping for anything other than reality.

The sculpture could have been called life-sized, if metal had a life, and in this case I guess it did, as it was supposed to stand in for the artist. Angular and whimsical, it looked like a satellite designed by Dr. Seuss, something one could imagine in orbit above Whoville.

"I wonder if it gets good reception?"

"Funny," the author said, as in funny ha-ha, banging on the armrest of her borrowed metal conveyance with her good arm. "I wonder if I do."

That cracked us both up, and after we had a good snigger I did a little pirouette with the wheelchair, then steered her toward a collage that I suspected she would appreciate: the artist had assembled old photos, postcards, and letters, then arranged them haphazardly. Floating on the surface of the canvas, on individual pieces of gauzy paper, were eyes, ears, nose, mouth, and hands—the parts of the body one uses to experience the world.

"It's interesting, isn't it?" I offered.

"It's a lot of crap," the author said, craning her neck and squinting at the self-portrait. "She wants to kill us with symbolism."

"Well, there are worse ways to go."

She sniggered again. "Death by ornithology would be worse."

I didn't even try to figure out what word she really meant.

Lying prostrate with her eyes closed, the Mother Superior heard the supplications of Sisters Abélard and Evangeline and the cries of Sister Bernadette. She felt the ministrations of Jeanne D'Arc, who was gently swabbing her face with a wet rag. But mostly she sensed a large darkness crossing over her. She sensed a darkness and she knew she should pray to Jesus for salvation, but she didn't want what he had to offer. She didn't want to be cushioned in the hands of God; she wanted to be rocked in the arms of Ignatius.

She didn't know who she was any more, and the only anchor she had was the rosary she'd taken from Ignatius's pouch while she bathed, and which she now wore around her neck, under her vestments, like an amulet.

CHAPTER 17

After the students packed up and drove home for summer vacation, towing their U-Hauls filled with stereo equipment, computers, and mini-refrigerators, I tossed a few folders, my Rolodex, and my Daytimer into a briefcase and moved back to the archives room. It was a temporary respite; the archives librarian who'd replaced me was on her honeymoon in Peru, where she and her archaeologist husband were sifting through Incan dirt. Her assistant, a twenty-two-year-old just out of college, had broken his leg in four places doing some sort of daredevil mountain skiing. What was it about spending one's days in an archives room that made people want to take up absurd, risky pastimes? Was it a need to breathe air that wasn't musty or climate-controlled?

And just what had I done that was so risky? Was I a daredevil to have loved the people I loved? Was it taking a chance to sport a punky, spiky haircut at the ripe old age of forty-eight?

"You know, you could assign someone else to keep an eye on the archives room," the associate library director said to me. "It doesn't get much traffic in the summer; anyone could sit in there, even a work-study student."

But I'd insisted on doing it myself, perhaps out of some sort of nostalgia, perhaps because I thought it would spur me to take up hang-gliding or the study of obscure arachnids found only in the rain forests of countries with questionable human rights records.

Or maybe I just wanted to go back to where I came from, a pilgrim from the fancy glass-and-steel library addition coming to pay homage to the bricks and mortar and sturdy oak.

The dust felt familiar as rain on my skin.

Even though I'd brought along my current project, the budget for the next fiscal year, and even though my phone calls would track me down through the maze of wiring in the walls, I did feel a bit like an anthropologist visiting some outpost of society, a place where people existed solely for the purposes of antiquity. What's the use of having memories if there's no one to sort through them, to assign them the proper numbers, the proper place on the shelf? The archives room had changed little since my early days in the library, though of course technology had gotten the better of the small circulation desk, which was now top-heavy with monitors, one linked to the card catalog system and one to the internet or, as the author called it, the infinity.

The author had gone high-tech, too. Following a period of initial reluctance, she'd taken to cyberspace like a nun to holy water after Gigi showed her how to check Amazon.com for her ranking and reader reviews. Even better was email, which she used to keep in touch with her agent and her publisher and to augment her several daily phone calls to me. I'd programmed her cell phone with my cell number so she had her own personal hotline, one she used indiscriminately, sometimes just to notify me that she was sending an email.

"Billie, I'm going to E you on the infinity," she'd say.

"Okay," I'd say. "Is everything all right? Did Gigi take you to physical therapy?"

"It's all in the E," she'd say, and then invariably drop the phone so I'd have to wait for Gigi to come, pick it up, and promise me she'd try to keep the author occupied so I could get some work done. But really, I didn't mind the distractions—budgeting sucked and the college controller was only going to chop me back to last year's figures, no matter how much time I put into my proposal. And—how do I say this?—the author was seducing me all over again. Not in a romantic way, though those feelings never entirely dissipate, but in a collegial way. We were, after all, alumni of the same crazy, wonderful, and hopelessly flawed love affair, and I hadn't realized how much I missed her until I had her back again.

Inexplicable, eh?

That from Suzanne Pleshette, who was still popping in from time to time without benefit of email or cell phones.

Since school was out and it was too early in the summer for teachers to be planning their fall classes, I was mostly alone in the archives with my budget, my thoughts, and my imaginary playmate with the 1970s' outfits and shag haircut. But from time to time during that week, my pulse would quicken and I'd find my gaze pulled to the door, as if I were expecting the author to walk in and slip me a note with a date on it, or an address.

Well, this is where you met her, Suzanne noted. *And in case you hadn't noticed, you're the same age she was when she sashayed in here and looked you up and down like you were some new invention.*

Yeah, best thing since sliced bread. Imagine the nerve of that, walking into a room and selecting your new plaything. And I swear I felt it again, her eyes on my turned back, until I realized I was sitting directly in the path of a ray of sun that shone through the leaded glass window.

She'd managed to stop my heart with that first look, then start it beating like crazy, like it had a mind of its own and was in no way connected to my brain, which should have known better.

You were only twenty-two. Give yourself a break.

And she was seductive as hell, and I did love her.

Yes. And you still do.

Yes. And I still do, and look at the choices I've made because of it.

Bob would say, 'Why don't you go with that?' Suzanne slipped into Emily Hartley persona.

Bob sucked as a psychologist. None of his patients ever got better.

That's because he didn't listen to me. But you should. Bob's patients were odd and eccentric, but they were okay. They had each other. Why do people think their lives need to follow a certain outline to be acceptable? You made the choices, so you must have wanted them.

Or they must have wanted me.

My sojourn in the archives room was a lovely respite, it turned out, from the life I'd hopped on and ridden into like a city slicker on her first horse. Or maybe more like a Boston heiress escaping her corseted life by stepping into dungarees and chaps and swaggering as if she knows how to swagger, I thought, remembering my namesake Billie and her first tentative steps in the shoes of another gender.

The first day of archives sitting was plagued by interruptions from the staff and minor annoyances like phone calls from salespeople and the like. The second day I made it known, in my no-nonsense library director grownup-in-charge way, that I needed to concentrate on the budget and should be consulted only when absolutely necessary. It wasn't really a lie; I did need to lasso the numbers and wrassle them to the ground. But mostly I wanted to be alone with history—mine, the author's, all the facts and fictions and conversations contained in the fading volumes on the shelves. By the end of the first week, I was coming to work incognito, in jeans, T-shirts, and running shoes, the kind of clothes Billie might have worn had she been born in the 1960s rather than the 1840s. Back then, as a girl itching to get out of skirts and into britches, she would have been called a tomboy. Now, she would be an LGBTQ, or whichever initials applied. Every couple of years, a new letter was added, and I'd started to think of the acronym as something served on rye with mustard. I didn't mind. There was plenty of room in the sandwich for all of us outlaws, even a supposedly respectable librarian who, unbeknownst to most people, harbored a tattoo of the sun under the sleeve of her T-shirt.

One day, toward the end of the second week in the archives room, I was absent-mindedly tracing its rays when the door opened and the author hobbled in, leaning on her spider-legged cane. "I've always thought that was a lovely gesture," she said, indicating my tattoo.

"Hey, it's my favorite movie star!" I rolled my sleeve down and jumped out of my chair. I hopped across the room to give her a hug, but instead of falling into my embrace she held me at arm's length, looking me not up and down as she had that first day in the archives, but directly in the eyes, and I was suddenly acutely aware of the color green. Then she leaned over and kissed me quite tenderly.

I settled her into the sturdy chair at the oak table, her usual seat, as if it hadn't been two dozen years since the last time she sat there, then took the chair across from her.

"What happened during those ten years?" I asked her.

"After you left me, you mean."

I looked at my hands. My thumbs were twitching with their individual pulses.

"I went back to my life, that's all."

"You stopped going to church." It came out sounding like an accusation.

She cocked her head. "I didn't know you were so attached to my spiritual life."

"No, I'm not. It's not that. But you're different now, and not just from the effects of the stroke."

"I don't kiss so well any more. Out of practice."

"You do just fine." I could still taste the lipstick from her slightly crooked mouth. "But I want to know—did you decide God doesn't exist, or did you just give up on him?"

"Can God exist if one doesn't believe in him?"

"That's very deep, Little Grasshopper," I said, not at all unkindly, "but it doesn't answer my questions. Please, I'm really interested." I didn't say, I don't want it to be about me, because maybe I did want it to be about me, just a little bit. Maybe I wanted to have been so important in her life that she lost her faith when she lost me.

"Don't you want to ask me why I came here?"

"Oh." The clock on the wall ticked audibly behind me. "Because your cell phone battery is dead and the infinity is down? Or did you just miss me terribly?"

She looked at me patiently. "Yes, of course, I always miss you, even though I see you nearly every day. You know that, Billie."

I swallowed.

"I've decided to give all my papers to your library, as a way to thank you for being my muse all these years."

I felt suddenly dizzy. "Wow! I don't know what to say. I mean, thank you. I mean, that's wonderful. Thank you, really."

This was an incredible coup for the college and the library, and for me as a librarian. I'd always assumed she'd give her manuscripts and correspondence to the well-endowed Seven Sisters school that had given her an honorary doctorate several years earlier. This was the kind of gift an archivist lives for. And I was too bowled over by the rest of her statement to fully appreciate it.

"Have I really been your muse?"

"Who else?"

All those conversations I'd had over the years with the imaginary counterparts of historical figures, and it had been me perched on the author's shoulder whispering into her ear. How about that. I was grinning stupidly when Gigi poked her head in.

"I guess you got the good news," she said.

I got up and gave her a big hug, then reached around to hug the author from behind, as well.

"I don't mean to rush you," Gigi said, "but Jeff's waiting out in the car. We're on our way to do some filming at the Historical Society. She insisted on stopping here first."

We agreed Gigi would bring the author back the following week so we could talk about the details of her donation, then Gigi gave the author her arm and helped her up. As they ambled to the door, I stopped them.

"My first question," I said. "It was the nuns, wasn't it?"

She turned and gave me that sad half-smile, then walked out the door.

> The Mother Superior is feverish, delirious, has been for two days. Sister Ignatius Loyola is afraid to stop; they're so close to their destination and have only enough water to get them there. And where would there be? A town, or what passes for a town in the scrubby Southwest—an outpost, really, one trading post, a couple of taverns, and not one church.
>
> The irony of the landscape—the ramshackle buildings muddying a quality of sunlight she would not have thought possible—is not

lost on Sister Ignatius as she walks down the one street, leading the two horses that pull the wagon carrying the novices and the Mother Superior, who lies supine beneath the canopy, a damp cloth over her eyes. She, the older nun, is seeing things, but the young sister does not want to hear about this. She does not want the Mother Superior to be a martyr or a visionary. She wants only for her to get well, because she is tired of losing people she cares about to the will of God. She knows now that God's will is only an excuse, something people say so they won't be overwhelmed by the randomness at the heart of creation. She doesn't want to be overwhelmed by it, either, and so she continues saying her prayers, her Hail Marys and Our Fathers, and the sounds of the words bring some comfort to her even though she understands the words themselves mean nothing.

The Mother Superior is reciting, too. Psalms: Yea though I walk in the valley of the shadow of death. They're her mind's default, something to fall back on in times of fervor. And so the novices, who are tending to her, pick up her chant: Thou anointeth my head with oil, my cup overfloweth.

Sister Ignatius, coated in dust and breathing dust, hears the plaintive voices of the novices and wants to cry but finds even her tears have turned to dust, and so instead she fills the air with curses.

Anyone who set down his whiskey long enough to listen to the sounds outside the taverns of this God-forsaken outpost would have heard what may have been mistaken for the voices of angels reciting the Twenty-third Psalm. And anyone who bothered to push away from the bar and swagger through the swinging doors would have seen a nun dressed in tattered robes that were once white leading two horses and a covered wagon to the far end of the street. Anyone who walked apace of the nun would have heard her strange prayer: Damn the dust, damn the sun, damn the heat, damn the Psalms, as she tied the horses to a hitching post. Anyone who followed her around to the back of the wagon and climbed inside would have seen her kneel beside the Mother Superior and kiss her directly on the mouth, not a kiss of friendship or healing or co-conspiracy in the elevated language of God, but a kiss of longing.

EPILOGUE / 2003

One year after the stroke redirected the author's nervous system and reset her thought processes, she was nearly back to her old self in body, only a slight limp and a delicate ivory-handled cane to show for her ordeal. Her brain, and her life, however, had been permanently rerouted. After Jeff's documentary hit the film-fest circuit, the author was suddenly hot property. Baby-dykes from the college came shyly knocking on her door, carrying with them battered paperback copies of her novels that they'd rescued from their mother's attics; queer studies journals ran incomprehensible articles about the reclamation of female desire in the context of fictional history; and her books were selling like hotcakes, especially *Conestoga Sisters*, which had been published, finally, by the gay and lesbian imprint of a major publishing house.

The old author, the one who finished the nun story but could not bring herself to publish it, would have been mortified by this kind of attention, by the fact that her new generations of readers considered her work campy. The new author was campy herself, larger-than-life as ever but now conducting business from inside the subculture, as if she'd always lived there, as if her readers had simply traded in their housecoats and bouffant hairdos for tattoos, eyebrow piercings, and same-sex partners.

I had my fifteen minutes of fame, too, if only for my proximity to her. My on-camera description of unzipping the author's red red dress had once made an entire theater full of women gasp; after the documentary was screened in town, I noticed my staff giving me odd looks from time to time, and students paraded past my office throwing pseudo-casual glances through the glass window. It even got me a few dates and an email from Max, who was suddenly thrilled to have been the "other woman."

Constance would be in our lives again in a few months; she'd pocketed her graduate degree, spent six months doing gopher jobs in Hollywood and learning about the kinds of films she did not want to make, and was coming back to camp out in Jeff's spare bedroom and develop her own projects for Moon Tattoo Productions.

And Gigi was now a permanent fixture in the author's house. The author didn't need nursing care anymore, though she was willing to accept help with the infirmities that went along with being elderly. She'd had enough of living alone, and got a kick out of being squired around town by a tough broad in a motorcycle jacket, and so she paid Gigi handsomely to take care of her house, handle correspondence, and coordinate her social calendar.

It also turned out that Gigi played bridge, and the two of them roped Jeff and me into a weekly foursome. "How hard can it be?" Jeff said. "It's just bluffing, and we've been doing that all along."

He was right, of course; it's all a matter of who's sitting across from you at the card table, who's North and who's South. It's a matter of a wink, a knowing glance, a kick under the table.

Okay, so we suck at bridge. The author and Gigi win every time. We go for the little cream cheese sandwiches, no crusts, cut into triangles, and the two-olive martinis. We go because this is, after all, our family, like them or not, and we do like them.

What I'm saying is that my story has caught up to me. I can't write what happens next because I don't know.

"My life has no plot," I say to Jeff when I tell him I have written down the salient episodes of my relationship with the author. "It has no theme, unless longing is a theme, and it can't be because themes are supposed to be complete sentences with subjects and predicates and verbs and denominators."

"You've got characters," he says. "You've got that bird-shaped scar on the back of your head. Plot is highly overrated. Longing is what counts, and nobody longs in complete sentences."

And I hand over my bundle of journals to him, because if I've shared my life with anyone, it's been Jeff, and because he's been the archivist of my longing all along.

Then we go out on the porch, sit down in our lawn chairs, and put our feet up on the railing, waiting for the next thing to happen.

ACKNOWLEDGMENTS

Parts of the opening section of *The Story So Far* appeared in the *Harrington Lesbian Fiction Quarterly.*

Huge thanks to so many people who encouraged me through the journey of this book, including the earliest readers, Patricia Spitalniak, Tatiana Schreiber, and Heather McKernan, along with Kate Gleason's Thursday morning writing crew. Thanks to Julie Simons for taking the cover photo and Clare Innes for an initial version of the cover design. I much appreciated thoughtful comments and support from Lynn Tryba, Brendan Tapley, Jane Miller, Gail Piche, and two dear people who are no longer with us, Linda Kent and Walter Clark, among many others. Thanks to agent Malaga Baldi, who believed in this project, and to Sarah Bauhan, Henry James, and Mary Ann Faughnan at Bauhan Publishing.